S M O O T H

O P E R A T O R S

Roshanda
Your light is
shining bright
I hope you enjoy!

Zink
5-16-03
WordDiva73@aol.com

SMOOTH OPERATORS

a novel by

Olayinka "Yink" Aikens

BROWN BOOKS PUBLISHING GROUP
DALLAS

Smooth Operators

Author photo by Ellery Harris

For information please contact
Brown Books Publishing Group
16200 North Dallas Parkway, Suite 170, Dallas, TX 75248
972-381-0009   www.brownbooks.com

First Printing 2002
ISBN 0-9720865-0-1
LCCN 2002094807

DEDICATION

This book is dedicated to the memory of:

Linda Denise Boyette

Shani Marie Fountain

Marsha Satterfield

and

Tupac Amaru Shakur

Rest in Peace.

WHAT IS IN THE BEGINNING WILL BE THERE IN THE END.

ACKNOWLEDGMENTS

Thanks to the Lord above for guidance, patience, and forgiveness. To my mother Ester L. Tyler-Aikens, my dad Charles E. Aikens, and my sisters Rosie and Dawn.

Thanks to the Aikens, Roberts, Tyler, Gordon, and Brown families and everybody in between. Thanks to all my peeps in Oakland and the Bay area, Chicago, and New Orleans; Texas, Mississippi and North Carolina. And to everyone else in between. Special thanks to all my little cousins (Yink loves the kids)!

A special thanks to Milli Brown and the Brown Books All-Stars: Thanks to Kathryn Grant and Zetta Wiley and thanks Alyson for all your hard work! To my publicist Yvonne Gilliam. Thanks to Chandra Sparks Taylor, Gwynne Forester, Deidre Savoy, Carl Weber, and Tracy Thompson-Price who I enjoyed meeting in North Carolina. Thanks to Emma Rodgers at Black Images Book Bazaar, To Beverly Jenkins for the best historical romances ever written. To Zane for saying what most people are afraid to! Thanks to Mark Anthony in the ATL for hooking up my do! And an extra-special thanks to Theodore Kloski for encouraging a young writer to pursue her talent.

Thanks to Terrence Clark, LaToiya D. Aikens, Tonya Aikens, Dana J. Oubre, William "Big Will" Brooks, Cheria Beal, Monica Koonce-Brooks, Teresa N. Anthony, Kaija D. Jones, Adam S. Benson, Mike Woolridge, Michael "Jug" Stephens, Brandi Taylor, Christina & Rodney Hudson, Shawn & Tyrone Frazier, Ellery Harris, Cedrick Jones, Ashley Saunders, Kendrick "Drack" Muse, Kimani Green, Carmen Woods-Caldwell, Jermaine D. Moore, Adrian Jackson, Oliver "Ollie" Allen, Melvin K. Smith, Quinn & Rashida Stephens, Brent Wade, James "Trippy" Haynes, Norley Jackson, Brian Steptoe, Jerrell Nelson, Marc Gordon, Kwame Satterfield, Charles Douglas, Marcus Douglas, Beanie Jones, Vera Jones, Kenny Jones, Mesa & Brian Jefferson, Danette Cross, Rosalind Griffis, Julia Williams, Artis Gordon, Chris Pitre, Brenda Jackson, Ashanta Williams, Keisha Frank, Jamaika King, Vanessa Johnson, Nicole Harper-Cotton, Cianci McDaniel, Zahira Sims, Tootie & Jimmie Byrd, Eric Sutton, John Drain, Joy Myrick, Crystal Martin, Annette Bettis, Scheresia Russell, Sidney & Carolyn Beal, Brandon Beal, Derrick Vernon, LaTisia Brumfield, Lizanette Howard-Stokes, Rod Stokes, Doris Williams, Eric Morris, Dawn Campbell, Robert & Pat Campbell, Shedrick Taylor, Edwyna Elzie, Rian & Danielle Townsend, Millie Collins, Daryl Washington and Sunday Players Sports Management, Marcia Graves, Dallasblack.com, NTheKnow.com, Houston "H-Dub" Harris, Vernon, and Rudy (Showtime at the Apollo), Clue Entertainment, CAAPCO, and to J. M. from Chicago, the handsome inspiration for my next novel, *Tackled By Love*.

Thanks to the Bay Area Chapter of the Links, Southern University Alumni–Dallas Chapter, the *Oakland Tribune*, the *Oakland Post*, Romance Writers of America, Prolific Writers Organization, Romance In Color and the Black Writers Organization. And to all of the schools in the SWAC (Southwestern Athletic Conference). An extra-extra special thanks to Mocha Funk Productions.

If I forgot your name, please forgive me and print it here:

——.

CHAPTER 1

Monday morning hit Monica Holiday like a bag of nickels. She rolled over in her full-size bed and realized she was almost late for work. If it weren't for her alarm clock and the bright Georgia sun seeping through the blinds, she would have kept on sleeping. The weekend had come and gone like spring rain. She forced her slender, mocha-colored frame out of bed and pulled her gown over her head. Hopping in the shower, she let the steamy water spray her as she washed. When she finished, she oiled her skin, glided on the deodorant, and hopped into a sexy, pink bra and panty set.

"Damn, these are tight," she said, referring to her panties. She looked at her butt in the mirror and slapped it. "Too many baked potatoes." She finished primping and pulled on her dress. It was almost nine o'clock.

Monica wanted to get through the day drama-free, but she knew the idea was far-fetched. The life of a music industry publicist is never free of anything. She learned that lesson fast when she signed on at Handle Up Records a few years earlier. She jumped straight out of the classroom at Clark Atlanta University into the conference room of the record company's Midtown Atlanta offices. She didn't complain one bit. It was a dream come true. Monica longed to be in the entertainment industry, and since she couldn't sing, she felt she was better off working behind the scenes.

When she got to work, she grumbled at the pile on her desk. She sat down and finished her sesame bagel with honey-almond spread while scouring through her to-do list. She rested her head on her hand. She had too much to do. The list was full of pen marks, corrections, and a bunch of squiggly lines. She'd completed just about everything on it but had a few more things she needed to finish (CD reviews, press releases, bio updates). She was swamped with work. Not one to become frazzled when things got hectic, she relaxed and sipped her tea.

A ringlet of hair dangled from her upsweep. I should have slicked it back, she thought, staring at the loose strands. It was hard for her to keep her long, relaxed mane tame. It dangled to the middle of her back, a few inches from her butt. As she sipped the last bit of her tea, she tried to avoid staining her suit.

The pile on her desk wasn't getting any smaller. She sorted through the stack in her in-box and came across a photo of her ex. Rodney "Double R" Robinson was the company's top-selling, triple-platinum rap artist. She tossed his picture aside and organized everything into neat piles. Still aggravated by the memory of their relationship, Monica hadn't realized it had been nearly four months since he'd dumped her. The two of them were considered the ideal pair in the eyes of the local paparazzi: he, the charming, high-profile rap star; and she, the beautiful, trophy girlfriend and working woman. Their peers envied them. For a while, they even moved in together. At times, Monica felt like her life was a downtown Atlanta billboard. When the press learned about their breakup, they labeled it one of the biggest disappointments in hip-hop.

Big Bill started Handle Up back in the early nineties. He'd had a successful tenure as the vice president of marketing at a record company in Nashville. He had more than twenty-five years in the music business. He'd made more money than he could spend and he lavished it on his staff. He rewarded them with gifts like Rolex watches, cars, trips, and bonus checks. Anyone who worked for him would definitely be happy.

Right now, Monica was far from happy. Rodney had been hounding her for days to write the press releases for his new single, *Terror*. Monica felt the title aptly described him. Almost every day he demanded something else. His list of wants was as long as his list of hits. She'd been putting off tending to him because she simply didn't have the time. She was promoting a hot new girl group, the Prima Donnas and their single, *Keep It Hot*. She was trying to push them into superstar status so Handle Up could have a female platinum-selling group in its realm.

However, Rodney believed her personal feelings about him breaking up with her were affecting her job, at least where it concerned him. He could have been right. She was bitter. You just don't dump someone in a newspaper article. Rodney didn't care. The world had turned him into an icon, and he felt that no artist should come before him.

Monica enjoyed working for the company, but wished she had more help. Her duties had doubled since the former artist and repertoire director, Carlos Weaver, was sent to jail a few months earlier. Carlos had been convicted of sexual assault and fraud. He used his position to lure aspiring female singers to his home and con them out of thousands of dollars. He'd even gone so far as to rent a Corvette for one woman, telling her she could have it if she did what he wanted. Big Bill pleaded with Monica to make the scandal go away and salvage the company's reputation. As a brilliant PR rep, Monica did just that, and Big Bill rewarded her with a shiny, new, black CLK 320 Mercedes coupe. It was an expensive gift, but Big Bill wouldn't take it back when she refused to accept it. "Money isn't an issue," she remembered him saying. It never was.

She hated giving the intern, Patrice, so much work, but things had to get done. She tried to keep the load as light as possible, but hoped the new A&R director would be there soon. Since he would be her immediate supervisor, she hoped he would take some of the load off.

"Monica?" Beverly Taylor, the head receptionist, buzzed.

"Yes?" she answered as she cleared her desk.

"Rodney's manager called again. He says Rodney's tired of you putting him off." George Peters was Rodney's obnoxious manager.

She sighed and shook her head. *Well, tell him to tell Rodney to jump off a bridge and do us all a favor.* "I'll take care of him later on this week. I'm too busy right now. Plus we've got this party. . . ."

"Okay, but you know George. He's going to keep on calling."

"Let him. Rodney will get over it."

Beverly laughed. "Oh, the manager from Taboo said you can come by and check things for tonight when you're ready."

"Great. I'll do that on my way to the cleaners."

"Okeydokey, chile."

Monica checked herself in the heart-shaped mirror that hung on the wall by her desk. Tonight would be the first time she'd be in the same room with Rodney since he embarrassed her in a newspaper article a few months ago. He told a reporter for *Vibe* magazine she was too high-maintenance for him, and he needed someone more down-to-earth. Monica was devastated. She'd never considered herself to be a snob. She liked the finer things in life, but what woman didn't?

Rodney had been vacationing in Jamaica, but came back for the Prima Donnas' party. Monica wished he had stayed in Jamaica. It was storm season. She hoped the success of the Prima Donnas would bring his ego down. He was becoming that jerk of a star that people loved to hate. He'd been so cocky lately, not many people at the office wanted to be around him.

"Chop-chop. Time is money, honey!" Patrice Williams yelled

as she stuck her head in the door. "You ready for tonight?" she asked.

"As ready as I'll ever be." Monica delicately reapplied her wine-colored lipstick. "If you've seen one record industry party, you've seen them all."

"Well, I'm excited!" Patrice chirped. "I get to meet some big stars. The Prima Donnas' single is blowing up the charts too."

"Yeah, and we have to make sure it stays there. I'll be glad when this new A&R guy gets here so he can take some of this load off my back."

"I hear ya," Patrice agreed. "Well, Bill says he's just what the company needs, so maybe he'll do a good job."

"He better. Lord knows we can't afford any more screw-ups."

Monica pulled her khaki-colored blazer over her matching sheath dress.

"I am so tired of these parties. I wish I could play Jimmy Hoffa and just disappear."

She pinned the rest of her fallen curls back into the upsweep. The hairstyle accented her striking cat-like eyes and perfectly arched eyebrows. She could have easily been a model with her long legs and clear skin, but sitting still was never her forte. She liked being on the go too much. Sitting in front of a camera, like a piece of meat, was not her thing.

"Jimmy Hoffa, huh?" Patrice's laugh filled the office. "You'll be fine. You always do a great job planning these parties. I can't wait until tonight!"

Monica jumped up from behind her desk and reached for her purse. "That, my dear, is because you're twenty years old and all of this is new. Trust me, stick around long enough, and you'll see what I mean."

Patrice shrugged innocently, "I guess so. Are you on your way to Taboo?"

"Yeah, I've got to check to make sure everything is where it's supposed to be and pick up my dress."

"What's on the menu for tonight?"

"Ah, let's see." She flipped open the file folder on her desk marked "PRIMA DONNAS." "Tonight we are having . . . hot wings, lemon chicken skewers, cosmopolitans, strawberry margaritas, and, of course, Cristal. We're trying to keep up with the pink theme, so the drinks have to reflect that."

"Monica, you are good. I think when I turn twenty-one, I'll have you plan my party."

"You're so young. I remember those days. Enjoy it while you can dear."

"You act like you're an old maid or something."

"I'm not a maid, but I am older than you. Twenty-six ain't exactly a walk in the park."

"You're not old, Monica," Patrice insisted.

"Well, I feel old. Maybe it's all this work I'm doing."

"Maybe," Patrice said shrugging.

They walked out into the hall. Patrice followed closely behind Monica and was nearly blinded when Monica swung around with a pointed finger.

"Do me a favor," she said. "Order a gift basket from Potpourri's and have it sent to Janet Stokes over at the *Journal-Constitution*. Write a note telling her how sorry I am about not being able to get her passes to the last party we had. Make sure to enclose passes for tonight and have it delivered ASAP by messenger."

"Anything else?" Patrice waved her pen as if she were casting a spell on Monica.

"Nope, that's it. Thank you."

"No problem."

Monica turned to head out the door.

"Hey, Monica," Beverly yelled. "You know that new A&R director will be here tonight?"

"Yeah, I know." She opened the door and paused for a moment. "And?" she asked, tilting her head and raising an eyebrow.

"Oh, nothing." Beverly smirked and put the folders she was holding to her chest. "He's really . . ."

"Cute," Patrice interrupted. "Very charming, well-dressed, and smooth."

"How do you know?" Monica asked sarcastically.

"We met him a few weeks ago when he was here. He's very, very handsome." Beverly cooed like a schoolgirl.

"Um-hmm," Patrice nodded. "I think you were out the day he came."

Monica waved good-bye, "Thanks, but no thanks, ladies. I'm not in the mood for romance right now."

"Bye," they chimed in unison.

♫✍

Drayton Jamal Lewis was sweating. It was mid-January in Chicago, and here he was in his Hyde Park loft pacing. He hoped he wasn't forgetting anything. The gleam of his bronze skin rivaled the sun but was much easier on the eyes. His faded Polo jeans hung loosely off his athletic-looking behind, which he got courtesy of three years of playing football at Jackson State University. He was a city boy with country-boy looks, which added to his mystique.

His FUBU boxers peeked over the waistband of his jeans as he stood shirtless in the middle of the living room floor. He skimmed the room for any other holes he might have missed filling with putty. He wanted to make sure he got his deposit back. Since he accepted the job in Atlanta, he had to move in a hurry. It was almost noon, and he still hadn't finished cleaning up.

♫✍

Patrice and Beverly were funny, but little did they know, dating was the farthest thing from Monica's mind. It didn't matter how handsome the A&R rep was, she wasn't having it. She figured work and men didn't mix after the Rodney debacle. Besides, she had a party to oversee, bills to pay, and a group to groom. If everything wasn't picture perfect, it would all come down on her. Most people think all publicists do is write press releases and show up at press conferences to make their clients look squeaky clean. But that is just not so. However, Monica was a Jill-of-all-trades. And her parties were legendary in Atlanta.

One of her most lavish events was a birthday party she threw for the then fiancée of a high-profile Atlanta doctor. The theme was "Diamonds Are a Girl's Best Friend." The doctor's mansion was decorated with huge silver streamers, sparkling white and platinum balloons, and a see-through dance floor that was constructed over the swimming pool. Once the event was over, her phone was ringing off the hook. People were begging her to throw their bashes. She promised herself one day she would start her own event-planning business. It had always been her dream, but for the moment, she was content being a publicist.

The decorations for the Prima Donnas' party were fabulous. When she walked inside, the restaurant, Taboo, was covered in pink. Huge crystals hung from the ceiling, accenting the color scheme. Streamers and balloons in all shades of pink billowed around the room. Each table was decorated with a huge pink candle, mini faux crystals, and vases filled with floating candles. It was a lot of pink for a crowd that would consist mostly of men, but it didn't matter. What Big Bill wanted Big Bill got.

After double-checking the setup for the party, Monica headed to Ethel's Dry Cleaners in the West End. She'd been a loyal customer since her days as a student at Clark Atlanta University and didn't have a reason to go anywhere else. Ethel always cleaned and pressed her clothes just the way she liked, and it was worth the drive from Midtown to get her clothes cleaned.

With the Prima Donnas' promo CD pumping from the speakers,

she pulled into the pothole-ridden parking lot next to the cleaners. She was careful not to hit any potholes mindful of the flat tire she got last time. It was a shame how the city of Atlanta neglected to fix the streets in the poor neighborhoods. Even with five colleges nearby, the streets were still in horrible shape. Things hadn't changed much since Monica's days in the Atlanta University Center. But if the residents didn't complain, why would she?

Her white strapless number hung neatly beneath the clear plastic cover. With slits on each side, Monica always turned heads when she wore it. Besides, every time she put the dress on, something special happened. The last time she wore it, she met the guy who introduced her to the Prima Donnas' manager. The time before that, she met a singer, Tyrone Steele, delivering packages for a living. Big Bill signed him after hearing his a capella rendition of LTD's *Love Ballad*. Ever since that day, Monica vowed to keep the dress until she couldn't fit into it anymore.

"Well, Miss Monica, looks like you made out just fine," Lucille, Ethel's oldest daughter, said as Monica came towards the counter. She was a bit on the heavy side, and her caramel complexion was marred with scars. As Ethel once put it, they were "love wounds." Monica had no idea what that meant and didn't want to find out.

"It looks good," she said, placing a ten-dollar bill in Lucille's hand. She picked up the dress from the garment rack near the counter.

"Yeah, it's a nice dress," Lucille muttered. "Here you go," she said, wiping her brow. "It's cool outside and hot in here. Lord, have mercy on me."

Monica took the change. "Thank you. See you guys later."

Lucille stopped her before she could get out the door. "You're such a tiny thang. You eat much?" she asked.

Monica grinned, "Any and everything in sight."

"Lucky you," she said. "Lucky you."

Monica cruised toward I-85 headed for the office. If everything went as planned, the party would be a success, the Prima Donnas would be on their way to super stardom, and she could have some peace of mind. Things always got stressful when new artists had to be promoted. Bill expected everyone to work magic. Monica tapped the steering wheel while she listened to the music, maneuvering her way through the morning traffic. As she stared at the black Range Rover beside her, she thought about Rodney. He had one just like it, courtesy of Bill, of course. With all of her hard work, he got what he set out to get: a record deal, women, and money. She'd been blinded by his charm. The smooth delivery he had on "wax" wasn't a front. Monica never saw it coming.

Rodney was only with her because of her position at Handle Up. He figured if anyone could convince Bill to sign him, she was the one. They met at a celebrity basketball game. And for months, he wined and dined her and lavished her with expensive gifts. She wondered how could she have been so stupid. With all her intelligence and wit, she never imagined getting played. Rodney had been around the music scene for a while but hadn't had much luck until Handle Up came along. Unfortunately, Monica suffered emotionally.

As she drove, she couldn't help but wonder about the new A&R rep, Drayton J. Lewis. His name sounded sophisticated enough. Monica just hoped he lived up to the intriguing reputation that preceded him. If he was half as good as everyone said he was, she could stomach him. For weeks, Bill had been ranting about how fabulous Drayton was. He was an aspiring songwriter with a degree in music who worked as a disc jockey at a hot Chicago radio station. If it was so hot, why was he leaving? Monica didn't care how good he sounded on paper, she needed help. Hopefully, he'd be the one to give it to her.

No one had to tell Dray he had it going on. He was the man and was about to let everyone know it.

"Atlanta, here I come."

Dray was on his way to becoming a music executive, something had always hoped to be. His position would enable him to learn the ropes of the music business, his passion. But more than anything, he wanted to make music. Babysitting a bunch of flighty entertainers with stars in their eyes wasn't his idea of fun. He had much more to offer, and it wouldn't be seen from behind a desk. He wanted people to hear his music, feel his music—while he made money in the process. At least Atlanta would offer him job stability and more income. The music scene just wasn't happening up north. Nor was anything happening professionally or romantically in Chicago. As an A&R rep, he'd be responsible for finding new talent and developing artists. That would be exciting.

He finished packing the last of his belongings for the movers and stood in the middle of floor. The nearly empty loft he once shared with his ex-girlfriend, Lisa Griffin, had been his residence since he graduated from Jackson State. Now that she was gone, he had no reason to stay. A good friend of his who was close to Big Bill's accountant got him the interview. The thought of moving to Georgia never crossed his mind, but the offer was too good to resist. For the first time in his life, he could see clearly and wanted to make the best of it.

Lisa was a woman with nothing more than greed and lust in her heart. An aspiring model who wanted someone to take care of her, she didn't think Dray had enough money. It didn't matter that he was handsome, educated, and talented. As soon as a guy with money came along, she was gone. She moved in with New York Jets linebacker Warrick Peters.

Dray was going to miss the Windy City: the L-train, gyros, stepper sets, and Michigan Avenue. He'd grown up here and never thought he'd see the day he would leave. But no matter what happened in Atlanta, Dray would take it head on.

"Okay! You ready to roll playa, playa?" His boyhood friend,

Adam Miller, surfaced from the bathroom with his usual giddy expression.

"Yeah, man." Dray rubbed his goatee. He knew he was forgetting something. "You seen my saxophone case?"

"There it is." Adam pointed to a group of boxes in the corner. "On top."

"Make sure these fools don't break it. That thing cost me two grand." His raspy voice echoed like running water.

"Man, you don't have to tell me. I was with you when you bought it. When's the last time you played?"

Dray threw back his head. "So long ago I can't remember."

"You should sell it."

"Nah, too much history."

They stood quietly for a moment and quickly caught each other's eye.

"You thinking about playing again?" Adam asked, folding his arms.

"Maybe when I get a reason to I will."

"Yeah, I bet some sweet little Georgia peach ass will make you play." Adam patted Dray on the back. "Well, I guess that's all, dawg. Time to roll on out."

Dray took a deep breath, "I guess so." He gave his friend a quick hug.

"I'll miss you, man," Adam joked. "I won't have nobody to go to the strip joint with." They laughed, and Dray picked up his bags.

"You need to keep your ass out of those strip joints."

"You know how I like my women: fast, easy, and no attachments. Maybe one day I'll square up and fall in love like you."

"Nigga, I ain't never been a square. You better believe that shit."

"Come on, man. We better get you to this airport before you miss your flight. I'll make sure the movers handle their business."

"Cool," Dray agreed. "Let's ride."

CHAPTER 2

The plane landed on time at Atlanta's Hartsfield International Airport. The cool weather was an indication of the evening ahead. Dray made his way to baggage claim and gathered his things. He stepped out into the brisk Georgia air. Luckily for him, it wasn't as bad as January in Chicago. And he was glad he brought his leather jacket with him. As he waited for his ride, he loosened his tie and was about to take a seat when a limo driver approached him.

"Drayton Lewis?"

"Yeah, that's me."

"Right this way, sir. I'm Robert Whitfield, your driver. How you doing this evening?" he asked with a thick southern drawl. Dray wasn't expecting a limo ride, but he wasn't about to complain.

"Just fine, Mr. Whitfield," Dray said, smiling. "I guess this is what it feels like to be a big baller," he mumbled, sliding into the back seat.

"Call me Rob, please. Is it cool enough for you?" he asked.

"No, I'm from Chicago. This is nothing compared to what I'm used to." Dray nestled himself into the comfortable leather seats.

"So," Robert began, "Big Bill tells me you'll be his new A&R

guy. You gonna be living here alone, or you bringing a wife with you?"

"It's just me," Dray said wryly. "I just got out of a relationship, and I'm not looking for another one. I need a break from women."

"Don't let the past mess up your future. Lotta good women down here would love to have a man like you. You're young, good-looking, and apparently successful because Mr. Sanders is a millionaire, and I know he takes care of his people. Know what I mean?"

"Yeah, I dig that. You married, old man?"

"I was. My wife died in seventy-six. I couldn't replace her with twenty women, and I promised my children I'd never remarry."

"She must have been really incredible." Dray could only imagine a woman special enough to make him never want another.

"You don't find many women like my Josephine. They only come 'round once in a lifetime."

"I don't know, man. Women cause too much trouble. I don't know when I'll give one the time of day," Dray mumbled.

"You will. Just wait and see."

Dray pulled out his Motorola Timeport as the limo pulled onto the freeway. He missed all of his messages during the flight. Three of them were from Handle Up, and one from Lisa. She wanted the boxes of shoes she left. Too bad. They were out with the rest of the trash. He read the other messages reminding him about the listening party in Buckhead that evening. It would be good not to have to stand in line to get in parties anymore. Working for Handle Up would grant him VIP access to all the Atlanta hot spots. He knew he would have to be fresh and clean when he stepped in the party and decided to hit up Lenox Square Mall as soon as he got settled.

Dray's temporary residence at the Wyndham Hotel in Midtown, compliments of Handle Up, was fit for a king. There was a huge king-size bed, a living area, a kitchenette, and a Jacuzzi tub. The whole place was covered in earth-tones. Dray stood in the middle of the suite and set his briefcase down on the tan Berber carpet. He sighed deeply. He was finally here. A bellboy came up shortly after to bring his bags. He thanked him with a $20 tip.

"This is phat," Dray said, walking around the room.

He took off his tie and went to the window. ATL, here I come. The view was spectacular. He could see Downtown Atlanta in the distance. The city seemed calmer than Chicago. There were lush, green trees, and the sky was a sparkling shade of baby blue. The Windy City had one hell of a view from Lakeshore Drive, but the hills of Georgia offered a sense of peace and calm. The only other state that could compare was California, and for Dray, moving there was out of the question.

After unpacking, Dray had Robert drive him to Lenox Square. As he walked through the mall, casually dressed in jeans and a T-shirt, he caught the attention of several women. It was something any heterosexual female with sense had to do these days in Atlanta. Dray heard how the local women complained that a lot of the "good" brothers were going both ways. It was scary. Many of the women didn't know if they'd end up on a date with a guy who wore more eyeliner than them.

Dray's good looks were the first thing to grab the women's attention. The second thing was his clothes and his style. He was smooth without trying to be.

He slipped into one of the pricier men's stores, and after trying on a number of ensembles, he decided on a stone-gray, four-button suit. It fit his slightly robust physique perfectly. He found a steel-blue shirt and tie, and he was ready to go.

"This is an excellent choice," the salesman said, "one of our better garments." He carried the outfit to the counter and thanked Dray with a firm handshake.

"Good choice," the bubbly cashier agreed. She batted her long eyelashes that hovered over her slanted blue eyes.

Dray smiled coolly, ignoring her flirtation. Having grown up with a beautiful and hard-working black mother, he could appreciate the black woman's struggle. There was nothing like a sistah's love and support.

He watched his total appear on the register's small black screen in turquoise numbers. It was a large amount compared to what he was used to paying for a suit, but well worth it.

"Your total comes to $656.18," the clerk said.

Dray counted the crisp hundred dollar bills he'd pulled from his pocket. I've got to get some cologne, he told himself. Got to smell good for the honeys. He owned more than fifty colognes, but another one wouldn't hurt. Since money wasn't going to be an object, he didn't mind the splurge. He would be seeing a lot more of it now that he had a real job. Being a deejay for Chicago's 92.3 radio station had finally paid off. If everything went well, one day he'd be a CEO for one of the big powerhouses like Sony or BMG, or even start his own label.

"Will you be needing anything else, sir?" the cashier asked. "We have some fabulous new loafers." She smiled, flashing her pearly whites in a poor attempt to up the salesman's commission.

"Thanks, but no thanks." Dray scanned the store one more time. I'm done here, he thought. He'd reached his spending limit for the day.

He handed her $700 and collected his change. She slid a dark brown plastic cover with the store's name over his suit and placed the shirt and tie neatly in a bag.

"Have a good evening, sir. Come by and see us again," she said, handing him the bags.

"Thanks," he said, checking his watch. Only a couple more hours to go.

After making a few more stops in the mall, Dray rode back to the hotel. He checked his Timeport again to get the exact location of the party. He read his message from the company's receptionist. The party was being held at Taboo, a chichi restaurant in Buckhead. He'd been hearing a lot about the party from Bill since his last visit. He wondered if the new group would live up to all of the hype they'd been getting. There were already established groups like 3LW and Destiny's Child topping the charts. Who was to say another girl group would sell a million copies? Time would tell. Dray just had to make sure he took care of his business. The trio of young girls from Memphis would be his pet project, and he had to represent.

Robert pulled the limo in front of the hotel. "I'll be back for you around nine."

With that, Dray exited the limo and gave Rob some dap. He admired the old man's feistiness and optimism. He handed him a fifty-dollar bill.

Robert looked insulted. "Oh, no. Save that for those honeys tonight. I'll see you in a few."

Dray smiled. "Check you later, old-timer." He waited for him to pull off before going inside. He stopped at the counter to check for messages before going to his room. There weren't any, so he hopped in the elevator and rode up to his room.

After a nice, hot shower, Dray smoothed on some cocoa-butter lotion, sprayed on his Versace Blue Jeans cologne and trimmed his goatee. He brushed his teeth and took a swig of mouthwash. If he were to make a great first impression, it had to start with something as simple as hygiene. He'd seen a lot of guys lose women just because they didn't floss or smell good. And that definitely wasn't a good thing for a debonair young man.

Fully dressed and lookin' good, Dray did a once-over in the mirror. He grabbed his wallet and headed downstairs to meet Robert. On the drive to Taboo, they engaged in stimulating conversation about life, women, love, and sports. Drayton learned Robert was a man in his late sixties. He was a retired postal worker who kept busy chauffeuring people around. Most of them were in the entertainment business or athletes. As they veered through the evening traffic,

Robert told Dray he got a kick out of listening to his drunken passengers' conversations. He heard more confessions than a Catholic priest.

"I hear Bill throws some fabulous parties," Robert chuckled. "Watch those young girls. They're trouble for a young man like you."

"I know, but I'm not looking for one. I'll just see what I can see."

"That shouldn't be a problem. There's a lot of pretty women here. Just watch yourself."

The limousine pulled in front of Taboo alongside a number of luxury cars double-parked in front. A red Bentley and a pearl white Escalade occupied the space near the front door. There were matching blue S600 Mercedes double-parked near the entrance too. Damn, Dray thought. This is baller heaven. He popped in an Altoid and smoothed his jacket. He examined himself in the mirror, a vision of perfection. His slightly curly hair complemented his strong bone structure and smile. He was sure to knock em' dead. He sprayed on some cologne from the sample he had in his pocket and prepared to get the night underway. The line trailed around the corner, but he knew he wouldn't have to wait. He adjusted his tie once more and stepped out.

"Enjoy yourself," Robert winked. "It's gon' be a hot one." He nodded toward the gawking females.

"Thanks, old man. I'll check you later."

Dray caught several eyes as he strolled up to the door. His broad shoulders and broad chest made him look every bit the former college football player he was. A group of women near the front whispered in one another's ears as they checked his assets. He lowered his head smiling. He hadn't been flattered in a while. They seemed focused on his alluring presence as he made his way towards the entrance.

"Damn, baby is working that suit," one woman yelled. Dray smiled as he peered over at the line of people, but he didn't see who had said it. It was probably best. His grandfather told him once if you hear a woman before you see her, leave her alone. Definitely words to live by.

Other women, and men alike, sized him up. His suit and striking steel-blue shirt and tie complemented his bronze-tinted skin. He was tipping scales tonight. There were gasps from the female admirers and envious stares from the men as he strutted confidently to the door. Paying them no mind, he approached the attractive hostess who was sheltered by a bodyguard.

"Good evening, Mr. Lewis." The greeting caught him off guard. He didn't expect anyone to know who he was.

"Good evening," he mumbled hesitantly. He stared at the petite honey dip before him. How in the world does she know my name? Her face looked familiar but he couldn't remember where he'd seen her before.

"Here is your badge . . . and oh, Mr. Sanders wants to see you. He's in VIP already."

"By the way, what's your name?" Dray asked in his deep, syrupy voice. She smiled as he clipped the badge on his lapel.

"I'm Patrice. I'm an intern for the company. Remember, I was at the office when you visited a couple of weeks ago?"

"Oh, yeah." He didn't remember meeting her, but he didn't want to hurt her feelings either. "Nice to see you again, Patrice. Thanks for the badge."

"Sure thing," she winked.

Dray stepped inside the noisy building, nodding his head as he made his way through the ambiguous crowd. He passed several scantily clad women, many of them whispering names of who's who. Dray offered a dry smile as he made his way toward VIP. He felt over-dressed as he stepped up to the small area with a number of familiar faces, most of the people worked for Handle Up. Many of the VIPs were in jeans, T-shirts, and flashy platinum jewelry. Better safe than sorry, he thought.

"Dray, my man, glad to see you finally made it." Cameron James was the vice president of Handle Up, and Big Bill's right-hand man. He was also an ex-NFL player.

Dray greeted him with a hug and a pound. "What's up, man? It's good to see you."

"I'm glad we got you here in one piece. So far, so good?"

"Yeah. Where's Bill?"

"He's relaxing. Come on, I'll show you around. Did you get a chance to meet the Prima Donnas yet? They've been asking for you all night."

Dray followed Cameron down the steps to the floor.

"No, I haven't had the pleasure. All I've seen are pictures."

"Well, believe me, they're much prettier in person. If I was eighteen again, I'd be in love with them like the rest of these dudes."

The pair crossed the room, running into a few celebrities along the way: the boxer Roy Jones Jr., DMX, Vivica A. Fox. Everyone seemed to be having a good time. The medium-sized restaurant had turned into a snazzy club, filled with thumping music.

"So this is how they do it in Atlanta," Dray muttered. "Still ghetto fabulous, I see."

Cameron smiled. "Don't let the canapés and champagne fool you. This is all work. Shoot, I've got to punch a time clock when I leave here," he joked. "Mr. Sanders is all about business. He takes care of his artists, and they take care of him. I'm sure you'll like working for him."

"I'm sure I will too," Dray replied as they approached a group of people huddled around small tables.

Big Bill Sanders was seated in a plush red chair, surrounded by ladies, in a corner of the club. The older gentleman with salt-and-pepper hair looked every bit the ladies' man dressed in a thin, smoke-colored, silk sweater and matching slacks, socks, and shoes. He looked like a genuine ol' school player. A Rolex Presidential encrusted with diamonds and a platinum link bracelet adorned his wrist. He cocked his eye as Cameron and Dray made their approach. He smiled as they greeted him.

"How you doing, Mr. Sanders?" Dray slapped him five.

A wide grin came across the old man's face. "Fine, son, just fine. Have a seat. I see Cam's been taking good care of you. Did you enjoy your flight?"

"It was alright. I really dug the limo ride," Dray grinned.

"Figured you would. Get used to it. Things like that happen every day around here. Have you met Monica? She's our publicist." Bill snapped his fingers. "Somebody pour this young man a drink."

"No, I haven't met Monica yet." One of the ladies next to Bill handed Dray a glass of champagne. He thanked her and smiled.

"Well," Bill said, "you will. Have a seat, son. Monica's a very beautiful woman . . . intelligent too. I depend on her a lot. She keeps the media off our backs. Those people can be vultures. You'll definitely know her when you see her."

Cameron nodded. "She is fine and has long, pretty hair."

"Will I be working with her?" Dray asked, before realizing how dumb the question was.

"Of course, you will. You're her boss. You all have a meeting set up for Monday morning, bright and early." Bill looked around the party. "Cam, see if you can find the girls. Bring them over here so they can meet their new A&R rep."

"No, problem," Cam said. "I'll be back."

Bill set his cigar in the ashtray. "The Prima Donnas are young, starstruck, and naive. I have Monica working with them on etiquette, you know. They can sing but they need more nurturing and guidance. Moni's done a fine job so far, but I need a young man's opinion as well. We want to go all out. Their album drops tomorrow. The single's been doing really well."

"Yeah, they're playing it back at the crib."

"Good. That's good to know. Chicago is a good town, and full of surprises."

Definitely, Dray thought. Too many damn surprises. He rubbed his chin as he saw the trio of young ladies making their way over. The glamorous looking seventeen-year-olds were clad in similar outfits in shades of pink. Their hair weaves flowed lushly down their backs, their complexions ranging from café au lait to mocha.

"Ladies, this is your new A&R rep, Dray Lewis."

"Hi!" they said simultaneously. "He's so cute," one of them whispered.

"These are the Prima Donnas: Rochelle, Amber, and Kim. Mr. Lewis will be your daddy from here on out, musically, that is."

"It's a pleasure, ladies." Dray held his hand out to greet each of the girls. They gushed, epitomizing their youth as he smiled at them.

After a brief chat with the group and a few pointers from Bill, Dray loosened his tie. Bill urged him to mingle and get a stronger drink. Dray ordered Hennessey on the rocks with a twist of lemon. He scanned the room, seeing several artists whose CDs were in his collection: Ludacris, Jay-Z, and a few others. He didn't realize the position he was in until some hot starlet who lived in Atlanta tried to hit on him. He graciously declined her invitation to meet later. He wasn't in the mood for flirting; Lisa had made sure of that. He finished his Hennessey and ordered a cranberry martini.

With his drink in hand, he decided to go back to VIP. He sipped it as he made his way through the crowd, caught in a swarm of dancing partygoers. As they bounced up and down, squirming from side to side, he strolled towards the VIP booth. He maneuvered fine until someone bumped him, and cold liquid dripped on his hand. What alarmed him even more was the face of the screaming culprit.

"Damn!" she huffed. "Look at my dress! I just got it out of the cleaners!"

She was talking so fast, it took him a minute to understand what she was saying. Dray stood baffled as he looked at the petite beauty clad in all white. She had smooth mocha skin, glistening wine-red lips, and piercing sable eyes. He knew who she was without even hearing her name. Cameron was right. Her long ebony tresses were beautiful. They dangled in corkscrewed ringlets all the way down her back. He couldn't help but stare; she looked like a ravishing lioness in the midst of stalking her prey. Even with all her feistiness, she was the most exquisite creature in the room.

"I'm sorry!" Dray uttered, struggling to maintain his cool. "I didn't see you." As she fussed, he tried to help absorb the stain with his napkin.

She shot him a cold look. "Don't touch me! You've already done enough. Just get away from me."

"It was an accident, baby. My bad."

She lifted her head, revealing the rage in her eyes. "Well, maybe you should see a doctor if you're prone to having accidents. And I'm not your baby."

Not yet, he wanted to say, though a look of defeat came across his face. "I said I was sorry. Can't you just let it go?"

"Let it go? Do you have any idea how much this dress cost?"

"No, I don't," he snapped. "But I'm sure you're going to tell me."

"Six hundred dollars!" She pointed her finger at him. "That's probably more than you have on right now and more than you make in a month."

Hardly, Dray thought. And just who did this snotty little chick think she was talking to in that tone of voice?

His curt voice lashed at her, "You don't know what the hell I make in a month. Money is probably all some little gold digger like you cares about."

He'd just blown $600 on the suit he was wearing. How dare she insult him like that. He threw his hand up as they stood in the middle of the floor. Everyone around them was staring. Dray didn't like being a spectacle.

"So what the hell are you gonna do, condemn me to hell for messing up your little stanky ass dress? Damn, gold-diggin'. . . ."

She put her hands on her hips. "I am not a gold-digger, nigga. I make more money than any broad in this room."

Damn, she was feisty!

"Look, I said I was sorry for the last time. If you can't accept my apology, that's your damn problem." His voice was firm and left no room for discussion.

She rolled her eyes. "Whatever," she mumbled.

His eyes blazed with sudden anger. "I don't have time for this."

As they looked into each other's eyes, an erotic wave passed between them. They both turned away in embarrassment. As the temptress in the white dress ranted under her breath, Dray realized no matter what he said, it would never please her. She was mad at the world right now and everyone in it. He wondered what type of woman would spend $600 on a dress anyway. But she was the prettiest woman in the room, so she deserved to wear the dress. And like she said, she made more money than any other woman in the room. Who was he to argue?

Despite her melodramatic behavior, there was something fascinating about her. As she stood in front of him, he noticed her flawless face and full, heart-shaped mouth. The way her lips curled in frustration excited him. He wanted to kiss her.

"Here," he said, handing her another napkin. "This may help."

She snatched it from him. "Just leave me alone, please."

Dray had made a mistake, but he wasn't about to be insulted, not even at the hands of a beautiful woman. "You know, your attitude is . . ."

"Ah, I see you've met Monica," Cameron said, as he approached them.

Dray sighed, "Yeah."

Monica's eyes widened briefly, before narrowing. "He met me with his glass," she mocked. "You know him, Cam?"

"Nice move, Dray," he joked. "Yeah, I know him. This is Drayton Lewis, our new A&R director."

Dray extended his hand.

"Yeah, yeah," Monica said angrily, ignoring it. She had had just about enough of him for one evening.

While Dray and Cameron talked, Monica took in his exquisite, compelling ebony eyes. She admired his neatly trimmed goatee and full lips. She loved handsome men with facial hair. But quickly remembered her "no men, no problems" policy and focused on the matter at hand.

"Cameron," she began, "could you tell our new A&R rep that he needs to take some classes on how to hold a martini glass properly?"

Dray couldn't believe how simple she was being. He'd done all the apologizing he was going to do for the night. "Cam, could you tell Miss Holiday she shouldn't have worn white to a party like this?"

Stumped for words, Cameron tried to ease the tension. "Hey, hey, guys. Relax. Hopefully the next time y'all bump into each other, it will be under less excruciating circumstances." He patted Dray on the back and nudged Monica's arm.

"Are we cool now?" Cameron asked.

"Yeah, we're cool." Dray decided to be the bigger person. "I'm sorry about the dress, Monica."

"I'm sure," she said rolling her eyes. "Where is Bill? I need to make sure he knows what he's doing hiring people like him."

She stormed off and headed for the rest room, rattling along the way. Dray watched her hips sway as she walked away. A part of him was turned on.

"Damn, she's cold," he mumbled. But Bill was right, she was beautiful.

"Don't sweat it, dude," Cameron said, putting his arm around Dray's neck. "Moni's always like that. She can be real funky sometimes. Been that way since her boyfriend broke up with her."

"Really? I wonder why?" Dray smirked.

"Very funny," Cam said, shaking his head at Dray. "But seriously, he used her. You've heard of Double R, haven't you?"

"The rapper?"

"Yeah. He's the top cat on our label."

"Damn. He doesn't seem like her type."

"He's nobody's type. As soon as he made it big, he left her. That fool's around here somewhere. That's probably why she came down on you so hard. She hates to be in the same room with him. Can't say that I blame her though. He's an asshole and a little cold around the heart. When they were together, he did all kind of shit for her; then one day he tripped out and that was the end of it."

"That's too bad."

"Fucked up, ain't it?"

"Yeah," Dray said, looking over the crowd toward the rest room where Monica had gone. Fucked up.

CHAPTER 3

Saturday morning Monica woke up bright and early. She showered and fixed herself a latte with extra sugar. She opened her blinds wide, glaring down at the Atlanta skyline. The view was one of the things she loved about her luxury high-rise condo in Buckhead. She pulled out her clothes for the day's outing and called her best friend, Robin Golden, a social worker. Monica still hadn't gotten over Friday night's disaster. The white dress was literally priceless. She'd gone to a boutique on Peachtree Road looking for a pair of jeans when she came across it. The boutique wasn't frequented by average Jane's. It was a store that catered to uppity women like Monica. They served tea and crumpets while you shopped.

"Girl, can you believe my white dress is ruined? It was damn near one of a kind. There were only three sold in the South. No one else in Atlanta had my dress. Damn him."

She paced the floor of her bedroom, garbed in her pink bathrobe.

"Who spilled the drink?" Robin asked.

"That damn fine-ass, smooth-talking Drayton Lewis."

"Who's he?"

"The new A&R director. He's a handsome son-of-a-bitch, but I could kill him!"

"Is he that handsome?"

"Girl, he has the most beautiful ebony eyes, and his lips . . . full and soft like cotton candy."

"So you kissed him?"

Monica snapped out of her spell. "Hell no! They just look like they taste good!"

"Um-hmm, you really do need a man."

"No, I don't. I'm not into the relationship thing anymore. They're not made for people like me."

"People like you are exactly the ones who need them."

"Well, you can stop holding your breath because I'm done with that crap. I'm focusing on my career, and that's it."

"I know that's bull shit, Monica. But if you take pleasure in telling me about it, so be it. You know you want a good sticking!"

"Yeah, a good stick without the ignorant bastard attached to it would be lovely." Monica refused to talk about it any further. She held her dress up again, and pouted. "That stupid Negro ruined my dress."

"Get over it, girl . . . shit! It's just a dress."

"It is not just a dress."

"You can afford to buy another one, can't you?" Robin mocked.

"Yes, I can, but that's not the point. I love this dress."

Robin sighed at her friend's misfortune. "You really need a man to take you away. You're trippin'. You've been like this since Rodney left you. I've never seen you dwell on something so frivolous. Get a grip. Burn the shit and let's go eat somewhere."

"I don't need a man to make me happy, Robin. I keep telling you that."

"No, but you need one to help you release some of that tension. The right man can cure all that shit."

"Not necessarily, freak mama. I can go to a spa for that."

"Ain't no spa going to feel like a big, black, strong . . . body pressing up against yours."

Monica couldn't hold her laugh. She plopped down on her plush Natuzzi leather couch. "Maybe you're right," she said, looking out the bay window. She coiled the cord around her finger. "I hate almost every minute I'm alone now, thanks to Rodney." There was a brief silence.

"Forget him, girl. You deserve better. Hell, you've had better. Mr. Right will come along, you'll see. And when you least expect it."

"I guess so."

"So are we still going to eat and head to Lenox or what?"

"Yeah. I'll be over in a few. Please be ready, Robin. You know I hate waiting," Monica pleaded.

"Yes, Queen Bee. I'll be ready."

Monica threw on her denim Capri pants, a white T-shirt that read Diva across the front, and black slides. She gathered her Gucci hobo bag and sunglasses as she trekked out the front door. A good salary and a killer client list allowed her to indulge in the finer things in life like designer handbags, expensive sunglasses, and spa trips. Robin was a bit more laid back. She preferred jeans to slacks, wore mules instead of heels, and liked to keep her hair natural. She had a neat pile of micro braids on top of her head. Her tawny colored skin was glowing and free of make up. Today, she was wearing a tie-dyed tank top, khaki shorts, and white deck shoes. Despite their fashion differences, Monica and her bohemian friend had one thing in common, they loved to talk.

Monica pulled up to the valet. She greeted him and slid out of the seat while another guy opened the door for Robin. The ESPN Zone was packed as usual. As they made their way to the door, they hoped the wait wouldn't be too long. They used their waiting time to sit down and see who's who. After fifteen minutes, Monica pleaded with the host to get them a table. She'd even sit on the patio, something she never liked to do. She was only able to get bumped up to the number ten spot on the waiting list. She and Robin took the beeper and went to sit outside on a bench in front of the restaurant.

"So what's this new guy like?" Robin asked, pulling a cigarette from her silver case.

Monica frowned, "What new guy?"

"The A&R rep." Robin crossed her muscular legs in a mockery of Monica's innocence and put the cigarette in her mouth.

"How should I know? I just met him last night," Monica griped.

Robin lit the cigarette. "On your men scale of 1 to 10, visually what is he?"

Monica reapplied her lipstick. "Probably a five. He's clumsy as hell."

"Seriously, Monica."

She smiled big. "I am serious. He's a klutz. A handsome one, but still a klutz" She took a deep breath and watched Robin's eyes narrow. "Okay, okay. He's about six-one or two, smooth bronze skin and a nice body."

"Would you date him?"

"If you paid me?"

"That's your problem, Monica. You always think with your wallet. Let a man just love you how you need to be loved. Stop worrying about his money."

"I never worry about a man's money. I have plenty," she sighed. "I just want a man who will sweep me off my feet and not be so damn serious all the time. Is that too much to ask?"

"No," Robin said. "Not really."

"The men I've dated are either too ghetto or too stuck up. I don't want a man who folds his socks before he gets into bed or one who can't eat without using hot sauce on everything. Why can't I have an intelligent man who can bring it in bed?"

Robin was laughing. "Because if life were that simple, it wouldn't be any fun. And I wouldn't need to smoke." She took a drag from her cigarette.

Just then a silver Mercedes-Benz stretch limo pulled up. Onlookers at the restaurant were breaking their necks to see who it was. The driver got out and walked to the back. When he opened the back door, a crisp pair of white tennis shoes hit the pavement. Monica gasped and turned away.

"Damn!"

"What?" Robin asked, puzzled.

"You know that's nobody but Rodney. Why does he keep doing this?"

"Doing what?"

"Showing up everywhere I go. If I didn't know better, I would think he had my phone tapped."

"Maybe he does have your phone tapped," Robin joked. "He's definitely got enough cash to do it."

"That was cute, Miss Golden. But I'm serious."

"I am, too. Is that him?"

Sure enough, Rodney "Double R" Robinson emerged from the limousine. He wasn't alone. His entourage exited the limo with him. Dressed in a FUBU denim ensemble, he stood proud like new money. A group of females popped out moments later. They looked like they were missing pieces of their outfits. Rodney took the hand of a fair-skinned one who was enjoying her five minutes of fame. They paused as a group of admirers flocked around him.

"Who's the girl?" Robin asked.

Monica shrugged. "Who knows? She's probably just one of his groupies. He seems to like things cheap and easy."

"You weren't cheap and easy, Monica."

"You got that right!"

"Don't let him know he got the best of you, even if he did."

Monica felt her heart sink again. He may as well have. Every time she looked at him, she wanted to cry. If only he hadn't been so unmerciful about their breakup, she would be able to cope. Embarrassing her in public was the worst thing he could have ever done. It took a copy of the *Journal-Constitution* for Monica to know she wasn't his girlfriend anymore. On top of that, he escorted another girl to an awards banquet that Monica had gotten him tickets to.

There wasn't anything special about him. Rodney was average looking, but he was vain. He was one of those guys you might dismiss at first glance, but once you got to know him, he was alright. He was tall like an athlete, and covered with coffee-colored skin. And his goatee neatly surrounded a full set of lips. Monica twitched nervously as their eyes met. He waved and offered her a phony smile as he embraced the young woman he was with.

"Moni, if you want, we can leave."

"No. I'm not going to run every time he shows up. I live here, too." Just then the beeper went off. "Time to eat. Come on, Robin. This one's on me." She shot Rodney a nasty glance and exhaled.

After lunch, Monica and Robin made their way to Lenox Square and Phipps Plaza. Robin settled for a pair of sandals, a dress, and shades. Monica opted for a new handbag, a coat, and three pairs of shoes. She knew she'd spent too much when the clerk in Saks asked her if she wanted to sign up for the shop-by-appointment-only program. She politely refused while Robin giggled. She'd never seen her shell out so much money in one day.

"Girl, you are really special. Just make sure you will some of that stuff to me. I can't afford any Ferragamo pumps."

"Very funny, Robin. Maybe if you stop working for the people you can."

Offended, Robin lashed back. "I enjoy my charitable work.

Why do you bourgeois folk always look down your noses at people? I make money. I just don't wear it on my back, Miss Thing."

Monica sensed she hurt Robin's feelings. "I didn't mean it like that, Rob. I just happen to like my designer duds. And hell, you only live once."

Robin sighed as she and Monica got in the car.

"I'm sorry, girl," Monica said. "I didn't mean to offend you. I'm stressed out right now. Maybe I need a vacation."

Robin smirked. "You don't need a vacation. You need someone to seduce you and treat you like a lady. Call one of your old flames."

"For what? So they can aggravate me all over again? No, thank you. I can't stand to be around any of them for more than three minutes a day anyway." Monica turned the key and started the engine. There had to be a better solution.

Later that evening, Monica rested on her couch going through her clients' portfolios. She jotted down notes, revised their bios, and threw away outdated photos. Some of the artists needed new photos. Scheduling photo sessions was next on her to-do list. Right now, she had to focus on the Prima Donnas. She wanted to get them some advertising contracts, somewhere along the lines of make-up or clothing endorsements. They were young and hot and needed to represent something of the same caliber. She made a note on her calendar to call a local cosmetic company to see if they'd like the girls as spokes models. They had to compete with groups like Destiny's Child and 702, but they also had to be grounded. None of that diva crap some of the other girl groups were pulling. At least not yet.

If one of the girls was going to be paid for something, so would the others. If they wrote songs as individuals, only that individual would get credit. If any of them wanted to write a song, they would have the opportunity to do so. Luckily for the company, there weren't any family members involved with the decisions. It would only lead to trouble. Too many opinions equaled too much drama.

Handle Up's focus was to put the Prima Donnas in the public eye and keep them there. After preparing some herbal tea, Monica made a few phone calls: one to her hair stylist, another to the bookstore, and the last one to her mother in Dallas for mother-daughter chitchat.

"So dear, how are you?" her mother asked. Helen Holiday was always prim and proper. She'd taught Monica to be the same way, but sometimes her daughter's choices didn't please her.

"Fine, sort of."

"Well, dear, you can't be sort of fine. Either you are or you aren't."

"Things could be better."

"That goes without saying." Her mother took a deep breath. "You know your sister Melody showed me a copy of the newspaper article. I can't believe Rodney would do such a thing."

Monica exhaled. "Well, he did. It's been awhile, and I couldn't believe it either."

"I knew he wasn't right for you. I never understood what you saw in that fool anyway. As beautiful as you are, you need a strong, handsome man. Not some cheap Negro who curses every other sentence. I don't understand you young girls. This would never have happened in my day."

"I know, ma, I know. Please don't start. I'm too tired to fuss."

"You're not fussing, I am. I do want grandchildren, you know?"

"Yes, ma. I know. And I'm doing the best I can." Monica sighed heavily.

"Have you been on a date lately?"

"No. But I did meet this cute guy at our party for the Prima Donnas."

"Is he a rapper too?" Helen asked dryly.

"No, he's our new A&R director."

"Is he cute?"

"Gorgeous," she said smiling in spite of herself.

"Well, if he's an A&R director, that means he's financially stable. Good-looking, too, that's a plus."

"Anyway," Monica said, knowing her mother could go on and on about her love life, "I'll call you later on in the week."

"Okay, dear. I'll talk to you later."

♫

It was Monday morning already and Monica was running late. She'd overslept — again. There was so much going on at work. She'd been lagging on her responsibilities. She showered quickly and threw her clothes on. It was a good thing she had ironed the night before. She fled the apartment and headed for work. She pulled her car into a space marked Handle Up and grabbed her bag.

It was already 9:45. She knew Bill hated tardiness, so she was prepared to apologize. Usually meetings weren't formal, so she was surprised to see everyone in suits. Luckily she was wearing a navy sheath dress with her heels and could blend in. It was too hot for a jacket, so she had opted for a sweater.

When she entered the boardroom, she was greeted with a dose of sarcasm. "Nice of you to join us, Ms. Holiday," Vera Leaks, the company's account manager, said. Vera gave Monica a dirty look. She always had an attitude and was more than a little jealous of Monica, and anyone else who looked better than she did.

"You missed some of our new A&R director's presentation," she added.

Monica flashed a toothless smile and took a seat next to Cameron. She wasn't in the mood to entertain Vera and her scoffing remarks. She leaned over and tapped Cameron for an update.

At first, Dray didn't mind the lateness, but Monica's whispering in the middle of his presentation was unacceptable. He waited for her to stop before he continued.

"Are you done, Ms. Holiday?" His dark eyes flashed a firm warning.

She looked up at the handsome man who'd ruined her dress and frowned. "Excuse me?"

"Are you done with your conversation so I can continue?"

Her gaze pierced him. "I was trying to get briefed on what you were talking about."

His expression grew still and serious. He wasn't intimidated to say the least. "If you have a question, then ask me."

The group held their breath. Dray didn't know Monica well enough to talk to her like that. She could have a bad attitude. Sure she'd been late a few times, usually because of some disaster with an artist. But it was always overlooked. She was extremely busy, and no one wanted to step on her toes. Even Bill would let her slide now and then. Monica decided to let the remark go, and tapped her fingers lightly on the desk as she ignored Dray. She seethed with anger. For the first time in a long time, a man had left her speechless.

As Dray went on with his agenda, Monica looked over at Bill. He was leaning back in his chair at the end of the table. He smiled and shrugged. She looked back up to the front and paid no attention to the small portfolio that was lying in front of her. Who did this guy think he was talking to her like that? She'd been at the company much longer than he, and he was treating her like a child. She definitely had to make sure it didn't happen again. No, he wasn't going to get away with this.

When the meeting was over, Monica waited for the room to clear. She had to confront Dray about what he'd done. He couldn't possibly understand the seriousness of his mistake. Hand on hip, Monica stood patiently by the door. As everyone exited the room whispering, she felt her heart pounding against her ribs. She was so nervous she was shaking. Be cool, she told herself. Dray gathered his things, preparing to head back to his office. As he turned toward the door, she stepped in front of him, her face flushed.

"Excuse me, Mr. Lewis." She tried to keep her fragile control.

"I need to talk to you." Damn why does he have to be so fine. He's almost perfect.

Dray set his things on the table and folded his arms. His onyx eyes narrowed. "About what?" he asked.

Somewhere she found courage to speak. "I . . . I just wanted to let you know that I didn't appreciate you putting me on the spot like that. Your tone of voice was totally inappropriate when you addressed me and . . . "

He put his hand up to cut her off. "Well, I didn't appreciate your tone of voice when we were at the party the other night either. Maybe if you hadn't been so rude to me, we wouldn't be having this conversation."

He leaned over and picked up his belongings.

"Too bad you messed up, Ms. Holiday. I may be new in town, but I'm not about to deal with your old bullshit," he warned.

She stared, motionless. She couldn't believe what he just said. "Excuse me?" she said, hand on hip.

Dray looked up, his face perilously close to hers. She fought to catch her breath when she got a whiff of his sandalwood. He moved to straighten his tie.

"I think you might need a course in punctuality and grace. Now, if you'll excuse me, Ms. Holiday, I have a job to do. Have a nice day." He left the room.

Bastard! Monica wanted to scream. Her heart was still pounding from their moment of closeness. And she struggled to catch her breath. *Who the hell does he think he is? He's so damn sure of himself he thinks he can just make me look like a fool!*

Drayton Lewis had made her look like an idiot twice — in less than a week. There wouldn't be a third time so she made a pact with herself to avoid him. She picked up her things and stormed out of the room. Damn him, she thought. Damn him.

"Hey, Monica," Patrice said, nearly losing her balance as Monica brushed past her.

"Hey!" she yelled, furiously walking into her office and shutting the door behind her. There was no way Drayton Lewis would have the last word again.

Later that afternoon, after a couple of meetings, Dray took a moment to relax. He hadn't had time to himself all day. He popped two Advil into his mouth and leaned back in his chair. When he swallowed the pills, he sat up again. He decided to return his boy Adam's call. Adam had already left three messages.

His friend was excited to hear from him. "What's the deal with the job?"

"It's cool. I'm tired, man. I've been working my ass off. We're busy trying to get this thing going with the Prima Donnas. They're supposed to go on tour in a couple of weeks."

"Sounds good. What's up with the women in the ATL?"

"Man!" Dray felt a chill go up his spine just thinking about Monica. She'd been on his mind since their first meeting. "There's one in particular."

"Who is she?"

"The company publicist, Monica Holiday."

"Cute name. What's the deal with her?"

"Man, this girl is fire. She's fine as hell. But she has a smart-ass mouth." Dray pounded his fist on his desk. "She's trippin' on me because I spilled a drink on her white dress at the party. Bourgeois broads make me sick. If she was a dude, I'd probably choke her ass."

He shuffled through a stack of photos and tapes on his desk, balancing the phone between his ear and shoulder.

Adam laughed. "Damn, D. She had you buggin' like that?"

"Man, you just don't know. She ain't like these other women. She'll tell you where to go and where to stick it!"

Adam chuckled. "Where's she from?"

"I'm not sure yet. But I think she went to college down here."

"Maybe she's giving you a hard time because she likes you."

"I don't know what her problem is. But she better get her shit straight if she's gonna work for me."

"Damn, you're lucky. I'd kill to be around intelligent, beautiful women every day. These vultures up here get on my nerves. All they want is money, money, money. Hands always out."

"You like that, though. You've always liked hood rats."

"Fuck you, man. What's your honey's name again?"

"Monica."

"Well, go easy on her, dawg. She's not Lisa."

"Yeah, she's definitely not Lisa. She's a whole different breed." If Lisa had had half the class Monica had, maybe she would have been a bit more tactful when she dumped him, he thought. Now it didn't matter. He was on to bigger and better things. And hopefully the better part would include a decent conversation with one lovely publicist.

Dray leaned back in his chair and closed his eyes. He was starting to feel the effects of the music business already. He was scheduled to meet with the girls the next day to talk about their tour. He'd only been on the job one day and was already beat.

"Man, I've got to get out of here," he said, opening his eyes. "I'm tired as hell."

"You know where you wanna live yet?" Adam asked.

Dray sighed deeply. "No, I will soon, though. My room's paid up for the rest of this week. I think I'm going to check out these lofts at lunch tomorrow."

"Can't get that Chicago living out of your blood, huh?"

"Never." There was a deep silence. "I'll buzz you later on during the week, dawg."

"Cool, man. Later."

Dray piled some files into his briefcase and grabbed his jacket. He didn't realize how late it was until he looked at the sunset outside the lobby's window. Damn, he thought. It was time to go home already. He had so many things to do and still hadn't finished them all. Hopefully. tomorrow would go a little smoother. If he played his cards right, he'd be organized by Friday and able to devote his time to pursuing some other acts, if Bill didn't mind.

He pulled his blazer on and grabbed his briefcase. When he went out into the hall, all he heard was silence. The receptionist was gone, and every office was dark except for one. He strolled down the hall quietly to peek inside. He was surprised to see the vision of loveliness that had caused him to step out of his usual humble character, working diligently. He wanted to interrupt her and tell her how sorry he was and that he wished they could start over. Neither of them had given each other the chance to be friendly.

Monica mumbled to herself quietly, and it made him smile. He was tempted to apologize, but feared his efforts would cause another argument. She was hunched over her desk listening to Billie Holliday. Dray liked the fact that she had such good taste. Not only in music but clothes too. He would never tell her. Complimenting her would be the kiss of death. She was far too opinionated and would probably offer him nothing but heartache.

CHAPTER 4

The Prima Donnas arrived for their meeting with Dray like teenage celebrities. They complained about not having enough sleep and hating the outfits they wore on their album cover. Once they were seated, Dray had them each write out the things they hoped to accomplish and things they needed for their tour as artists. He wanted to make sure he and the girls got off to a good start developing their business relationship. He read each girl's list. Amber, the shy one, wanted to write some of the songs. Kim, the outgoing caramel beauty, wanted a new set of luggage; and Rochelle, the funny one, wanted a personal hair stylist. Dray thought their demands were minor for girls of their status. But they were cute. He stapled the papers and placed them into a file folder. His first goal was to make sure all of them were intelligent enough to know what was going on around them. Beautiful, dumb girls had no place in the music industry. They would only be setting themselves up as prey to the vultures in the business. He'd start with some Q and A time.

"Can I have spring water?" Rochelle, the fair-skinned one, asked. "I'm thirsty."

"Have you eaten?" Dray asked, holding his clipboard.

She batted her pretty little eyes. "Nope. We had some doughnuts, that's it."

Dray buzzed Patrice and told her to get some bagels and cream cheese from Einstein's on the corner for the Prima Donnas. She came in and got each girl's preferences, and Dray handed her the money. As their meeting got underway, Patrice left the boardroom quietly. Dray was chatting with the girls when Monica popped her head in the door. When she saw Dray, she tried to close the door quickly.

"Monica!" Amber called quietly. "Come here!" The chocolate-coated beauty had the full makings of a diva in training. She was dressed in a fitted denim dress with a pair of white tennis shoes. An anklet enclosed her tiny ankle.

"Yes, Amber?" Monica mustered sarcastically. She could tell Amber was up to something. There was a mischievous look in her eyes.

Amber pulled Monica in the door by the arm and whispered, "Don't you think Mr. Lewis is cute? I think he's cute." She fingered her ponytail.

Monica shrugged as she shifted her eyes toward him. "He's alright."

Dray looked up, and their eyes locked for the first time since their spat in the boardroom. She could feel the power he exuded. He was strong, articulate, and attractive. It wasn't going to be easy to deal with him. One look into his coal-black eyes, and she'd melt like butter in a hot cast-iron skillet. She tried to relax so the girls wouldn't sense her jitters.

"What's up, Monica?" Kim asked, smiling. She was the mature one of the group. She stood about five-eight and had striking green eyes that complemented her tawny skin.

"Nothing much, just work," Monica answered.

"I'm getting some new luggage," Kim said proudly. "Louis Vuitton or Gucci. Mr. Lewis is gonna get it."

Monica's brow rose. "Oh, is he now?"

Dray sat at the table, observing her. Monica was dressed in a cute little beige suit and matching heels. She had a pair of long legs that complemented her slender frame. She was very well put together. Her almond-shaped eyes were a perfect match for her dainty oval face. Dray couldn't keep his eyes off her. One look at her, and she'd be on his mind all day. He wanted to greet her, but her defensive expression indicated she didn't want to be bothered. The girls seemed to have most of her attention anyway.

"We want you to help us pick out outfits," Rochelle whined. "You have such good taste."

"Yeah, Moni, come on!" Amber yelled. "The ones we had on our cover were terrible."

Monica's eyes fell on Dray. "I'm sure Mr. Lewis has a stylist to help you do that. That's what he's here for."

Dray took her comments as an opportunity to make a new start and break the ice again. He knew she despised him, but he had to follow his instincts.

"Actually, I'd like to find them their own personal stylist, in addition to Rochelle's hair stylist," he said. "I was hoping you could help me with that. I don't want them to look like anyone else." He anticipated her response and searched her eyes for a sign of compliance. There was none.

Instead, she gazed nervously back and forth. "Patrice can help you with that. I'm working on something right now." She met his eyes with an icy glare.

"Fine," Dray said firmly. He rose from his chair and ushered the girls back to their seats.

"I'll see you later, girls," Monica said.

"Can I talk to you outside please, Ms. Holiday?"

"Sure," she said dryly. She sucked her teeth.

What did he want now? Another chance to bite her head off?

The blood began to pound in Monica's temples. She wasn't in the mood for chit-chat, especially not with him. He came from behind the table and walked toward her. She knew he was upset. He seemed to be huffing as he got closer. She folded her arms as he pulled the door open. When they stepped outside, she leaned on the wall and looked at everything but him.

He was angry, and it was hard for him not to approach her the wrong way. She'd been against him since they met. But he was still attracted to her. And he couldn't understand why. She pasted on a smile of nonchalance. He knew she was dying for a chance to chew him out again since he'd embarrassed her at the staff meeting.

"Listen, Miss . . ."

"Ms.," Monica corrected.

"Ms. Holiday. I know we got off to a bad start, but we're going to have to get along sooner or later."

"Maybe later then," she said smartly.

He groaned and placed his hands in his pants pockets. "Can you please get off your high horse and act professional for once?"

"Professional? Why don't you try being professional?"

Dray's eyes darkened. "Ms. Holiday, I am still your superior, and you will treat me as such . . . ."

She cut him off and put her hand on her hip. "The only thing superior is the chip on your shoulder. I've been here a lot longer . . ."

It was his turn to cut her off. "I don't give a damn how long you've been here, you will respect me. Do you understand?" Monica was a part of the PR department, and Dray was her boss. But that didn't quite sit well with her.

He continued, "I will not take this shit from you anymore. You're acting like a goddamn child. For someone who has such a nice face, you can be a real . . . " He was on the verge of insulting her. She was trying his patience. "I'm not going to ask you to stop this crap again!" he yelled.

Monica's face flushed in embarrassment. She looked deep into his eyes for a bit of humor. When she realized he was serious, she stood tight-lipped.

"Do you understand me?" he snarled. His brow crinkled as his mouth neared hers. Was he going to kiss her? He wanted to, and she wouldn't mind if he did.

Her heart fluttered as she swallowed.

"Yes, I understand you," she said in a low voice. *Now please get out of my face before I die. If you weren't so damn handsome, I would tell you to go to hell.*

She forced a demure smile and gave a defeated sigh. "Is there anything else I need to know, Mr. Lewis?" she asked, trying to be cool even though she was shivering inside. He made a dismissing gesture and turned around.

"Cocky bastard," she said to herself as he went back toward the boardroom.

He turned abruptly. "There is one more thing," he began.

What now? she wondered. "You might want to check that little attitude of yours at the door the next time we meet. I'm tired of your bad attitude."

Monica looked down the hall. Patrice and Beverly saw the whole thing. Dray walked back into the room and closed the door behind him. Monica stomped her foot and rushed back to her office. He'd embarrassed her again.

When Dray sat down, he clasped his hands together. He took a deep breath and hung his head for a moment. How long was it going to take him to stop finding her attractive? The tension between them seemed to do nothing but make him want her more. He couldn't explain why he was feeling confused and excited at the same time. He needed strength, and quick.

Rochelle sat in the seat next to him. "Mr. Lewis, you a'ight? We heard you yellin' out there."

He smiled and pinched her cheek playfully. "I'm fine. We'll continue in a minute."

After his meeting with the Prima Donnas, Dray took a lunch break. He drove a few blocks to Eatzi's, a trendy market that served fresh foods. He placed his order for a turkey sandwich and retreated outside to a table alone. As he sipped his ginseng tea he looked across the patio. There was Monica, sophisticated and sassy. She was reading and munching on a sandwich, enthralled in her book. He desperately wanted to make things right and win her approval. But she seemed determined to keep her distance. She was so cold and indifferent that he knew he didn't stand a chance. Not since junior high had a woman had him questioning his confidence. This wasn't junior high. They were both adults. "Fuck it," he said, "I'm Drayton Lewis. I can have any woman I want."

He watched her closely, observing the auburn streaks throughout her mane. He figured beneath her brazen exterior she might actually have heart. It would be just a matter of time before he got her to show that side of herself. It was now or never. He had to break her down and win her trust. Nervous as a rat at a catfight, he took his tray to her table. At first, she ignored him and continued reading her book. When he cleared his throat, finally she looked up. Her mouth fell open and her eyes darted to the tray and then up at him. With his good looks and charm, she couldn't ignore him for long. Dray didn't wait to be asked to sit down.

"What are you reading?" he asked as if they were old friends. He took a bite of his sandwich.

She looked up and then rolled her eyes at him. "A book."

"What kind of book?" Her rudeness annoyed him, but he kept his tone polite.

She sighed and held it up for him to see.

"The Maintenance Man', by Michael Baisden." Before she could say another word, he said, "You know, maybe if you took that chip off your shoulder we could have some peace between us, Monica. All I'm trying to do is be a gentleman."

"I didn't know there was anything between us," she blurted, not taking her eyes from the book.

"There isn't, but I'd still like us to be cool. I don't see the point of us being adversaries since we have to work together. I know it would give me peace of mind."

"Well, there are plenty of foreign countries that you can make peace in." Her sarcasm caught him off guard. *I don't see what the point of your talking to me is anyway. You've already made me feel like a fool. Do you have to keep trying?* "Why don't you read my mind?" she suggested.

Dray chuckled, "I'm afraid to. I might see something I don't like — or something that doesn't like me."

"You might," she said coolly.

She continued to read her book as they sat in silence. And Dray continued to eat his food. Their eyes didn't meet once. Even though she hadn't meant what she said, she had to keep her guard up. She wasn't up to having her heart broken again. Dray was aggravated by the brooding silence. He wasn't used to Monica's type of harsh treatment. Women were usually pleased to be in his company. Other than his ex, Lisa, no woman had ever gotten under his skin. Why was Monica doing it? When he knew the answer to that question, his problem would be solved. But he didn't. And he wasn't about to let some uppity PR exec get the best of him either. When he finished his meal, he disregarded her determination to ignore him.

"You always this snippy?" He moved his chair closer to hers. "Or do I have to act like a gangster to get your attention? Is that what you like? Gangsters?"

Her mouth dropped open. "How would you know what I like? You don't know anything about me."

Dray ignored her comment. "Men who treat you like shit and

don't say what they feel. Is that what you like? You must be the sadistic type."

Monica closed her book and met his eyes with a glare. "If I did like those kind of men, what would that make me?"

"Human, I guess," he said softly, "but definitely a sadistic one."

"Why do you keep trying so hard to get close to me? To get another cheap jab in?" She took in his handsome features. "Every day it's something new. What is it with you?"

He decided to lay his cards on the table. "Maybe I like you."

Monica quivered at the rumble of his strong, masculine voice. And the thought of his lips against hers ignited passions she'd long forgotten.

Flustered, she ignored him for a moment. "Why are you so interested in what I do?" she asked nervously.

"I'm not," he lied. "I'm just trying to bring you to your senses. Why are you so defensive all the time?"

"I'm not defensive."

"Yes, you are. Anytime I say something to you, you're ready to bite my head off."

Her eyes slanted with fury. "I'm not defensive. I just don't like you."

He laughed. "It's obvious somebody's done something to you in your life to make you so vigilant. Is that the reason you're upset with me all the time?"

"You don't know what you're talking about," she said, stuffing her book in her purse. She'd had just about enough of his presumptions.

"Oh, but I think I do. You want to take all your bitterness out on me because of what some man in your past has done. It's been bottled up so long, you don't know how to deal with it."

Monica wanted to admit what he was saying was true. But her pride kept her from doing so. "The only problem I have is you. That, and your ability to watch where you're going in a crowded party." She covered her mouth to hide her faint smile.

He threw his head back and grinned. Her gesture was cute.

"I told you I was sorry about the dress. How many times do I have to apologize? I was trying to get through the crowd, and I was pushed into you. Maybe you shouldn't have worn the $600 dress if it pissed you off that much."

"I don't . . . "

"I don't know why I'm even wasting my time with you."

Her eyes fell to the ground. Maybe she had been a bit cruel. She chuckled and looked across the street. How could she ignore a man this fine? She decided it wouldn't be so bad to be cordial, and that she wouldn't lose any respect by doing so. She had been acting childish lately. Besides, his cute dimples and poster-boy smile were riveting. Still, she wasn't sure of his motives, so she kept her guard up.

"Okay, fine," she said. "Whatever makes the new A&R rep happy. I guess I'm not allowed to be myself around you, huh? Since as my superior you want me to submit, I guess I will."

"No, I don't want you to submit." At least not yet, he heard a voice say. "I like you when you're mad. You're easier to tame."

Monica blinked. "Tame? So you think you can tame me?"

"Oh, yes," he said in his slick Chicago drawl.

She slammed her purse on the table. "I think I'm done here."

"Can't take a little heat, Ms. Holiday? People need criticism every once in a while."

She met his eyes. "You know, if you spent as much time worrying about you like you do me, you might get some work done."

"I already have."

He smiled and put his drink to his lips as she rose from her chair. She straightened her suit and snatched her purse.

"Good day, Mr. Lewis."

He nodded, "Good day, Ms. Holiday."

She cut her eyes at him and dashed across the street into the mid-afternoon traffic. Dray shook his head and clapped his hands together. Such a feisty little thing, he thought. Just the way I like em'. He caught a glimpse of her looking back and snapped his fingers. Got her, he thought as she pulled her car into the traffic.

Later that day, Monica couldn't focus. Drayton Lewis was on her mind. What was so special about him? Nothing, she tried to convince herself. But she knew that was a lie. He probably had plenty of women falling at his feet. Not Monica, no way. She'd never thrown herself at any man, not even Rodney. She wasn't about to lose control now. She would resist Dray no matter what.

Despite getting the Prima Donnas an interview with Spice Cosmetics company, Monica still had work to do. She swept through the files on her desk. They were filled with photos, receipts, articles, and memos pertaining to her clients. First on her list was a press release for the Prima Donnas second single, *Just Enough*, and another for her former beau about his plans to do a movie. The latter was the least important on her to-do list. She examined an e-mail Rodney had sent her instead of telling it to her face-to-face.

> From: RR [rr1269@doubler.com]
> Sent: January 31, 2001, 3:10 p.m.
> To: Monica Holiday; missholiday@handleup.com
> Subject: My business
>
> Hope we can get over this bullshit we're going through. I'm tired of this.

She deleted the e-mail and trashed it. Rodney's attempts at an apology were just that — an attempt. What was she thinking dating a rapper anyway? The relationship was doomed from the start. He was always on the road, surrounded by groupies, or throwing parties for tons of people. They never had any real quality time, and when they did, it usually resulted in sex. She vowed not to let a man or his career hurt her again. As she checked the rest of her e-mail, Patrice walked in.

"Are you alright, Monica? You were a little iffy the other morning when you walked past me."

Monica got up and walked around her desk to get a file from her cabinet. "I'm fine," she said, sighing. "Just trying to keep up with the Prima Donnas, that's all."

"Good, I had to make sure." Patrice turned to walk out. "What do you think of Mr. Lewis?"

Monica gave her the once-over. "Professionally? He's arrogant and cocky and any other word that describes a jerk."

"And romantically?" Patrice asked. Monica tried to hide her smile.

"He's strong, sexy, handsome, everything you would want in a man. I would never tell him so. It might go to his head."

Patrice giggled. "You're always so together, Monica. I don't know how you do it." Patrice sounded like a talk-show host. "If I had to deal with something like that mess Rodney pulled, I think I'd just die."

"No time for mourning," Monica said. "Only the strong survive. I'm successful, I'm happy. Do me a favor, fax these contracts over to this number on the bottom, and make sure Bill gets these today, please. And order a small pepperoni pizza for my dinner. Have them deliver it."

"No problem. How long are you gonna be?"

"I'll be here until at least nine or so. It's supposed to rain tonight." She looked out of the window. "I hope it doesn't."

"No problem, I'll let security know. I think Mr. Lewis is working late too."

Monica shrugged. It was obvious Patrice was trying to play matchmaker. She gazed out the window at the light drizzle that had started to come down. Before their eyes, the rain started to pour.

"Let me get that pizza."

As the thunder and lightning crashed, Monica returned to her office. She turned on her CD player and slid in her Isley Brothers disc. As Ron Isley moaned over the sensuous track, she slipped into her chair. If she had a man who could sing to her like that every night, maybe half of her problems would be solved.

Around seven, the office was extremely quiet. Everyone had gone home or to happy hour, a Thursday ritual for most of the staff. After the pizza arrived, Monica finished printing out the expense account for the Prima Donnas. Once Vera, the vice president of finance, took a look at it, she would give the final copy to Bill. Dray would also get a copy in the morning. She read over it carefully, she wanted to make sure the girls weren't spending money on things they didn't need. Just as she began to examine the report, the lights went out.

"Shit!" she groaned. She slid out of her chair and felt her way to the door. She made small steps until she hit her knee on the file cabinet. "Ouch," she fell back in her chair and rubbed it. She felt around in her desk drawer for her flashlight. When she found it, she pushed the button and tried to turn it on. Nothing. "Damn."

There was no way she could make it to the supply room to find batteries for it. She strapped her purse across her shoulders and put her car keys in her jacket pocket. She felt the desk for her letter opener, just in case she needed protection. She clutched it firmly and opened the door to her office. The hallway was dark, not even a streetlight came through the windows. She felt her heart pounding. What if she couldn't get out? Would she be stuck in the building until daylight and have to sleep on the couch in the front lobby? She walked along the wall, feeling her way to the front door. Hopefully the generator would provide enough light for her to make it downstairs. Just as she passed the receptionist's desk, she bumped into something and felt a hand cover her mouth.

"Shh!" the voice whispered, as the scent of a familiar cologne faintly filled her nostrils.

The strong body hugged her to him, as she shivered with fear. As he pulled her along, she leaned against him. Unsure of her fate, she decided to make a bold move and use the letter opener as a weapon.

"Ouch, woman, you trying to kill me!" he yelled, clutching his hand. "It's me, Dray!"

He'd been working late and didn't have a flashlight either. Like Monica, he decided to take a chance and make his way out.

"Damn you!" Monica yelled, punching him. "You scared the hell out of me!"

"I'm sorry, I didn't want you to scream." He reached for her. "I didn't mean to scare you."

"Well, you did!"

"You caught me off guard, Monica. I thought I was alone."

"Well, you're not," she groaned, pulling away from him.

"Damn," Dray griped. "You are the most difficult woman I've ever met."

Monica was all set to complain again when she realized she might have stabbed him.

She called to him. "Are you bleeding?"

"I don't know. I don't feel anything yet. You must be crazy swinging that thing like that. What's wrong with you?"

"Look, you're the one who scared me half to death! Sneaking up on people can get you in trouble, Mr. Lewis."

Dray wanted to strangle her, but at the same time, he could easily take her in his arms. More or less, the strangling was more desirable. Even in a time of need, she was disagreeable.

"You know what? If I had a flashlight, I'd shine it in your face right about now!" he yelled. "Are you always such a . . . never mind."

"A what?" Monica snickered at his frustration.

"Brat," he said plainly. "I was going to say brat."

"At least I'm not the one sneaking up on people in the dark."

"Unbelievable. Just get away from me," Dray muttered. He had all he could take. She'd struck his last nerve. It was then that he remembered something he'd heard earlier that made him smile.

"So, you think I'm arrogant and pushy, do you?"

He could hear her gasp, and he smiled in the darkness. It was a good thing she couldn't see his face.

"I don't know what you're talking about." *I'm going to kill that girl! I can't believe she told him what I said.*

"Come on, Monica. You can tell me. I won't be mad. It won't be the first time I've heard a woman say it."

"So, I guess you're like one of those fiendish men who like it rough?"

Does she know how sexy that sounds? he wondered. "It depends on what type of mood I'm in," he said seriously.

She sucked her teeth, realizing her choice of words. "That's not what I meant. Damn it! I'm getting out of here. You're driving me crazy," she said.

"Fine, suit yourself."

What was he saying? Something could happen to her. Despite her tough façade, she was still a woman.

"Come on," he said grabbing her wrist.

She tried to pull away as he led her through the dark office. "Let go of me, I'm fine." She yanked her arm away and tossed her hair out of her face.

"Fine with me!" he said, letting go. As he huffed in confusion, he heard a stumbling sound, then a loud moan.

"Oww!"

Her cries echoed in the dark. She'd fallen up against the marble statue in the lobby and hit her back.

"Monica! Monica! Where are you?" He followed her groans until he bumped into her foot. He knelt down and felt his way to her.

"Are you alright?"

"Y-yes," she groaned. "I'm over here," she cried as Dray slowly stepped toward her. When he found her, he slid his hand underneath her back. "Ouch!" She was in terrible pain. She hit the middle of her back on the statue's sharp edge.

"Don't move. Tell me if this hurts." He moved his hand up and down her back until he found the tender spot.

"Ouch!" she wailed. "That hurts!" She held on to his shoulder.

"Okay. I'm going to pick you up."

"No! Please don't."

"Relax, baby. I've got you." Monica could have sworn he called her, baby. What was that all about? "Just grab my shoulders," he said, reaching for her. "I'm gonna pick you up slowly."

"Okay," she agreed.

She was scared to death, figuring something was broken. She wrapped her arms around his neck as he lifted her effortlessly off the ground. He pushed her purse out of his way to get a better grip on her and stepped slowly toward the wall. She rested her head on his shoulder as he made his way in the darkness toward the door.

"Damn, it's dark in here." It was hard for him to see, but the backup lights offered some light as he entered the hallway. He carried her to the stairwell and rested her body against the railing.

"Are you okay?" he asked, moving strands of hair from her face. "Tell me where you're hurt." He lowered his gaze.

Her dazzling eyes mystified him as she met his. "My back and my ribs."

"You might be bleeding internally. We've got to get you to a doctor."

"No! Please don't take me to a doctor, just take me home."

"Why, are you scared?" he asked with a slight grin.

"Yes," she said, putting her head to his chest. "I don't like doctors." She felt light as a feather in his arms. She wasn't the tough, ferocious creature he'd met a few nights ago. He comforted her for a moment, trying to figure out his next move.

"If you're hurt, I've got to get you to the hospital."

"No!" she cried.

"Hold on tight, I'm taking you downstairs."

He carried her effortlessly down two flights. Once they got to the sixth floor, he stopped. As she rested briefly on his shoulder, the lights came back on.

He tried to lighten the mood. "Well, I guess playtime is over." Monica was in too much pain to laugh. He lifted her momentarily to readjust her body.

"Ouch!" she cried again. "That hurts."

Dray was scared for her. "I'm taking you to a hospital."

"No, Dray, I'm fine, really." She was lying and he knew it.

"Okay, get up and walk then." He gave her a derisive look.

She contemplated the idea for a minute, but knew it was impossible. "I can't."

"I know you're in pain, I can see it in your eyes. So just hold on to me. I'm taking you to the hospital, and I don't want to hear anything else about it."

The words were music to Monica's ears. There was no sense in arguing. He'd won round two. She was in awe of his concern for her, and his insistence on getting her some help. The gesture made her feel special. Right now, all she wanted was to lay on a nice soft bed, and she wouldn't mind if he was in it. Dray reached into his pocket for his car keys. He gathered her in his arms and carried her to the elevators. When they made it downstairs, he had security call his driver to take them to the hospital. He held her in his arms if she weighed two pounds, not even wincing once.

"You know you need to eat a little more. You're a little light in the ass," Dray joked as Robert pulled the car up to the building. She gave him a dirty look. How could he be joking at a time like this? She clutched his shoulder as Robert helped him put her inside. It was going to be a long night.

After X-rays and a few motor skills tests at the Atlanta Medical Center, Monica's exam was over.

"Well, Miss Holiday," the doctor said, "you're going to be fine. You have a minor back sprain, and a little bruising." Monica was relieved. "Your chart says you were here a year ago for broken ribs. What happened?"

She was surprised he would even mention that. "I fell — off a motorcycle. I was riding with a friend of mine."

Dray, who'd been standing next to her bed, lifted his head in wonder. What friend? He wanted to know. He didn't say anything. Now wasn't a good time. He stared at her for a moment and then focused his attention back to the doctor. His main concern was to make sure that she got home safely and took a few days off.

"Well," the doctor began, "I'm going to give you some crutches. I've seen how you've been hobbling around here all night. You might want to take it easy for the next few days. Your fall may have triggered the pain in your ribs again."

"I'll make sure she stays in bed," Dray said, not taking his eyes off her. She was a bit embarrassed by his concern.

"Well, that's all," the doctor began. "Here are your prescriptions. One is for pain, the other is to help the swelling. The nurse will bring in your crutches and help you out."

CHAPTER 5

After a trip to the pharmacy, Dray and Monica arrived at her place. Robert was nice enough to wait downstairs until Dray summoned him. Monica sat quietly on the bed as Dray pulled off her shoes. He placed them neatly beside her bed.

"You want me to take your clothes off?" he asked in a serious tone.

Yes, but this isn't exactly how I pictured you doing it, Monica thought. "No, that's alright. I can manage."

"Are you sure? I don't want you to hurt yourself."

"Too late for that," Monica said, struggling to unbutton her shirt.

He looked in her eyes and reached to help her.

"I think I can get that," she said softly, pulling away.

He nodded. "I'm sorry. I don't know what I was thinking." He took a few steps back to catch his breath as he got a glimpse of her shoulder.

"I don't know what you were thinking either," she grinned.

She peeled off her blouse, revealing a pink Victoria's Secret demi-cut bra. Her dainty, round breasts peered over it, shooting a dangerous venom through his veins. He could have snatched her off the bed and taken her right then. But he remembered her condition, and quickly resumed his position as assistant. Stumbling a little, she held his shoulder.

"Thanks," she said, almost in a whisper. She felt a little embarrassed as she stood in front of him in her bra and panties. "Could you hand me my gown?"

He did, and tried hard to ignore her svelte body. She clutched the gown tight to her chest as he slid her skirt to the floor. When all of her clothes were off, Dray helped her put on the nightgown and pulled the covers back on the bed. She was still using him for support as she placed her hand on his shoulder.

"This is so hard for me. I'm not used to being taken care of."

"That's too bad. You should be." She looked astounded. "I mean you should have someone take care of you . . . if you need it."

Dray wanted to kick himself for letting his true colors show. Once she was dressed comfortably, he helped her into bed.

"You think you'll be alright tonight? Or do you need me to stay?" he asked.

Without thinking, Monica replied, "Oh, yes . . . I need you to stay. I mean, if it's not too much trouble," she muttered.

Her request was the sweetest he'd ever heard. "No, it's no trouble at all. It will give us a chance to talk." Monica would like that. Since there was no pressure from work, they would be able to be who they were. No masks, no games.

"I'd like that, Dray."

He broke into a mercurial smile. "I'm going to have Robert take me to pick up your car and then I'll be back, okay?"

She nodded and pulled the sheet up to her neck. "Can you bring me something to eat please? I'm starving."

His laughter floated up from his throat. "Didn't you eat pizza at the office?"

Monica's eyes widened. "Patrice told you that, didn't she?" Note to self: kill Patrice.

Dray rolled up his shirtsleeves. "Don't worry, that's between me and you," he grinned. "Take your pain medicine. I'll be back. I'm gonna get some clothes for tomorrow too. Get some rest while I'm gone."

Once she heard the door shut, she threw the covers back. Of all the ways she could think of to have a man wait on her hand and foot, she had to take a fall to find out. She closed her eyes as Dray's scent lingered in the air above her head. It was cool and tantalizing, almost like he was still there. If she had the strength, she might have undressed him and pulled him into bed with her. There were no words to explain what she was feeling. All she knew was that she was coming to like this man. His warm body felt so strong when he carried her from the office. She'd never been lifted off her feet with such ease and finesse. How was she going to be able to resist him if they were close again? She didn't know. But she was eagerly waiting to find out.

♫

Dray sat quietly in the back of the limo as Robert headed back toward Midtown. He ran his hand over his goatee and checked his watch. It was almost midnight. What a day, he thought. He put his head back and closed his eyes. Usually, at this hour he was tossing and turning between his sheets. He didn't mind helping Monica. It would give him a chance to spend more time with her. She was beginning to loosen up. Maybe, if he kept trying, he could get her to relax a little more around him. He couldn't blame her. Dray amazed himself sometimes. After he got a change of clothes, he got her something to eat. He had Robert take him back to work to get Monica's car.

Robert watched him every so often in his rear-view mirror. "You alright, son? I hope you're not letting baby girl's little spill get you down."

"No, I'm alright. I'm just worried about her. We didn't really hit it off at first, but now I can't stop thinking about her."

"Women will do that to you. They mess your head up, chew you up and spit you out, and then you fall in love with them," Robert smiled. "Happens every time. Even to old cats like myself. She'll be fine," he reassured him.

"I hope so."

"She will. Don't let it get to you. I'm sure she's a strong woman if she's dealin' with you."

Dray caught the old man's eye in the rear-view mirror. "I guess you're right."

"Of course, I am."

When Dray got back to Monica's apartment, she was asleep. She was even more beautiful. Still and quiet. He wished he could be the mattress she was lying on. He felt comfortable with her, like he'd known her forever. He placed her food in the microwave. He didn't want to disturb her. If she wanted to eat in the middle of the night, it would be there. When he finished in the kitchen, he hung his garment bag on the doorknob of her hall closet. He made his bed on her couch, throwing a blanket over his legs for cover. He propped his head up on a pillow and folded his arms behind his head. He closed his eyes momentarily and said a prayer for Monica, and one for himself.

It was almost two o'clock in the morning, and way past his bedtime. He tried to sleep, but found himself thinking about Monica with every breath. Usually when he was tired, he could go right to sleep. Tonight was different. There was a beautiful woman in the next room that he wanted to get to know. He knew he shouldn't be having those thoughts. But they remained. He reached for the television remote but paused when he heard Monica groan.

He sat up. "Monica, are you okay?" She didn't respond. He walked into her bedroom to check on her. She was lying on her side, with her legs uncovered and her arm across her stomach. As he knelt down at her side, she opened her eyes.

"Are you alright?" He moved hair from her face.

"Did you bring me something to eat?" she asked grumpily.

He laughed, and studied her for a second. "Yes, but could you ask in a nicer tone?"

"I'm sorry. Did you bring me something to eat?" she asked sweetly.

"Is that all that's wrong? You're hungry?"

She tried to sit up. "Ouch. No, that's not all. My back is hurting."

He placed his hand on hers. "You'll be alright. You want me to bring your dinner in here?"

"Yes. Thank you."

She watched him leave the room. Damn, that man was fine. When he returned from the kitchen, he was holding a Styrofoam container. He sat on the edge of the bed with it and looked at her.

"I hope you like this," he said with uncertainty.

Monica didn't know what he was talking about, but it sounded good. She noticed the strong muscles in his forearms, and thought about being wrapped in them. His large hands pulled open the container.

"Catfish?"

"What, you don't like catfish?" Dray asked, "I'm sorry, I didn't know."

"No, no, I love it. It's my favorite. Thank you." She broke off a piece and started to put it in her mouth. "You want some?"

"Are we talking about the fish or something else?" Dray couldn't help but laugh. Monica punched him in the arm playfully. "I was talking about the fish!"

"Oh, I just wanted to be clear. Let me taste a piece."

Monica broke off a small piece and put it in his mouth. He opened and took it in slowly. A flash of humor crossed Monica's face.

Dray chewed the fish and licked his lips. He'd rather be tasting something else.

"You like it?" she asked.

"Umm-hmm." And he wasn't talking about the fish. "Are you comfortable? Let me fix your pillows." He got up from the bed and adjusted them. Monica leaned back and continued to eat.

"How's that, Ms. Holiday?"

"Fine, thank you."

"Your back should be a little better in the morning. You'd better hurry so you can get some sleep."

"I thought we were going to talk. Shouldn't you massage my back?"

He smiled, thinking about it. "Monica, if I touch you right now, I'm not going to stop, so I have to decline your request. Is there anything else I can get you?"

"Yes."

"What?" he asked softly.

"Would you bring me some lemonade, please? It's in the fridge by the milk."

"Sure," he replied. *I'll bring you anything you want. I'd love to rub you down with some warm oil, but it will have to wait.*

He went to the kitchen to retrieve her beverage. After gathering some ice from the freezer, he took the lemonade from the fridge and poured into it a glass. Monica had a nice kitchen. It was painted in a soft yellow. Her canisters on the counter matched, and there were several small paintings on the wall next to the fridge. He placed the pitcher back inside. He hadn't been in a woman's apartment in so long, he'd forgotten how much they liked to decorate. He walked back to the living room, but stopped at Monica's desk. He came across a poem, and read the first couple of lines. "Love is like the weather. You don't know when it will change, but you always look forward to it." He smiled approvingly, and returned to the bedroom.

"I didn't know you wrote poetry," he said, sitting on the bed. He handed her the glass and looked at what was left of her food. She definitely wouldn't be a salad eater on a date.

"Yes. How'd you know?"

"I read your poem. I hope you don't mind." His eyes glowed. "I couldn't resist."

Her eyes took in his powerful presence. "Most men . . . I mean — most people can't."

He chuckled. "Where are you from, Monica?"

"The Bay Area, but my mother lives in Dallas now. My parents divorced when I was eight."

"Brothers and sister?"

"One sister. What about you? Where are you from?"

"I was born in Monroe, Louisiana, raised in Jackson, Mississippi, until I was nine, and then we moved to Chicago. My mother died when I was young. My father lives in Chicago."

"No siblings?"

"Nope, it's just me. You mind if I take my shirt off?" he asked, standing up. He started to unbutton it before she could reply.

"No, you can hang it my closet if you like." She watched him until the last button was undone. When he removed the shirt, Monica nearly choked on her drink. His chest belonged to that of a god. Even with his muscle shirt, Monica could see how fine he was.

"Are you okay?" Dray asked.

"I'm fine," she lied. Her temperature had risen twenty degrees. She fanned herself and placed the glass on the nightstand.

Dray returned to the bed. Is it okay if I lie back? I'm a little beat."

"Sure, go ahead." Monica put her empty container in the plastic bag it came in. She tied it in a knot and set it on the floor. "You may want to scoot up, Dray. I don't think you'll be able to sleep with your feet hanging off the bed."

He moved to rest his head on the soft pillow. He let out a tired sigh and folded his arms behind his head. "You believe in love, Monica?" He turned his head to look in her eyes, hoping she wouldn't think he was being corny.

Monica wondered what he was getting at. "Yes, I do. But sometimes I think I'm the only person who does." She dropped her eyes before his steady gaze.

"Don't think like that. I believe in it too."

They both looked away from each other.

"I think I need a bath. I feel kinda sticky," Monica said. "Would you run my water?"

"It's a little late to get wet." Dray wished he could take back those words. "Are you sure you want to take a bath now?"

"I'm sure," she grinned. "I'm used to soaking in the tub before I go to bed, it relaxes me."

"Well, I'll run your water then. And I'll put some Epsom salt in there too. It may help ease the pain." Dray got up and went into the bathroom.

Monica moved herself up on the pillows. "Thanks."

Dray threw Monica's food away and came back to help her to the bathroom. She leaned her small five-foot-five frame against him for balance.

"Thank you," she said once they were in the bathroom.

"You're welcome."

Monica rested on the toilet and stuck her hand in the water. He made the water just right, and even added a capful of bubble bath.

"You need me to help you undress?"

This time she did need his help. "Yes, please," she said, clutching her side.

Dray helped Monica remove her clothes and then he put them in her hamper. She was wearing her bra and panties. But she didn't seem to mind him staring, or maybe she didn't notice. His eyes caressed every inch of her softness. Monica clipped her hair on top of her head and reached for the towel that hung on her rack.

"Let me get that," Dray said, grabbing it. He held it open for her while she tried to stand. "You need help?"

"No, I've got it." Biting her lip, she looked away. "Can you close your eyes? I have to take off my bra and panties."

"Sorry." He was ashamed for not thinking of that himself.

After a moment she said, "I'm ready."

He opened his eyes. Monica struggled to keep the towel up as she held his arm. "Oops," she said, as it fell open.

Dray felt his manhood stiffen, getting a glimpse of her feminine curves was enough to set him afire. He quickly looked elsewhere, and nervously stepped backward.

"I'm sorry," he said.

"What for?"

"Never mind," he said, approaching her from behind. Monica leaned back against his hard chest. No man should be this strong. He lifted her gently into the tub. He turned the other way until she was covered in bubbles. "Thank you."

"You're welcome," he said not looking at her. "I'll just be in the other room, straightening up or something. Holler if you need me."

"I will."

When he left the bathroom, he leaned against the wall in the hall. He was fighting to maintain her honor by not taking her from the tub and doing provocative things to her. What was he thinking letting himself get this close? His hands shook as he slid them in his pockets. He had to get her off of his mind. He went into the living room and then out onto the balcony for some air. Right now, he needed every molecule of the Georgia air to keep from pulling Monica Holiday into bed.

When Monica finished her bath, Dray helped her onto the bed.

"I think I'll take the couch." *Lord knows if I stay in here we'll both be in trouble.* He walked to the door.

"Are you sure?"

"Yes, I'm sure. See you in the morning."

Dray returned to the living room. After covering herself with scented oil, Monica eased into her chemise and slid under the covers. She closed her eyes, wishing he'd come back to check on her once more. She wanted to look into his eyes again, and rub her fingers across his full lips. She wondered if he was feeling the same way.

In the next room, Dray was having his own flights of fancy. Slumber wouldn't come easy tonight. As he lay down, he traced the curve of her lips in his head over and over. If only she knew how badly he wanted to take her in his arms. He would hold her close and tell her everything would be okay. She had no idea what she was doing to him, but the bulge in his pants was a firm reminder.

As the sun drifted between the blinds, Monica groaned in relief. She felt much better, even though her back was still sore. She could hear Dray in the shower and made no attempts to get out of bed. He was getting ready to go to work, she assumed. She looked over at the blazing red numbers that read 7:03. It was still early, so she lay quietly until he finished showering. When he emerged from the bathroom, Monica gasped. He stood before her with nothing but a towel wrapped around his waist. Monica examined his chiseled chest and board flat stomach. "Oh my God," she said to herself. He stood in the middle of her room towel drying his hair.

"Good morning," he said, smiling.

Monica swallowed hard. "Morning." She couldn't keep her eyes off him. She had half a mind to jump out of bed and pull the towel loose.

"Did you sleep well?" he asked, walking back to the bathroom.

"Fine, thank you."

"You're mighty beautiful when you sleep. I was tempted . . . to disturb you."

She had to fight the overwhelming need to be close to him.

"You were watching?"

A mischievous look came to his eyes. "Yes."

"You little devil!"

"I couldn't help myself," he said, getting dressed. He went back into the bathroom. "I'll be back to check on you later," she heard him say as he brushed his teeth.

By the time he emerged from the bathroom again, he was fully dressed. He was wearing a tan suit with an indigo shirt and tie. He looked impeccable in his get-up, every bit the debonair gentleman Monica had met nearly a month earlier.

"I want to go to work today," she said. "I'm not used to being idle."

He straightened his tie and sat on the edge of the bed.

"You can't go. And don't be hardheaded by trying to come in to work either." That was her plan exactly. "There's nothing in the office that needs your immediate attention anyway. Do you want to end up back in the hospital again?"

"No, but . . . "

"Well then, relax, Monica. I'll be back to check on you at lunch."

He leaned forward to kiss her forehead, but kissed her nose instead. A spark flickered between them.

He didn't want to leave her. "I better go," he said. "I'll call you in a couple of hours. I've got to figure out how to explain this to Bill."

She folded her arms across her chest. She wasn't happy with his request.

"Come on now, Monica, don't pout. You'll be alright." Silence. "You need anything?"

A kiss would be nice. She shook her head no. Then he was gone.

"Good, I'll see you later."

CHAPTER 6

When Dray arrived at the office, he still hadn't figured out a way to break the news. Bill wasn't a difficult man, but he wasn't exactly easygoing either. Finally, Dray just decided to rely on the truth. It wasn't an easy task. Bill couldn't comprehend how in the world the lights would go out in a multimillion-dollar building. In his mind, everything should have been working perfectly. As much money as Handle Up spent on electricity bills, the Georgia Power Company should have been able to light up all of the city. Call it crazy, or just plain unreasonable. William Sanders had to have his way.

"It's no one's fault," Dray tried to explain. "It was Mother Nature, that's all."

"Mother Nature doesn't need to screw around with me. Why did Monica fall?" Bill asked. "She just fell?"

"It's a long story, Mr. Sanders, but she's fine." The situation seemed hopeless. Bill was as stubborn as an ox.

"What did the doctors say? Is anything broken?"

"No, she just had a slight sprain and mild swelling. The doctor said she'll be fine."

Bill nodded and placed his fingers to his lips. "Be sure to have Patrice get her some flowers or something, ya hear?"

"No problem, I just wanted to let you know what happened personally. The lights went out, neither one of us could see. It's really not a big deal. Things happen."

Bill relaxed a little, but he still wanted to make sure she would recover, fully and fast. He couldn't have one of his best workers disabled. She was part of the reason the company had so many platinum albums. Her extensive efforts to boost sales had them higher than they'd ever been. He was all set to send one of the other employees over to take care of her. Just as he reached for the phone, Monica appeared from behind the door. She was leaning against a crutch, and dressed almost exactly like Dray in a tan business suit and blue shirt. The surprise showed on Dray's face.

"Monica?" Dray said, as Bill stared with wide eyes. "What are you doing here?"

"What are you doing here?" Bill repeated, rising from his seat.

Monica hobbled to a chair to sit.

"Shouldn't you be at home resting?" Bill asked.

"You shouldn't be here," Dray said, helping her into a chair. "I told you to stay at home."

"I'm fine, really, guys." She looked up at both gentlemen as they stared in amazement. "Come on, Bill. You know a little bruise isn't going to keep me from working. Besides, I have too much to do here."

Bill sat down and leaned back, clasping his hands together. "You know I love you like a daughter, Monica. But I want you to take a few days off."

"I can't. The girls need me." She avoided looking at Dray. She knew he was upset. Right now, she didn't care. And she had other things to worry about.

"Come back on Monday," Bill said. "Dray has everything under control so you can relax."

"I'm trying to get the girls a contract with Spice Cosmetics. I need to do that this week."

Dray shook his head. *This woman is so pigheaded. Can't she see I'm trying to help her?* "You really don't have to do that, Monica, I can handle it." He sat down in the chair next to her, watching the flustered expression on her face. "You really need to rest. As much as I loved taking care of you . . . "

Bill interrupted. "Taking care of her? What the hell is going on?"

Monica's eyes darted toward Dray. "Nothing," they said in unison.

"It was nothing. I just wanted to make sure she was okay."

"And I asked him to stay," Monica offered.

Bill hesitated, measuring them for a moment. "I don't want to have to tie you up to keep you from coming to work, Monica," he said.

"No, Mr. Sanders, you won't. It's my fault. Dray was just being a gentleman. Everything is fine, really."

Bill cut in. "No, it's not, Monica. Take a few days off. That's an order. And I'll dock your pay if you show up after today!"

"I'll be over to check on you," Dray said. "And I'd like to see you in my office, Monica," he said sharply. "Is there anything else, Mr. Sanders?"

Bill rubbed his chin and sat down. "No, that's all. I'll talk to both of you later, individually."

"That's fine, sir," Dray said. "Come on, Monica." He left the room faster than a bullet.

When she followed him down the hall and into his office, he offered her a seat. Then he lit into her like Christmas lights.

"What the hell are you doing here?"

She was too stunned by his tone to give him attitude. "I was . . . I was just trying to get some work done."

"What did I tell you before I left your house? I specifically asked you not to leave. You're in pain, you're on medication, and I think you're just determined to go against everything I say."

"No, Dray, that's not it."

"Well, what is it then? You know you shouldn't be here."

She couldn't answer or offer an excuse. And she realized she'd made a mistake ignoring his request. The last thing she wanted was for him to be angry with her. It was obvious he had her best intentions in mind. But being told what to do wasn't easy for her. She liked to be in control. But how could she resist Dray's effort to make her life easier? She looked up at his brown eyes and wanted to say yes, she'd do what he'd asked. But it wasn't her style to shy away from her responsibilities. Frustrated, she struggled to get up from her chair. Dray reached out quickly to help her.

"I've got it," she snapped. She made her way toward the door. She stopped suddenly before she opened the door. His dark eyes were full of anger. "If we're done, I'm going to get my things."

"Yeah, we're done," he said turning his back.

Dray met Bill in his office thirty minutes later. He was still seething from his talk with Monica. Never in his life had he met a woman too smart for her own good.

"Is she always like that?" he asked, sitting in front of him.

Bill clasped his hands together. "Been that way since I've known her. She finds it hard to let go of things, even when she knows she should. Women like her are special. She's strong and loyal, not like some folks."

"Well, I'll help her as much as I can."

"Dray, I want you to remember one thing."

He listened closely.

"This is a business. There's a lot of beautiful women here, including Monica. I'm not telling you what to do, son. But if you get involved, keep your business to yourself. I don't want any soap opera drama here. Monica's a good girl, and from what I've seen you're a good guy." He paused for a moment. "Don't ruin my image of you."

Dray nodded. "I won't, Mr. Sanders. I respect Monica as a person. I don't want to do anything to hurt her."

"Good. Then we have an understanding. And don't pay any attention to that attitude you keep getting. You're exactly what Monica needs; she just doesn't realize it yet."

At six o'clock, Dray was on his way out the door. He had a party to go to at a club near downtown. Bill wanted him to check out the male singing group Extasy because he was interested in signing them. He placed a few files in his briefcase and reached for his jacket. He hoped he would have time to get something to eat. He locked the door to his office and walked down the hall. Monica was making copies. He knocked on the copy room door and stuck his head in.

"I see you're still here."

Without turning around, she said, "I was on my way out then I got a call. I needed to get some things done."

He knew she was lying. She just couldn't stay away. He admired her drive even though she had a head as hard as a brick. "You're supposed to be taking it easy, remember?"

She placed her hand over her heart. "I'm going to, Mr. Lewis, I promise."

"Well, good night. I guess I'll see you when you get back."

"I guess so." As he walked toward the door, Monica hobbled out of the room with her crutch.

"Dray?"

"Yes?" He stopped in his tracks and turned around. She looked at him as though something was on her mind and eased toward him.

"Listen," she began, "I really didn't get a chance to thank you last night for what you did. You really went out on a limb for me, and I didn't want you to think I was ungrateful or anything."

She looked down at the ground as if she was searching for more words. But her silence indicated she couldn't find any.

"No problem. And I must admit, you were less tart than usual."

She rolled her eyes. "So I was tart before?"

They both laughed.

"Nah," he said. "You were just a little harsh. But I'm a man, I can deal with it."

Monica shook her head. "I didn't mean to be so rude to you before. I had a lot on my mind . . . things were crazy. I know you didn't deserve that treatment." She shook her head and laughed. "I'm really sorry for being such a . . . well, you know."

He smiled, moved by her sincerity. Not only was she beautiful, she was honest. He ran his finger over her cheek. A soft gasp escaped her. Inside there was a flutter of emotions. Lust, pain, yearning. Was he getting under her skin? Didn't he know she was close to jumping into his arms? She stepped back.

"Please, forgive me for my behavior."

"I already have," he said warmly. "Good night, Ms. Holiday. Take care of yourself."

"Good night, Mr. Lewis. I will."

When Monica got home, she ran water for a bath. She was aching all over, and there was nothing more relaxing than being in a tub of hot water. She turned on her stereo and put in her Sade Greatest Hits disc. She stood in the mirror and peeled off her clothes. She thought back to Dray that morning, with the towel wrapped around his waist. "What am I thinking?" she asked herself as her clothes dropped to the floor. His firm chest pressing up against her breasts. That's what she was thinking about. Embarrassed by her thoughts, she grinned. She turned to examine the bruises on her back; they were still a deep shade of purple. She knew it would take a couple of weeks to heal. In the meantime, a soak in hot water and Epsom salt would have to suffice.

She surrounded the tub with red candles and submerged herself in bubbles. She thought about taking the rest of the week off, but wondered if Dray could really handle the cosmetic company negotiations for the Prima Donnas. She wanted each girl to have a hefty paycheck for her appearance in the ads. She wasn't just their publicist; she served as their financial advisor sometimes too. There was no way Dray would be able to ensure they would get a good deal. He didn't know a thing about beauty. Besides, she wasn't sure if he was experienced with business negotiations. She reminded herself to call Bill the next morning and talk to him about it. She wouldn't mind Dray helping at all.

♫

Dray got out of the shower in his new Midtown apartment and wrapped a towel around his waist. He was glad to have a place of his own. Now he could get settled and see the city. He looked at his well-toned physique in the mirror and oiled his chestnut skin. He pulled on a pair of Polo boxers and wind pants, his relaxation gear. After promising himself he would not do any work, he nestled down in a reclining chair to watch television. He hoped Monica was taking it easy. Her apology had compelled him to look at her differently. She wasn't the snooty woman he'd first had the displeasure of meeting almost two months ago. She'd become a woman he wanted to get to know better. Not that he was looking for romance, he just wanted to enjoy her company.

OLAYINKA AIKENS

CHAPTER 7

Two weeks after her accident, Monica made her way back to Handle Up with an armful of work. While she enjoyed her mini-vacation, she was happy to be back. She rode in the elevator up to the seventh floor. When she got inside the office, she was surprised to see Beverly wasn't at her desk. It was just nine o'clock, and Beverly always got there at eight. She went around the corner to her office. All the other offices were empty. Something wasn't right. As far as she knew, there wasn't a meeting, but she headed to the boardroom just to double check. She opened the door slowly and stuck her head inside.

"Surprise!" everyone yelled. She put her hand over her heart.

"Oh, my god!" She held her chest as Bill hugged her. "What is this?"

"Just a little something for our favorite PR person," Beverly yelled. She gave Monica a quick hug.

"It's good to have you back. We missed you." Bill hugged her once more as everyone scattered around the table.

"Welcome back, Monica," Patrice said, giving her a quick hug. She leaned close to whisper. "Mr. Lewis has a thing for you."

All of the employees clapped as Monica wiped the tears from her eyes. She was totally surprised. She was speechless as she saw Dray emerge from the back of the room with a beautiful bouquet of yellow roses and a beautifully wrapped pink box. He smiled as he stood before her, dressed all GQ in a slate-gray suit. His fresh haircut accented his striking eyes.

"Nice to have you back," he said, kissing her gently on the cheek. His tantalizing after-shave flustered her senses. Someone whistled at them. Monica blushed as Dray handed her the roses.

"It's nice to be back," she said, inhaling them.

"I have something else for you too," he whispered. He set the gift down on the table, resisting the urge to embrace her in front of everyone.

"We have cake too!" Patrice said proudly. There was a huge rectangular cake with white and pink icing on the table. Small, frosted yellow and pink flowers were on each corner.

"It looks delicious," Monica said.

"Let's cut it," someone else said.

"Too early in the morning," Vera snarled. "I'm on a diet anyway." No one seemed to care. They ignored her.

Monica and Patrice made eye contact and giggled. Vera could definitely stand to shed a few pounds. Patrice reached for the knife and began cutting the cake into small squares.

"Who wants cake?" she asked. Several people went for plates.

Bill stood in the center of the room. "Well, who says you can't eat cake in the morning?" he kidded. "I can enjoy something sweet twenty-four hours a day. Enjoy yourself, Monica. I've got a meeting to go to downtown. Get your cake and let's get back to work, everybody!"

As Patrice handed everyone a piece of cake, they emptied the room. Monica chatted with some of the other employees as Dray helped Beverly clean off the table.

Patrice started covering the cake, "Monica, you want your piece of cake now or later?"

"Oh, no, I haven't eaten yet. I'll have some at lunch, thanks."

Dray whispered in her ear. "Let me take you out for lunch." Monica couldn't hide her smile as she nodded her approval.

"Beverly, we better go," Patrice mumbled. "I think they need us to do some filing or something." It didn't take a rocket scientist to see Dray wanted Monica to himself. "I'll just put this in your office, Monica." Beverly lifted the cake box and followed Patrice to the door.

"Thanks, Patrice. Thanks, Bev," Monica cooed as she shut the door behind her. Monica could hear them giggling through the door. Now that she and Dray were alone, she could grill him. When she turned around, he was standing so close she had to reach for his arm for balance. He grabbed her arm gently and clutched her for a moment.

"Sorry," she said moving back from his arms.

"No problem. Are you alright?"

"Yes, I'm fine. I guess all the excitement made me a little woozy." She looked down at the floor.

He clutched her hand with both of his. "We can't have that. Can we?"

Her eyes came up to study his face. "No, we can't."
Dray folded his arms across his chest. "So, did you enjoy our little surprise?"

"Are you the reason I have this lovely cake?" she asked, not taking her eyes off him. "And these beautiful flowers?"

His smile was a mile wide. "Maybe."

"You didn't have to."

He studied her face, and put his hands in his pockets. "Well, it's done, so why don't you open your gift?"

"I can't believe you got me a gift. Why?"

"You ask too many questions, woman. Why don't you just take it for what it is?"

She moved close to assess him. "And what is it?"

He stared deeply into her eyes as if undressing her. "Just open your gift."

It was so nicely wrapped, she thought about letting it stay that way. "This paper is really beautiful, I don't wanna tear it."

"If you don't open it, I'll be very disappointed. Then I'll have to punish you." He moved closer. Her eyes froze on his lips. How badly she wanted to kiss him. His appeal was devastating.

"Punish me," she said. It was a statement, not a question.

He was intrigued by her challenge.

"So you're a woman who likes danger?" His deep voice was smooth and steady. He coiled a strand of her hair around his finger. "Humph?"

Her world was spinning. But somehow she managed to whisper, "Maybe."

"What are you waiting for?" The smell of his fragrant cologne made her flush. She smoothed her hair nervously as he put his hand on hers. "Go on, open it."

He guided her hand over the box. His warm hands made her tremble. She felt his other hand brush hair from her neck. Oh, my god, she wanted to scream. His touches were so warm and tender. Monica tried to calm the butterflies in her stomach as she pulled the bow off. Guiding her hand, Dray helped her tear the wrapping paper. Under his watchful eye, she lifted the top. Elation filled her heart when she saw a replica of her white Noviko dress.

"Oh, my God!" She lifted it from its box. "Where did you get this? And how did you know my size?"

"Patrice told . . . " Before he could finish, she wrapped her arms around his neck and gave him a quick hug. He dreaded his body's reaction to her softness. "Patrice told me."

She covered her eyes with her hand. She was so overcome with joy, tears formed in her eyes. She didn't want to cry, so she forced them back and blinked. Dray returned her embrace and then released her.

"I guess I'm not such a bad guy after all, huh?"

"No, you're not," she said. But she couldn't keep the dress. She already had one. Besides Ethel's Dry Cleaners got the stain out. She had to give it back.

"Dray, I can't accept this."

His brows flickered a little. "Why?"

"I have one. And besides this dress is too expensive for—"

"For what? A woman like you?" He slid the dress from her hands and placed it back in the box. "A woman like you deserves thousands of these."

His words turned her insides to butter. As he moved toward her, Monica stiffened. He put his hands on her arms. "You know, the folks at Noviko will be very upset if I return this dress. It was a special order. Why don't we exchange it?"

"Okay," she managed to say. "What did it cost you. I can give you the money."

He cupped her chin with his hand and lowered his mouth to hers. He kissed her hungrily, pulling her into his arms for a snug fit. Monica was shocked at her eager response to his lips. His kisses were warm, urgent, and tender. He pulled away only to return with one more quick taste of her. When they parted, she stood beneath him, lips moist and swollen as she throbbed with desire.

"Damn," he said, running his hand over his goatee.

"What?"

"Here I am thinking I could keep things all business, and I go kissing you like that."

"Ditto," she said, not meeting his eyes. "I guess we got carried away."

"I think it's my fault. I'm sorry." He wasn't really. Her kisses were sweet like berries. Even though Bill's warning was still on his mind, he couldn't pull away from Monica's charms. "So when do you want to exchange the dress. I'm free this weekend."

Monica watched his mouth, eager for one more kiss. She leaned forward and placed her hands on his chest. Dray held her close and tilted her chin upward. He kissed it, moved down to her neck and then back to her lips. They couldn't get enough of each other. Monica hadn't kissed a man in months, and here was the reason why. She'd been waiting for his lips, and his lips only. His mouth welcomed hers. He couldn't remember when he enjoyed kissing a woman this much. He slid into the chair behind him and pulled her onto his lap.

"If I keep kissing you, we'll need a motel room." Monica couldn't help but laugh. He continued, "We better stop."

"You know, you have the softest lips," she purred.

"That's the only thing on me that's soft right now!"

"Are you complaining?"

"Yes and no. But because I'm a gentleman, I'll forget you asked me that."

"I guess I should be grateful."

"Yes, you should. Come on, let's get back to work."

They stood, and heard a beep from the phone. It was Beverly.

"Mr. Lewis?"

"Yes?"

"There's a Lisa Griffin on the phone for you, she says it's urgent. Shall I put her through?"

Monica looked at him, but he avoided her eyes. "No, Bev. I'll take it in my office. Thanks."

"Okay."

"Excuse me for a moment, Monica," he said, rushing out the door. He left her standing alone in the room. Monica folded her arms across her chest and pouted. Who the hell was Lisa? And why was he rushing to answer her call?

Dray shut the door to his office and pressed the speaker button.

"What's up Lisa?" he asked dryly.

"Hey, Dray. How's Atlanta?"

"Fine. What do you want?"

She was silent and then spoke. "I need a favor, Dray."

"A favor?" She must have been out of her mind to call him and ask for a favor. "Maybe you need to ask your ball player boyfriend for a favor?"

"I would but he's out of town."

The gall of this woman. "Sounds like a personal problem to me."

"I'm serious, Dray. I need a big favor."

Dray sat in his chair and loosened his tie. "What?" He couldn't believe he was entertaining her.

"I need a loan."

Dray knew he was dreaming now. She didn't just ask him for a loan. "What?"

Lisa continued, "Well, I heard you got a big time job with Handle Up records, and I was wonderin' if I could borrow five hundred dollars."

Dray picked up the receiver. "Lisa, what the hell have you been smokin'? How the hell you gon' call me and have the audacity to ask me for anything? You break up with me, move in wit another nigga, and now you're asking me for money? What the hell is wrong with you?"

"I'll get it back to you soon. I promise."

"You don't need to give back anything you're not going to get. Bye, Lisa."

"But Dray!"

"No buts. Goodbye, Lisa."

Back in her office, Monica sat down to check her e-mail. She stared at the vase of flowers on the edge of her desk. The bright yellow blossoms added color to the room. But flowers were the last thing on Monica's mind. She could still feel Dray's lips, and his arms wrapped around her. But then there was the phone call from Lisa. Was she his girlfriend? The mother of his child? A close friend? Monica didn't know. But she wasn't going any further until she did. She stared at the screen. There were three e-mails from Rodney. What on earth did he want?

CHAPTER 8

At home, Dray wondered if Monica was upset by his phone call. He didn't see her for the rest of the day. She missed their lunch date, and she wasn't in her office when he left. Of all the times Lisa could have called, why did she have to call when Monica was around? He settled onto his sofa with his laptop. He was outlining his plans for the Prima Donnas. He had to give Bill some idea about how much more he would have to spend on promotions. Hiring a stylist for them was at the top of his list. They would need one when they started touring. And that would be soon. He would need Monica's help more than ever.

"I kissed him," Monica told Robin. They'd been on the phone for over an hour before Monica confessed the deed. She continued, "Then some woman named Lisa called."

"Who's she?"

"I don't know. But he rushed to take her call."

Robin tried to comfort her friend. "Maybe she's his sister," Monica sighed heavily. "Maybe you should have asked him."

"I don't wanna seem like I'm that concerned."

"You are. Maybe kissing him wasn't a good idea," Robin said.

Monica closed her eyes. "He kissed me first."

"Well, you did kiss him back."

"But it felt right. I've never lost control like that? What was I thinking?"

Robin laughed. "You weren't."

"I still can't believe he went out and found this dress." She held it up and looked at it.

"That is something." Robin was intrigued by the gesture. "Not many men would go out on a limb to find a replacement for a dress they'd ruined."

"Well, he did," Monica said softly.

"Maybe this Lisa character isn't as important as you think. It was his idea to throw that little bash today. And he did give you yellow roses. The rose of friendship. Clearly brutha man has something for you."

Monica went into her kitchen and put some water in her teapot. "So you think he wants to be my friend?"

"I'm not saying that. He did kiss you. I'm just saying that maybe you're worrying about the Lisa thing for no reason."

Monica plopped down on the couch. "Don't get all excited, it was just a kiss. And I'm sure he just meant well with the gift. The roses might have been Bill's idea."

"Please, if all he wanted was a kiss, he would have gotten it and left. But he stayed, you kissed him again. And if Lisa hadn't called, lord only knows what would have happened."

"Maybe you're right. I don't think if I ruined some guy's expensive suit, I would hunt down the manufacturer."

"See what I mean?"

"Yeah, I guess so." The teakettle was whistling. "Listen, girl, I've got to go. I'm gonna drink this tea and lay down."

"Alright. Call me tomorrow."

"Bye, girl."

Later in the week, Monica decided to make a bold move. She called Dray into her office to invite him to dinner. She decided on her favorite Chinese restaurant, Uncle Tai's. They had delicious cuisine. Dray agreed on one condition: he would pay and they would ride in the limo with Robert behind the wheel. Monica agreed and set the time at 7:30.

Dray arrived at her apartment on time. And when Monica opened the door, he was casually dressed in a pair of smoke gray slacks and a long-sleeved black silk sweater that hung just right on his athletic frame. On his feet was a pair of black Kenneth Cole loafers.

"Hey," she said, looking him over. "You look very handsome." She invited him in.

"Hey, yourself, beautiful." He grabbed her and gave her a quick kiss. She hadn't expected that. And she felt uneasy about it. He noticed her unresponsiveness as she pulled away. Dray could tell something was wrong. Perhaps the phone call from Lisa still lingered in her thoughts.

"I'll be ready in a second," she said, dashing to the bathroom.

She was dressed in a black one-shoulder slip dress that she'd gotten down in Miami and a pair of black sandals. She looked every bit the diva she was.

"You know, Mr. Lewis," Monica called, from the bathroom, "if you keep dressin' all stylish like me, I'm going to think you're up to something."

"I am," he said. He looked her over as she smoothed her clothes in the hall mirror. "Nice dress. Hopefully we can make it through the night without staining it," he joked.

"That shouldn't be a problem this time. Besides, black hides stains well," she said dryly. "Let me get my purse and we can go."

Monica picked up her black clutch and her keys. She pulled a sweater from the hall closet and said, "I'm ready."

Dray was smiling at her.

"What?" she asked.

"You know you very have good taste." He was staring at her like she was a piece of candy. "And I like that painting too." He nodded toward the wall. There was an abstract oil piece with two bodies intertwined over the fireplace.

"It was a gift from a client."

"At Handle Up?"

"Sort of. Rodney's lawyer gave it to me a long time ago. Let's go," she said. She didn't want to talk about Rodney. But she did want to find out more about Lisa.

Dray simply smiled and escorted her out the door.

The ride to the restaurant carried them through Buckhead. They sat side-by-side taking in the sights. They passed all sorts of stores and trendy eateries along the way. Dray wanted to know what was on Monica's mind. She'd been quiet since they left her place. Was she mad at him? He couldn't think of anything immediately. But then he remembered the phone call from Lisa.

"Dray, who's Lisa?"

He was right. That was what was bothering her all along.

He didn't beat around the bush. "My ex," he said looking at her.

Her eyes widened and then narrowed. "Oh. Why didn't you tell me about her?"

"Is that what's been bothering you?"

Monica frowned. "Yes . . . I mean, what do you mean bothering me?"

"Well, I haven't really talked to you since you came back to work. And that was the day she called when we were in the conference room. And you've avoided me ever since. That was the day we . . . "

"Kissed," she said, trying to keep from blushing.

"Yeah. The day we kissed," he said looking in her eyes. He looked down at her mouth and licked his lips. He wanted to kiss her again.

"Do you like Chinese food?" she asked, determined to get off the Lisa subject. In the back of her mind, she wondered if they were planning to get back together. But did it matter? She wasn't interested in him. At least that's the lie she kept telling herself.

"Chinese food is fine," Dray sighed. She hadn't given him a chance to explain the phone call from Lisa.

"Well, Uncle Tai's has the best walnut prawns I have ever tasted, except for this place back home called Shin-Shin. The kung pao chicken isn't bad either."

Maybe she didn't care about the phone call anymore. He put his arm around her. Monica relaxed a little. There was no sense in ruining the night. She invited him to dinner, and she didn't want him to think she was a snob. And being near him still gave her butterflies.

"How'd you get to be so worldly?" he asked. "I mean you know about good food, you wear Italian-made dresses that cost a fortune. Have you always been this way?"

"What way?" She glanced at his well-defined profile and laughed. "Are you trying to call me a bourgeois?"

Her reaction seemed to amuse him. "You are! You're like one of those Black American Princesses, a BAP. I bet you were a debutante, weren't you? Prancing around in a white dress, doing curtsies and afternoon teas."

"You know for someone as streetwise as you, you sure know a lot about bourgeois people. And yes, I was a debutante. I was presented in 1990 at the Links Cotillion, thank you very much."

"That explains a lot. You California folks are always into fancy stuff — the Hollywood lifestyle. I bet you know how to surf, too, huh?"

"See, now you're going too far, mister." She peeked out the window. "Here we are."

Robert pulled the limo in front of the restaurant. It was located in Phipps Plaza near Saks. He stepped out to open the door for them. Dray got out first and took Monica's hand to help her. When they arrived inside, the hostess seated them immediately. Monica made it a point to make reservations because the restaurant was always busy. Even with her pull, they would still have had to wait if she hadn't called first.

As they ate the kung pao chicken over steamed rice, wonton soup, vegetable-filled egg rolls, and walnut prawns, their enjoyment was evident. Dray was on his second helping. Their conversation covered everything from work to politics. Neither of them had ever had more fun over dinner. Dray finally had someone who could make him think and laugh. Sure, he and Lisa ate out, but they did more arguing than eating. With Monica he felt relaxed and was looking forward to the next time. There was enough food there to feed three people. Since both of them had huge appetites, nothing went untouched. Dray observed her as she ate her prawns, holding them delicately with her fork. He watched it slide into her mouth and wondered if she'd be willing to give him another kiss. The thought of it made him warm.

"I see you like those jumbo shrimp," he said.

"I love seafood."

"Me too. I haven't really had any since I left Chicago. My dinner lately has been nothing more than pizza and fried chicken."

They continued to eat. When they finished their dessert, Dray paid the bill and led Monica to the limo. He wanted to go someplace where they could sit and talk. Monica directed Robert to a park just off Piedmont, not far from the restaurant. Robert parked the limo and let them out.

"I'll be right here." He tipped his hat and pulled out a cigar. Dray and Monica strolled under the moonlit Georgia sky. It was full of stars, a perfect backdrop for a romantic evening.

"Can I ask you something, Monica?" Dray stopped his stride as they came up on a small waterfall."

"Sure."

He met her eyes with a concerned look on his face. "What happened with you and that Double R cat?"

Monica quickly looked away. "Who told you about that?"

"It's not exactly a secret, Monica. To be honest, I never paid any attention to Rodney or his music before I moved here."

She sucked her teeth and shook her head. "That was the biggest mistake of my life."

Dray lifted her chin. "If you don't want to tell me now, I'll understand. But does it bother you that I know?"

Taking a deep, steady breath, she stepped back. Her eyes narrowed, then met his.

"No, I just didn't expect you to ask me about it." She resumed her stroll and he followed. She wanted to leave the past just where it was. "He just used me to further his career."

Without commenting any further, she walked faster. Dray followed as they headed toward a bridge that crossed the park's small lake. Monica rested her arms against the rail and looked down at the water. Rodney was a touchy subject, and she definitely wasn't ready to discuss him with Dray. Sensing her tension, Dray took the opportunity to comfort her.

"He's a fool, you know," he said, staring at the moon's reflection on the water. "I would have never let you go."

"Oh, really?" she murmured glancing his way.

He turned to face her. "Yeah, really. Monica, you're the most beautiful woman I've ever known, inside and out."

"Gee, thanks," she said sarcastically. She was flattered by his compliment, but didn't believe him. She was too vulnerable. She'd heard words like that before and wound up being disappointed. Trusting men was on the bottom of her list of priorities, and she wasn't ready for a relationship. Even if it was with Drayton Lewis.

"You trying to get on my good side?"

"No, I'm not. You are beautiful."

"How do I know you're not lying?"

"Because I'm telling you. I don't have to lie to you, Monica. I like you as a friend, and I'm attracted to you. There's nothing wrong with that because I don't expect anything from you. I just enjoy being around you."

As he leaned to kiss her, she put her fingers to his lips. "Please don't. What happened the other day was a mistake."

"What do you mean, a mistake?" He put his hand under her chin, turning her toward him. "You know you don't mean that."

"Yes, I do." She tried to pull away but he held her wrist. "I can't be with you."

"Look me in the eyes and tell me that you didn't like the way my lips felt against yours."

She couldn't do it, and he knew it. "Please let go of me, Drayton."

He released her, and she started to walk toward the limo. He hoped he hadn't upset her. But the sound of her heels hitting hard against the pavement confirmed his presumption.

"Monica!" he called, trying to catch up with her.

She kept walking.

"Monica! Please wait."

He trotted after her. When they got to the limo, he pulled her gently by the arm. She eyed him sharply. "Just let me go."

He did. "Tell me you don't want me, and I'll leave you alone."

She stepped inside and slid over on the seat. If she told him what he wanted to hear, he might not be ready for it. Or better yet, he would be ready and it would change everything between them. No answer is the best answer, she convinced herself. He slid in next to her and took her hand in his. She pulled it away quickly and rested it in her lap. Robert shut the door and Dray gave her a quizzical look. If she was going to be like that, so was he.

"Hey, Rob. We're going back to Miss Holiday's place. She's not feeling well."

Dray caught the surprise in Robert's eye in the rear-view mirror. He shrugged and threw his hands up. Damn, she was hard on a man.

CHAPTER 9

Monica had been on Dray's mind since the first day they'd met, but never like this. He couldn't get any work done. And he couldn't understand why she'd said they made a mistake the other day. He hadn't done anything wrong. At least he didn't think so. She was so cold when she said it, he was beginning to wonder if it were true. Fast or slow, he wanted her like he'd never wanted anyone in his life. How could she walk away from him without even trying? She had more feelings toward him than she was willing to admit. She just didn't want to accept them.

"Man, I don't know what I did wrong," he told Adam, who'd called him from Chicago. "She's been avoiding me all week and won't even look me in the eyes."

"Damn, dawg, what'd you say to her?" Adam asked.

"I just asked her about Double R dumping her." Dray eased himself into the reclining chair in his apartment. He propped his feet up on the footrest and took a sip of his beer.

"She dated him? The rapper?"

"Yeah."

"Damn. And he dropped her?"

"Yep. I don't know what she ever saw in him anyway."

"Do I hear a little jealousy in your voice, man?"

"Hell, no. I ain't jealous. I just don't see why she would waste her time on such a loser."

"Maybe it was the money."

Adam had a point, but Monica wasn't a gold digger. She'd proven that to Dray once he got to know her.

"I don't think so. She has plenty of money and way more class than that. I guess shit just happens."

"No doubt. Maybe she didn't want to talk about it. Man, you know how sensitive women are about breakups."

"We talked about it for a minute, then she ran back to the limo. I had Robert drive her back home. She wouldn't even talk to me."

"Let it go, man, don't even think about it. It's not like she can avoid you anyway. Y'all see each other every day."

"I see her every day. She won't look at me."

"Ignore her like she's ignoring you, that'll get a rise out of her."

"Easier said than done. Monica is not a woman who can be easily ignored. She has this pull to her that yanks me every time I see her."

"She's probably in love with ya, punk ass! I need to write a book. I'm damn good at this relationship shit."

"Well, why don't you have a woman then, Dr. Love? You seem to always be able to give other people advice."

"That's because great men like me have to take our time with this love shit. Right now I'm just trying to please all the ladies. I don't want a woman right now. Get over it, move on."

"I don't know if I can. You know I thought after Lisa I wouldn't want a woman."

"And now?"

"Now . . . now I think I lied."

"You tripping, nigga."

"Fuck you Adam. I don't expect you to understand. I think I'm gonna send a message on her two-way and apologize."

"Apologize for what? You didn't do anything wrong," Adam scoffed. "She should be apologizing to you."

"Naw, man. I can't go out like that. I don't want her to think I'm a jerk."

"You are a jerk," Adam said. "Besides, she may already think that. I told you, act like it didn't affect you one way or another. Women go crazy when they find out they can't make you ass crazy. I guarantee it."

"Ay, man, I'm not listening to you. Your chicken-head methods don't work with real women."

Adam broke into a hearty laugh. "If you say so, man. But I know I'm right."

"Whatever, nigga." Dray sat contemplating for a moment. He couldn't forget about it. "I'ma talk to you later, dawg," he said.

"Alright, dude."

The next morning when Dray saw Monica, he realized getting over her wouldn't be easy. She was what he always wanted. Passionate, intelligent, and beautiful. He told himself he wasn't interested in a relationship. But was it the truth?

When he entered the office, she was the first person he saw. Their eyes drank each other up, but she was the first to look away. Had she forgotten what they'd shared the other night? Was it all just an act? As she and Patrice went through some papers, Dray came to the desk.

He smiled at Patrice and greeted both of them. "Good morning," he said, looking directly at Monica. She looked absolutely gorgeous in her red wrap dress. It clung to her petite frame as if it were made just for her.

"Good morning," she said.

"Hey, Dray," Patrice chimed in, "what's up?"

"Nothing much. Any calls for me?"

Patrice flipped through a stack of message slips on the desk, and pulled out one. "Here you go."

Monica watched as he took the message and looked at it. He was standing dangerously close to her. If she moved an inch, they would touch. It was too much for her to handle. She decided to cut her conversation with Patrice short.

"I'd better get back to my office," she said, stepping away. "I've got some . . . something to do."

She made a stop in the mailroom first.

Dray decided to follow her. "Thanks, Patrice," he said, fumbling with the message. "I've got to check my mail too. Can you hold all my calls this morning?"

"Sure."

"Thanks."

Dray went inside the mailroom and met Monica coming out. She brushed up against him and turned her head quickly. He paused and looked at her. She avoided his eyes, walked down the hallway and went into her office. She shut the door and sat down. Being around him was tough. She put her head back. How was she going to make it through the day without thinking about him? Could she convince herself that she didn't need or want him?

When Dray stepped inside his office, he was surprised to find Double R waiting for him. He was annoyed because Double R didn't have an appointment, and Dray hoped to spend the morning drafting a treatment for the Prima Donnas' new video. Rodney stood near a shelf that was decorated with pictures of Dray and people he knew back in Chicago. Dray moved in slowly, shutting the door quietly behind him. Rodney didn't hear him come in.

"Can I help you?" Dray asked in a skeptical tone.

"Oh, my bad, man, I didn't mean to just come in your office like this."

Well what the hell did you mean by bringing your ass in here without an appointment?

Dray set his briefcase on the desk, and the tall, thuggish guy turned around.

"What's up man?" Rodney greeted him with a pound. "Sorry about intruding." His voice indicated he was much older than he looked. He was an average-looking brown-skinned brother with cold, deep-set brown eyes. His rap skills were probably his most beneficial asset.

"Mr. Robinson." Dray shook his hand as he gave a quick smile.

Rodney's teeth were outlined in platinum, and he wore a huge matching chain adorned with a diamond scorpion reminiscent of a zodiac sign. Dray surveyed the man who seemed a bit too flashy and brusque for a sweet woman like Monica. Rodney made himself comfortable in a chair in front of Dray's desk. As Dray pulled off his jacket, Rodney shook his platinum-adorned wrists.

"What can I do for you, Mr. Robinson?" Dray asked.

Rodney looked up at the ceiling. "Well, as a partner in Handle Up Records, I thought it was time we met. I just came to see if you were enjoying yourself. You know? Making sure you're settled in and all."

Dray sat down in his chair. "Yeah, as much as to be expected. It's work, you know?"

"Yeah." Rodney pounded his hand on the desk. "I see they hooked this office up for you. The last cat that was here couldn't keep this son-of-a-bitch clean."

Dray nodded. Who cares? "So, you're the infamous Double R? I've heard a lot about you. Missed you at the party last week."

"Yeah, that's me." His voice was rough, just like it sounded on his records. "I'm sorry I didn't get a chance to meet you. I got caught up trying to entertain some fans. You know how this rap shit is."

"Yeah, I know." Dray could only imagine how "R" entertained his fans. "So what can I do for you, Mr. Robinson?"

"Nothing much. Call me Rod. I just came by to meet you, you know? Since I didn't get a chance to see you at the party, I wanted to see what the real deal was. Bill's told me a lot about you. I hear you're from Chi-town?"

"Yeah," Dray said sharply. "South Side."

"That's where my father's from. I grew up in Detroit, though."

"Is that right?"

"Yeah, had to get away, though."

"Really?" Dray had no interest in why Double R left Detroit, but obliged his ego anyway.

"Yeah. I was in to too much trouble. I had a couple of patnas who were into some thangs they shouldn't have been in to, you know?" Rodney was rambling. "I didn't want to get caught up like them. Understand what I'm saying?"

If you do. Right now, I really wish you'd get out of my office. Dray checked his watch, hoping Double R wouldn't keep him any longer.

After a spell of silence, Monica knocked on the door. "Excuse me." She saw the back of Rodney's head. "I'm sorry, Mr. Lewis."

"No, come on in Monica." Dray was relieved to have a break. She opened the door slowly. And walked inside with an armful of files. Rodney looked over his shoulder as she approached the desk. Monica caught his eye and quickly turned to Dray. What an idiot, she thought. It was bad enough she had to represent him. Why did he have to keep working her nerves?

"Mr. Lewis, I need your signature on these documents for the Prima Donnas, please."

The sight of Rodney made Monica sick. She wanted to throw the papers in his face as he sat grinning in the chair.

"So, how's your morning going, Ms. Holiday?" Dray asked.

She was caught off guard by the concern in his voice. "F-fine, so far. The girls want to go shopping for the promo tour. Can we arrange something for them?" She placed the papers in front of him.

"I don't think that will be a problem." He pulled his pen from his shirt pocket and read over the papers. They were mostly approvals for expenses for the girls' tour and upcoming video shoot. He stopped momentarily to compliment Monica. "You look nice today,"

She managed a smile. "Thank you, Mr. Lewis."

"You're quite welcome," he said, meeting her eyes. Rodney shifted in his seat. "Looks like things are coming along well for the girls," Dray continued.

"Yes, they are."

Monica moved each document away as he signed the next one. When he finished, she picked them up and placed them back into the folder. Rodney sat mum, fiddling with his jewelry.

"Is that all you need?" Dray asked. There were more ways to interpret his question.

Monica nodded, "Yes, that's everything. Thank you."

"You're welcome. So, is everything else in order?"

"Um-hmm. I'll brief you later." She shot Rodney a grim look and opened the folder again. "I'll get you copies as soon as I can. I have to get the rest of these to Bill before he disappears."

"Thank you, Monica."

"You're welcome."

Just as she reached for the door, Rodney blurted, "What's up Monica? You can't speak? You tryin' to act funny in front of Mr. Lewis or something?" Dray looked up from his copies. The urge to punch the jackass for taunting her was irresistible.

"Hey, Rodney," she said dryly. She rolled her eyes and walked out, shutting the door behind her.

Rodney wiped his face with one hand. "Man, she's a trip. I can't believe she's still acting like that."

"Like what?" Dray asked, pretending not to know what he was talking about.

"She's mad because I broke up with her." He shook his head and laughed. "I hate bourgeois ass broads like her. They think the world owes them something. So prissy and shit. They want you to eat at the Cheesecake Factory and shop at Phipps Plaza all the time."

Dray folded his hands together. "So what's wrong with that?"

"Nothing. It just ain't me, ya dig? I'm a real nigga. I ain't got time for all that shit."

Dray didn't "dig," but he nodded in agreement anyway. Monica definitely wasted her time with Rodney. He was just plain ignorant. And too stupid to realize it. He went on to burden Dray with some nonsense about his tour.

"I have some ideas for the shows. I want to do three a week." Dray sighed. He knew that was impossible, especially for a rap artist. There was no way Rodney could travel to that many cities in such a short time—unless the cities were close together. The shows would have to be scheduled during the week and that could be hard on people who held jobs or went to school. The tour was scheduled for Friday and Saturday nights in May. Rodney was greedy, pure and simple, and he wanted to piss a few people off. And he could do it. He was the label's only artist who owned a percentage of the company. Because of that, he could manipulate his way into anything.

"No," Dray said, "it won't work. You need to stick to the schedule you're on. We have too much to lose. A tour like that would mean nothing but trouble."

"Not really. I think it's cool."

"It has to be more than cool. Have you talked to Bill and Monica about it?"

"No, I don't need to. They'll do what I say, regardless. I make the most money at this camp anyway. What can they tell me?"

Just then Monica entered the room again. "These are the new pictures of the girls from their last photo shoot. I need you to take a look at them when you can."

Dray opened the folder as she turned to leave. "Okay. Oh, and Monica, have you heard Rodney's plans for the tour in May?"

She folded her arms and stood behind Dray. "No, I haven't," she replied. "What are they?"

Rodney waved her off and sucked his teeth as he figured out his rebuttal.

"Come on Rod, tell her," Dray teased. He wanted to make him look like an even bigger fool. "She may like the idea." He was meddling, but he didn't care. Next to seeing Monica smiling, watching Rodney squirm made his day.

"I want to tour three days a week," Rodney said sullenly.

Monica smirked. "Maybe that would work if you were doing a regional tour, but not a nationwide one."

"The original plan is better." Dray pulled the itinerary from his desk drawer. "Much better." He stressed, "If you change it now the company may be forced to shell out money for tickets people have already purchased. Some places have already sold out."

"I agree," Monica said, "we don't need anymore mishaps on the road like we did on the last tour. I'm not going to spend all hours of the night cleaning up your mess while you go get another aggravated assault charge."

"It's not your decision," Rodney snapped, "and that's what you get paid to do. Clean up my mess." He leaned back, sneering.

Monica ignored his comment. It was an attempt to get a rise out of her and it wasn't going to work.

Defending her, Dray put the arrogant rapper in his place. "She may not have the final say, but she does have some. It will be up to the rest of the executives as well to see if this idea will gel. Don't get cocky on me."

Rodney kept his comments to himself. Monica wanted to hug Dray. But instead she let her finger brush the back of his neck softly as she moved her hand in his hair. Her faint touch aroused him. She took the folder from him and left the office. He watched her exit. Those sweet hips he wished he could get between made his knees weak. Graceful and poised. She took a step down when she decided to date Rodney. Dray clasped his hands together and waited for Rodney to leave. Frustrated, he got up without uttering a single word. He reached and shook Dray's hand.

"Later, dawg," he mumbled.

At noon, Monica invited Dray to lunch. It was her way of thanking him for putting Rodney on the spot, and an opportunity to take in his smile again. And since she'd ended their last date on such a sour note, she wanted to redeem herself. She picked a small Italian restaurant in Buckhead, not too far from her apartment. She decided not to let her past with Rodney hinder any new relationships, so she loosened up. If she kept harboring her anger about Rodney, she would never be happy.

At the restaurant, a hostess showed them to their table. A few minutes later a waiter greeted them. He took their drink orders and then returned with the drinks, a small baguette, and butter. After they ordered they sat quietly looking out into the street. "I see you always know all the little hot spots," Dray said, trying to break the ice between them.

"Listen, Dray," Monica said as their salads arrived. "I'm really sorry about what happened in the park. I was scared. . . . I'm not used to guys like you. You've done everything in your power to look out for me, and I'm grateful. I just got scared."

He smiled, touched by her words. The last thing he ever wanted was to scare her. He knew the pains of recouping after a breakup and didn't expect anything more than friendship.

"I understand completely, Monica." His deep voice lowered, "From here on out, we'll take things slowly."

Trying to be serious, she asked, "Does that mean you won't kiss me again?" She covered her mouth, trying to hide her smile.

"If you don't want me to kiss you, I won't. But I had hoped that would be a part of our friendship," he smiled. "You won't be rushed into anything else unless you want to be."

Finally, he understood what she was talking about. It would be easier for them to move forward now that things were clear. They both harbored animosity from past relationships.

"My ex and I had a bad break-up," Dray said suddenly.

Monica set her fork down. "I'm sorry to hear that."

"Don't be. She just wanted more than I could give . . . financially anyway. I never knew a woman more concerned with how other people saw her. It was like she had to put on this façade for people."

Monica swore she saw pain in his eyes. She wondered if he still had feelings for Lisa. Her selfish side wished he never uttered her name again.

"I see you're enjoying your salmon and angel-hair pasta," she said.

He nodded, "I am."

"I'm glad. I've been coming here for years."

"You're a cultured woman, Monica. The average black woman your age hasn't experienced half of the things you have."

"Flattery will get you everywhere, Mr. Lewis."

"Good. I hope you keep inviting me to lunch. You have good taste in food, girl!"

Monica grinned. "That's not the only thing I have good taste in."

He knew exactly what she meant and smiled. "Thank you, bella," he said pulling her to him. In front of everyone at the restaurant, he planted a kiss on her lips that shook her to her toes.

"Thank you, Mr. Lewis," she muttered softly.

.

CHAPTER 10

After work, Dray followed Monica to her condo just off Peachtree. He felt a rush as they rode up in the elevator side by side. He admired her sexiness, even though she wasn't trying to be sexy. The sweet citrus of her perfume danced around his senses. He imagined seeing her with nothing on but perfume. The thought made his manhood stir. He covered himself as a satanic smile crossed his face. Just then, Monica turned and wondered what he was thinking about.

"Something on your mind, Mr. Lewis?"

Just the thought of my lips against your lips against mine, he wanted to say. "No, nothing at all."

"Are you sure?' she asked.

"Yes," he said. "Positive."

It was nice to be alone with her away from work. They needed to go over the plans for the Prima Donnas' promotional tour. Monica mapped out a ten-city tour, complete with radio and record store appearances. She wanted the Prima Donnas to perform on a couple of late-night shows on the major networks, but hadn't had any luck yet. She hoped they would at least get to appear on some of the cable music video shows. Along with Dray and Patrice, Monica coordinated the Prima Donnas' wardrobes, personal staff, and studying schedules. If everything went as planned, they'd be household names all over the globe in no time.

"Have a seat," Monica said once they were inside. Dray settled on the couch. "Would you like something to drink, Mr. Lewis?" she asked seductively.

He turned to find her in the kitchen. "What do you have? Let me guess, Chardonnay and Pinot Blanc?"

She pulled a beer from the refrigerator and grabbed a bottle opener. She flipped the top off and threw it in the trash.

"Oh, you're very funny, Mr. Lewis. I have Coronas in here too." She reached for one and grabbed her bottle opener from the drawer.

He reached for the television remote. "Oh, I didn't know they qualified for being a debutante's drink."

"Are you going to let me live that down? Can I help it if I was special?" She handed him the beer.

"Thanks. And I'm sorry. I was just kidding." He took a sip and turned on the television. "Let me see check out the sports news right quick."

Monica watched as he put the bottle to his lips. The thought of his kisses came flooding back. She returned to the kitchen to get her tea and joined him on the couch.

"These look great," he said, sorting through the pile of pictures. "I think we should have a couple of these made into posters and get them to the stores. They've got enough of Britney Spears and the rest of those folks in Wal-Mart nowadays."

"I know. Maybe we released the album at the wrong time," she said biting her lip. "You know Rodney is still riding high off the success of his album, and I'm wondering if the girls aren't a hit because he's still on top."

"Could be," he said, observing her. "But I don't think that's the problem. They just need exposure. They'll be fine."

"Which one do you like best?" she asked, referring to the photos.

"This one." He pointed to the photo where the girls were assembled in all black in front of a red background. "This is tight."

"Yeah, it is nice. Amber is coming out of her shell. She was so quiet when I met her."

"She has a lovely voice," Dray added, looking at her individual photo.

"Yes, she does. We'll have to check on that poster deal for them."

Dray lifted his nearly empty bottle. "Well, here's to long-lasting relationships and platinum records. Cheers."

Monica tapped his glass with her teacup. "If the girls' tour is a success, Bill will definitely fatten our wallets," Monica laughed.

"You've done a good job with them already, Monica. What more do they need?"

She set her cup on the table. "I don't know. Their lives are much better than mine was at seventeen."

"It couldn't have been that bad. All teenagers go through rough times."

"Try to juggle a job and college prep classes. Their life's a picnic compared to what mine was."

"Maybe, I guess you're right, but look at you now. You're successful, beautiful, and damn good company for a guy like me."

Monica blushed at his flattery. "A guy like you? What does that mean?"

"Nothing," he whispered. His nose flared in embarrassment. She peered at him inquisitively. "Why are you looking at me like that?" he asked, finishing his beer.

"Like what?"

"Like you want something." He grinned, softly.

Monica felt a ripple of excitement but didn't respond. She sipped her tea quietly. She glanced at him. *Like you want something*, she repeated in her head.

Dray set his empty bottle on the coffee table. He wanted to kiss her badly. Those silken mounds of supple flesh fired him up every time he looked at them. She couldn't know what she did to him inside. He was tempted to claim her lips but common sense prevailed. Almost as if they were reading each other's minds, their eyes met. Slowly they leaned forward. But before their lips could meet, the phone rang.

"I better get that." She got up and reached for the cordless phone. "Hello?"

"Hey, Monica, it's Cam."

"Hey, Cameron. Are you back in town?"

"Yeah. I was just calling to check on you. I heard about what happened to you at the office. Are you alright?"

"Yes, I'm fine. Thanks for asking."

"It was cool, all work and no play. I've been to so many meetings and parties. All I want to do is rest. Is your boy doing his job?"

"Who?"

"The A&R director, Dray."

Monica looked over at Dray, "Yeah, he's doing a great job. I'll have to tell you about him later on," she winked.

"Did I interrupt something? Is he there?"

"Why did you ask that?" she grinned. "And the answer is yes to both of those questions."

"So I guess that little incident at the Prima Donnas party sparked something in both of you?"

"Maybe . . . alright then, Cam." She had to get him off the phone.

"Tell him I said, 'What's up.'"

"Okay, I will. Bye." She went into the kitchen. "Would you like another beer?"

"Sure," Dray said.

She returned to the couch and handed him the beer. Their moment had been spoiled. She handed him the bottle. She jotted some notes down on her notepad. As her delicate fingers held the pen, Dray envisioned putting them to his lips and rubbing them along his face. He couldn't hold back any longer. He set his bottle down and took the pen and pad from her hands. Monica trembled at his warm touch.

"Can I have what you were going to give me before the phone rang?" he asked. He outlined her lips with his finger.

Her eyes closed. "Th-that depends." She savored the comfort of his nearness.

"On what?" He ran a finger across her cheek.

Before she could speak, he claimed her lips. She pulled away after a quick kiss. "We'll talk about it later."

It was almost eleven o'clock when the tour calendar was finished. The first leg would start in Charlotte and then on to Houston. From there the girls would go to California, back down south, and then up to the East Coast. New York would be the last stop. Monica didn't think it made sense to start in Charlotte, but that was what Bill wanted. It was a strange setup, but she and Dray were merely interpreters. Dray signed off on everything and finished his second beer. He didn't want to overstay his welcome and decided to head home.

"I better go," he said, stretching.

She didn't want him to leave. "No . . . I mean there's no hurry. Relax."

Dray didn't have to be told twice. Monica went to put on something more comfortable. He knew she wasn't the type of woman to sleep with him on the first date, but a part of him wanted her to. He was a man, so naturally if the opportunity presented itself, he would be glad. But if she had been easy, she would have succumbed to his charm a long time ago. He turned the television off and turned on the stereo. He threw his beer bottles in the trash and placed all the photos back in their envelopes. When Monica emerged from her room, he couldn't take his eyes off her. She was dressed in a short gray gown and a matching robe. The attire was far from sexy, but there was something about Monica's natural beauty that made her attractive. He could see her nipples protruding beneath fabric and a part of him stiffened.

"So are we okay?" she asked under his watchful eye. Somehow her attire and tousled hair turned him on. He rose from the couch and walked to her.

"Yeah, we're okay." He lifted a hand to her face. He slid his hand into her hair. It was soft like silk. He moved it back and put his mouth to her ear. "I enjoy your company," he whispered hotly.

Monica was melting. She closed her eyes, and his lips trailed along her ear. She clutched Dray's arms, and he pulled her closer. Her breasts pressed against his chest. She was so soft and warm. He ran his tongue across her ear and then moved his mouth to hers. She welcomed his kisses, his touch, and his strength. He slid her robe off slowly, and she didn't protest. He kissed her bare shoulders, tracing the angles with his fingers. Monica's blood was pulsing from his magnificent touches. When she felt the straps of her gown sliding off, her knees weakened. His hands glided gently across her warm skin. She closed her eyes when she felt Dray's mouth on the tops of her breasts. His hands slid down her thighs, kneading them softly like bread. She ran her fingers along his neck and bit his earlobes gently. He moaned, and felt warm all over. In one swoop he lifted her from the floor and put her legs around his waist. He carried her to the front door, still covering her body with kisses. Monica held his shoulders as he pressed her against the door.

"I've wanted to do this since the first time I saw you."

She broke into a lazy stutter. "Wh-what would that be?"

Greedily tasting her lips, he let her down on the floor. "Relax, you'll see."

Kissing her mouth again, he slid his hands beneath her gown. A moan escaped from her throat as he kissed the top of one of her breasts. He held her thighs while grinding against her. He lifted her gown and bent to kiss her between her thighs. She panted as he slid his fingers inside her panties. She was flowing. He licked the object of his desire until she gasped in delight.

"Dray . . . " she moaned.

"Yes?" he replied, pulling the gown up until it bared her breasts. His manhood throbbed with fire. "Do you want me to stop?"

She shivered as he moved to lick her belly button. Monica couldn't recall when she'd felt so alive, yet so lax. She tried to pull away but his grasp on her hips was firm, and she wasn't sure why she needed to escape.

"Let's go somewhere more comfortable," Dray said as he stood and kissed her nose.

Monica was too dazed to speak. Dray carried her to her bedroom. Gently he laid her down and stepped back to undress. When he was done, he moved toward the bed with smooth graceful strides like a cat. Monica couldn't take her eyes of the mahogany Adonis in front of her.

"I see playing football was good for you," she whispered.

Dray smiled bashfully. "I guess so." He knelt in front of her. "Take your clothes off for me," he muttered.

She did. Their nude bodies glistened beneath the Georgia moon. Dray lay on his back and pulled her on top of him. She sat up, straddling him. Her body fit his snugly, as if it belonged there. She was so hot, he felt scalded. He wanted her more than any words could ever say.

"I just want to look at you," he said softly.

She leaned over him a little. "Are you looking?" she purred, rubbing the sides of his face.

"Yes," he said, reaching for her breasts.

He rubbed the ebony jewels softly, outlining her nipples with his fingertips. He rose to kiss each one. Monica clutched him as he sucked and licked until she couldn't restrain from touching him. She wrapped her hands around his throbbing muscle and stroked it. He leaned back supporting them with his arms braced against the bed. She could see the pleasure in his dark eyes as she clutched him in her hands. She flicked her tongue playfully against his. Unable to sustain his desires any longer, Dray flipped her on her back and climbed on top of her. She was still stroking him, his mouth gaped open as he breathed deeply.

"Shit, Monica. What are you trying to do?"

She simply smiled and pulled him to her. "You like that?" she asked.

He nodded, moaning as he prayed for his desire to subside. She was toying with him, and seemingly enjoying watching his sweet agony.

Monica couldn't stop touching the man in front of her. Their bodies together seemed to cause a heat that rivaled that of the sun. She wanted to know every part of him, inside and out.

"I need a condom," he groaned in her ear.

She pointed to the nightstand. "Top drawer."

Dray found the protection and brought it back to the bed. Monica took the package from him and tore it open slowly. He watched her, his eyes filled with a longing she'd never seen. She slid the condom on him so slow he thought he would die. Gracefully, she stroked him until he gasped. He kissed Monica deeply as she lay on her back. He climbed on top of her and covered her mouth with his. He held her face lovingly as he gazed in her eyes. Tonight she was his, and nothing before it mattered. He took her fingers and kissed each one of them.

Monica felt as if her insides turned to pudding. Never had a man taken such intricate care with his lovemaking. For once, she had someone who wasn't in such a rush that he forgot what she wanted. She savored Dray's kisses on her neck and breasts. He eased his hand across the plane of her belly, each stroke as sensuous as the last. His dark eyes seemed to say all the words his mouth couldn't. She was so hot for him, she couldn't stand it. She reached for his throbbing manhood again, and he smiled.

Dray eased close to her again. He pulled her legs around his waist and traced her lips with his fingers. He tasted her sweet lips again. Fluidly, he made his way inside of her. Monica exhaled in ecstasy. The warmth of their bodies together was magic. She lifted her hips to meet his powerful thrusts. He moved like a jockey in a lover's race. As they rode the waves of passion, Monica felt her first climax coming on. She tried to hold back, but passion claimed her like a thief in the night. She clutched Dray tightly, and cried out in ecstasy as her body began to tremble. He filled his hands with her hair and pulled it gently. He continued his ride of love until she shattered once more. He pulled her on top of him and let her take control. It was only then that he submitted to the desire within. When the moment came, he clutched her hips tightly and let out a tormented groan. They rested.

Dray pulled Monica close as she lay beside him. He stared at her sweet face and asked, "Do you want me to leave now?"

She heard him, but she didn't know why he was asking such a ridiculous question. She lifted her head to meet his eyes. "Do you want to leave?"

He traced her lips with his finger. "No," he said, sliding his fingers into her hair.

"Then don't."

Dray kissed her once more, and sleep claimed them both.

CHAPTER 11

Monica wasn't able to concentrate. She and Dray had been spending an awful lot of time together since they made love a few weeks earlier. They ate lunch together, spent weekends together. They were hardly ever apart. People at work were starting to talk, so Monica kept a low profile. Fortunately, they were both extremely busy. Monica had some other projects she was working on, and Dray was busy handling business for the Prima Donnas. But she found it hard to get him out of her head. Every day she sat at her computer, remembering his kisses, his hands, his lovemaking. He seemed so sure of what he wanted when they were together. But she was afraid of giving her heart to him. What if it didn't work out? What if he turned out to be like Rodney? She'd be back to square one again.

"Knock, knock." Dray stuck his head in the door with a boyish smile upon his face. "Hey, beautiful."

"Hey, yourself, handsome," she said.

"Everything okay? I sent you an e-mail. Did you read it?"

"No, I haven't even checked my e-mails yet."

He eased his way inside and slipped into the chair in front of her desk. "Are you avoiding me? We haven't really talked that much this week."

"I'm sorry, Dray," she shrugged. "I've been so busy. And I figured you were busy too."

"I'm never too busy for you. I hope you aren't having any regrets about what happened between us."

She shook her head. "No, no. Of course not." She smiled. "I don't regret anything we've done."

"Good. So you won't have a problem accompanying the girls and me to kick off the promotional tour? I know sometimes publicists travel with their clients. I was hoping you wouldn't mind."

"No, I don't mind."

He smiled. "Good. I'll have Patrice make the reservations." He rose smoothly from the chair. "And also, Double R seems to think that you're not devoting time to his needs, whatever they are. He left a memo in my box saying something about a press release you were supposed to write for his upcoming single, *Million Dollar Nigga*."

Monica sighed. "Here it is. Honestly, the single isn't all that great. Bill mentioned Double R and the girls doing a remix."

Dray looked over the piece of paper. "I'll have to find out. I haven't even heard it yet."

Monica opened her desk drawer and handed him a copy of the CD single. "This is the edited version. The explicit version is a bit much. I don't know if it's a good idea for the girls to do the hook."

"I'll talk to Bill about it."

"Okay."

He got up from the chair and winked. "I'll see you later on. I've got a few things to take care of."

Once he was gone, she read his e-mail message.

From: draylew@handleup.com
Sent: Tuesday, March 20, 2001

To: missholiday@handleup.com
Subject: U
Missing you.

The shivers kicked in like a racehorse. Monica deleted the message and fanned herself. She closed her legs and remembered the way Dray's hot body dipped between her thighs. After double-checking to make sure the e-mail was deleted, she closed her eyes. As she drifted into her daydream, the phone rang. The voice on the other end was not one she wanted to hear.

"What's the deal, ma? Why haven't you done my shit?" It had been a long day, and a bunch of bickering was not on the agenda.

She held the phone loosely before putting it back to her ear. "I'm busy, Rodney, and I have taken care of that. Mr. Lewis has it."

"Are you trying to say you're too busy for me? You used to always have time for me."

"Well, I don't now."

"It must be because of Mr. Lewis. You let him get you that easy?"

"I don't owe you any explanations. And as always, you're wrong and tacky as ever. Don't you have anything better to do, Rodney?"

"Not really," he joked. "I know you're fucking him."

"Bye, Rodney."

"Hold up, Monica. What's the deal with my press release?"

"I just told you, Mr. Lewis has it. Don't you listen? It will be out this week. Now if there's nothing more, I have things to do."

"Yeah, whatever," he growled. "Don't let that smooth talkin' nigga make you lose your job." Monica wondered what he meant, but didn't dare ask.

"Goodbye, Rodney."

Monica stretched across the couch in her living room to read her mail. Most of it was bills, magazines, and invitations. There was one envelope she was particularly interested in. It was from Big Hits, a rival record company across town. They had a roster of major talent, too, and most of them were platinum artists as well. One of their rappers, Dirty X, had taken shots at Rodney in a song for something Rodney said about the guy on a past album. The animosity was so intense, he and Rodney nearly came to blows in a Decatur nightclub just outside Atlanta. Monica cleared up the mess with the media, even though she despised him. No matter how many times Rodney or anyone else screwed up, she fixed it. Bill just couldn't seem to get enough of the hoopla in which his company seemed to be engulfed. He said it boosted record sales, and of course, he was right. Each time an artist landed in the news, he sold another million. Who could argue with that?

Monica read the invitation from her company's rival. They were inviting her to an album release party for their new singer, Asia. She was an ex-model with mediocre pipes, but her killer body made you overlook it. More than once, Asia found her way over to Rodney's house in Sandy Springs while he and Monica were dating. Monica even found her in Rodney's bed once. He insisted it was a one time thing. But Monica saw them together more than once. She couldn't believe she allowed him to talk his way out of being busted.

She folded the invitation and placed it back in the envelope. Sometimes she hated when her personal and professional life collided.

This was one of those times. She would go, but not unac-companied.

Dray would be the perfect date. But it could be detrimental to their reputations if word got out they were seeing each other. People in the office already suspected. But they didn't have any real proof. Going to the party with Dray was a risk Monica was willing to take. She turned the lights out and wondered if he was still up. If he was, it would be a good time to ask him to the party. She dialed his number.

"Hello?"

"Hey, Dray. It's Monica."

"What's up, sweetness?" He was glad she called.

"Were you sleeping?"

"Nah, I was watching Shaft. But I dozed off for a minute. What's up?"

Monica took a deep breath. "I just wanted to hear your voice."

He sat up to make sure he'd heard correctly. "What?"

"I just wanted to hear your voice before I went to sleep," she spoke in a whisper.

The warmth of his smile echoed in his tone. "I'm glad you told me. I was beginning to think you would never tell me how you felt."

"I'm not good with words, Dray."

"Yes, you are. You didn't have a problem telling me to go to hell the night we met!"

She laughed. "I did not tell you to go to hell."

He laughed too. "May as well have. And I would never believe you didn't know how to express yourself."

"I do, just not where romance is concerned."

"Well, I'll have to fix that little problem." His silky voice held a challenge. "But what you have in mind will involve little talking."

Monica purred, "Are you asking for a repeat of what we did a couple of weeks ago?"

"Um-hmm. Are you saying yes?"

She chuckled, "Uh-huh."

"When are you going to come over and help me decorate my place?" Dray asked.

She sighed. "Ah, yes, the infamous bachelor pad. What more than your gorgeous body do you need to decorate?"

"Woman, you keep on saying things like that, and I'm gonna forget what a gentleman I am."

"Ha-ha, very funny. What exactly does your crib need?"

"Well, I need you to hook me up with some of those scented candles and artwork or something like you have at your place. I like that stuff."

"Most men don't."

"I'm not most men. I need my digs to be nice. How am I going to entertain some sweet little lady if I don't have candles and flowers and all that stuff y'all like?"

"Good point. Well maybe this weekend we can hit Pier 1 and Garden Ridge home store. I'll help you hook your place up."

"This weekend sounds good. Next week, we'll be heading out of town for the tour."

"Sounds like a plan to me." She sighed. "I won't keep you up any longer, Dray. Have a good night's sleep."

"You too, baby. Later."

CHAPTER 12

On Saturday, Dray picked Monica up in his SUV rental, a Cadillac Escalade. He hadn't been able to decide on which automobile he wanted Handle Up to lease for him. All of the VPs had their choice of luxury cars, complete with accessories, for as long as they worked at the company. Dray wasn't in a hurry, renting suited him just fine. It would give him a chance to decide what he really wanted. Like most men, he fancied the big sport's utility trucks like Yukons, Navigators, and of course, Escalades.

As he waited for Monica, he fiddled with the CD player. He turned the music up and nodded back and forth. Just then, she appeared, descending from the steps of her building. He marveled at her girlish beauty, her face was glowing and free of makeup. Her hair was pulled back in a slick ponytail, and diamond studs decorated her earlobes. She wore a fitted top, a denim skirt, and slip-on sandals. The smile in his eyes held a longing for her as she opened the door.

"Hey," she said cheerfully, climbing inside.

"Hey," he replied. "You look nice and jazzy."

"You too. I like your little ensemble." He was wearing a white

T-shirt with the sleeves cut off, a pair of baggy Roc-a-Wear jeans, and white tennis shoes.

"These old rags? They've been around longer than you."

"Ha-ha. But they still look good."

"Not as good as you."

"Thank you," she said smiling.

"You're welcome," he said. "Put your seatbelt on. I drive fast."

He turned up the music, and they were off.

When they finished shopping, they headed back to his place. He'd spent more than $800 to decorate the place with odds and ends. Most of the items would go in the bedroom and the living room. Monica got some artificial flowers for the arrangement she planned to make for his dining room table.

Once inside, Monica stood by the window. "Your view is so much better than mine," she said, gazing at the burnt-orange and purple sky. She closed her eyes and inhaled the fresh Georgia air. She could see downtown from Dray's windows. He opened the patio door for her and she stepped outside. It was a fascinating sight, the perfect end to their day together.

"I think my view is better," he said, standing behind her.

Monica turned around. Dray stood so close that his lips grazed the tip of her nose. It twitched in response, and she swallowed as his hands cupped her face. As she closed her eyes, he greeted her with a slow, delightful kiss. The way her lips caressed his mouth made him throb with desire. His hands rested against her spine, and she savored the tip of his tongue as it danced in her mouth. She felt the muscles in his back as she caressed him.

"I can't stop tasting you," he muttered against her lips.

"Then don't," she purred.

He pulled away and stroked her forehead. "I had a good time today," he said.

"Me too." She dropped her chin on his chest with a sigh of pleasure.

"You can stay the night if you want," he whispered in her ear.

"I'll even let you have my bed."

"That won't be necessary." She put her hands beneath his shirt and rubbed his chest. "I want you to be in your bed."

He quivered as her fingers stroked his nipples. "Oh, really now?" He took her hands in his.

"Yes, really." She kissed him quickly. "Let's finish this . . . "

"In the bedroom?"

"I see you like to finish my sentences, Mr. Lewis, but I was talking about the decorating."

He threw his head back and laughed deeply. "Oh, yeah, we can take that to the bedroom."

"You wouldn't be trying to get fresh with me, would you now, Mr. Lewis?"

He patted her on the butt and grinned. "Of course, I am."

Monica smiled and made her way to his entertainment center. She slid in a copy of Maxwell's Urban Hang Suite.

"I love this CD," she said snapping her fingers.

He watched proudly as she danced toward the bags from their shopping trip, swaying her hips like a sassy island dance. She stopped abruptly and darted towards the dining room table.

"Okay, let's see what we have here." She removed the fresh bouquet of tulips from the bag. Feeling frisky, she put one to Dray's chest and stroked him with it.

"I see you wanna take this decorating to another level," he said.

"Maybe later," she winked. "We have too much to do."

"Just one little kiss wouldn't hurt, would it?"

"No," she said, setting down the flowers. He lifted her from the floor and sat her on the table, easing between her legs. His warm hands slid up between her thighs as he kissed her lips. Goose bumps covered her with each stroke of his hand. She felt him move suddenly.

"What are you doing?" She looked to find him lowering his head between her legs.

"Finishing off where I left the last time we were alone like this." When his hand slid under her skirt, she almost fell off the table.

"Relax," he said, opening her legs. He moved her panties aside and kissed her hottest spot.

She felt one swift lick and closed her eyes. She had something to say, but the words seemed to have disappeared from her thoughts. He was too powerful to resist. With each stroke of his tongue, Monica felt her world spin.

Nervously, she uttered, "Let's finish, or we'll never get done."

She was lying about wanting to start the decorating. She just wanted his hands off her because she was afraid he would keep his word about satisfying her. He straightened her clothes and helped her off the table. She could still feel the dampness between her thighs.

"Let's see how this looks," she said, nervously reaching for one of the vases they bought. She set it near the window and placed the faux branches in it.

Dray backed away. "Looks good to me." And he wasn't talking about the vase.

"Very funny, Mr. Lewis. I'm talking about the vase."

"Oh, my bad. You were talking about that." He rubbed his chin. "Oh yeah, it looks good. Real good."

Monica poked him in the ribs. "You play too much."

He grabbed her around the waist. "I know," he grinned.

By night's end, Dray's apartment looked like something out of Metropolitan Home magazine. Monica transformed his plain bachelor's pad into a bachelor's paradise. He couldn't help but smile as he watched her whip up a snack in his kitchen. She prepared a Mexican appetizer that consisted of corn tostadas, refried beans, sour cream, cheese, lettuce, and tomatoes layered on top of one another. It looked like a pizza when she was done.

"Here we go," Monica said, bringing a tray over to the couch.

Dray was watching Sports Center. He looked at the snack she'd just prepared. "What's this?"

Monica went back to the kitchen to get napkins and the Jamaican ginger ale they bought from the Whole Foods market.

"Something I put together. Just taste it," she said, joining him on the couch.

"I'd like to taste something else," he said, rubbing her thigh.

She nudged him on his side as he shook his head. "Come on, seriously."

"I am serious."

"Dray!"

"Alright, alright. I'll taste it."

He lifted the tostada from his plate and examined it. She took it and put it to his mouth. She watched as he took a bite. He licked his lips sensuously and chewed the snack slowly. The strong flavor filled his mouth like a hot kiss.

"Not bad," he said. "Where'd you learn how to make this?"

"I saw some people back in Texas do it. Good, isn't it?"

"Yeah, it's not bad. Hand me a napkin, please."

She handed him the napkin and bit into her tostada. "Any games on?" she mumbled.

Dray cocked his head to the side, stunned by her interest. "You watch sports?"

"Sometimes. If there's a team I like playing."

"Okay, so who's your favorite team?"

"Basketball or football?"

"You like b-ball and football? Damn. A woman after my own heart."

Monica took another bite of the tostada. "Okay, for basketball definitely the 76ers. I love Allen Iverson, he's so cute."

"Oh, come on, Monica, you like the team because the star player is cute?"

"No! I've always liked him, even when he was at Georgetown. I like Chris Webber too, Latrell Sprewell and Gary Payton."

"Um-hmm, all the roughnecks. I bet you think Chris is cute, too, like all the rest of the women, don't you?"

"I sure do." She pinched his cheek. "But not as cute as you."

"Yeah, right." He fixed himself another tostada. "These are really good."

"I told you."

"Okay, so what about football players?"

"In football, I like the Tennessee Titans because Steve McNair is good. My cousin used to go to Alcorn State with him. Eddie George, is good too. I like Tampa Bay, the Ravens, and Ray Lewis. The Raiders are cool, and I like the Rams too."

"Tennessee is cool, I'll give you that. Tampa Bay ain't bad either. What about boxing?" He took another bite of the tostada.

Monica slapped her knee. "Mike Tyson and Roy Jones Jr. all the way."

"Why those two?"

"Nobody has a left hook like Mike, and Roy . . . let's just say if he crosses my path, there won't be any fighting."

Dray sneered. He didn't know why he was jealous of her little crush on someone she'd never met. He smiled to himself realizing how silly it was.

"What's the matter?" she asked.

"I've never met anyone like you," he said.

"I think you said that before."

"Well, I haven't."

She wiped his mouth with a napkin. "And you never will."

At that moment, Dray knew he had something special. A woman who could cook, decorate like Martha Stewart, and liked sports? She was a gold mine. He had to keep her around. They watched the rest of Sports Center and finished eating.

Moments away from midnight, they relaxed on the couch. Monica rested peacefully in his lap. He brushed her face with his fingers, feeling the softness of her skin. The sound of her breathing was music to his ears. It flowed smooth, just like she did. He liked having her so close. Wanting to make her more comfortable, he carried her to his room.

"Where are we going?"

"In here so you can lie down."

"I was lying down," she muttered sleepily as he held her.

"That deep slumber you were in, lying in my lap?"

"Yes."

He put her on the bed. "You'll be more comfortable here." He placed her on the bed gently.

She adjusted herself on the firm mattress and looked around the room. Her assistance with his decorum looked pretty good. The room was almost all white with a touch of beige here and there. It was neat, too, especially for a guy's place. The only sign of disorder was a small pile of clothes he'd left in a chair by the window. There was a cherry-wood dresser on the wall near the door, and two small, matching nightstands on both sides of the bed.

"We did a good job," she said, yawning.

"We did a great job," he said, looking around. "We work pretty well together, Ms. Holiday."

"Yeah, we do," she yawned. "I need something to sleep in," Monica groaned. She yawned again and stretched her arms out in front of her.

"Let me see if I have something." He opened the closet door. "You know, I'm a little big," he winked. "So you might be out of luck."

"Anything will work."

He flipped through a stack of clothes and found a Chicago Bulls T-shirt.

"I know you're not a Bulls fan, but this might work . . ." She was sitting on the bed in a very sexy pose. "I think."

Monica was wearing a red lace bra and panty set. Her delicate, round breasts peeked over the top of her bra, sending his hormones into overdrive as she reached for the shirt. He tried to hide the bulge in his pants. Whatever she was trying to do to him was working.

"Thank you," she whispered, setting the shirt on the bed. "Can I have a kiss good night?" *Where did that come from?* The words escaped before she could halt them. It was a bold statement, and it seemed even more so now that she couldn't retract it.

He smiled and licked his lips. "Is that all you want?" he asked, walking toward her.

"I don't know," she said demurely.

He put his finger to her lips. "I do."

Dray could feel the pulsing in his pants as he knelt to offer her the sweetness of his lips. Monica greeted them anxiously. He climbed onto the bed and swept her in his arms. He took a finger and stroked her bottom lip. She opened her mouth and sucked his finger. He pulled it only to pull her closer. He groaned as he caressed the soft curves nestled in his arms. Monica eased his shirt over his head, kissing his chest and nipples until he gasped. He let out a tormenting moan as she slid her hand in his pants. She could feel how much he wanted her.

"Somebody's happy to see me," she murmured. He didn't speak, but his eyes said what he couldn't.

He managed to unhook her bra in his tight embrace. His kisses explored her neck and breasts. She moaned as he tantalized her nipples with his tongue. With the moon offering the only light, Dray slid her panties off and tossed them on the floor. He kissed her navel and thighs, furthering her excitement. He drew circles on her belly, licking them, and blowing gently. The hot-n-cold sensations brought Monica close to the edge.

He groaned in her hair, "Now you're in my house. I've got to make sure I do you right."

She let her head fall back as his hand slid between her thighs.

He parted her legs and moved back to view her. She was panting from his fiery play. He couldn't push his desires aside now. To hell with the consequences. He wanted her. He got up from the bed to retrieve a condom from the bathroom drawer. He set it on the nightstand as Monica undressed him. She pulled his clothes off slowly, examining every inch of him. She stopped every few moments to kiss him. When she discarded his clothes, she examined his magnificent glory. She put her lips to it, and then licked it. Dray groaned. Nothing should feel this good.

When he climbed on top of her, Monica's body called. Her nipples rose as her eyes closed. And then there was that fluttering between her thighs. Dray answered it by sliding the tip in a little. He paused until she opened her eyes, teasing her with it.

"Are you sure you want me inside?" He gazed deep into her eyes.

His words made her hot all over again. She was flowing as she breathed, "Yes."

He waited patiently as she slid the protection on him. A sigh escaped from his throat as she ran her hands up and down it forcefully. She curled into his body as they kissed once more. They slid across the bed, embracing each other. It was flesh against flesh, man against woman. Dray stroked her nipples, watching her breasts surge at his touch. His tongue explored the soft mounds of skin. He pried her legs open gently and tested her. She was more than ready.

He began his strokes softly and rhythmically. Her silken walls clamped him for a perfect fit. He held the long strands of her hair in heated passion. As he plunged deeper, he had to bury his face in the pillow for a moment. The combination of her hot body and his own fire lust were more than he could stand. Her soft, delicate fingers were kneading his back. Her hot tongue, flicking in his ear. He grabbed her legs and pulled them around his waist. The warmth between her thighs scalded him. And he loved every minute of it.

Monica cried out from the rapture of ardent lovemaking. She was hotter and wetter than she ever remembered, and his body reacted accordingly. With each kiss he eased an inch closer to the end of her tunnel, stroking her sweetly. He rode her waves with grace. She purred as they teased each other's lips with their tongues. He moved down once again, allowing his lips to brush her nipples, his thrusts intensifying. She squirmed beneath him and tightened her embrace as her body began to shiver. She screamed as her pleasure reached its highest level, clutching his damp body to hers. In a fluid motion, Dray allowed himself to succumb to the same ecstasy, filling the room with sweet memories.

It was dawn when they drifted off to sleep. Monica settled in Dray's arms and slept peacefully. He stayed awake to watch her sleep, touching her face gently. He wanted her again. He needed her again. This was right. Somehow he managed to sleep, as the sun came up, wondering if she was in love too.

The smell of French toast filled the air later that morning. Monica opened her eyes, blinded by the forceful rays of the sun peeking through the blinds. As she turned away from the window, she focused on the familiar surroundings. She didn't want to get out of bed, not today. Last night's rendezvous still danced in her head.

"Morning." Dray entered the room cheerfully and made his way to kiss her. He dipped his tongue into her mouth and ran his hand across her breasts. "I see you're nice and perky," he joked.

She felt the bulge in his pants and greeted him with the same enthusiasm. "Good morning to you too."

"You better watch those hands, young lady. You're liable to get a repeat of last night if you keep it up."

"Well, maybe I need to grab it again."

"Come on. I made you brunch." His voice was still groggy from sleep.

"You didn't have to do that."

"Yes, I did." He pulled her out of bed. "Come on. I promise you'll like it."

She followed him into the kitchen. "Are we still talking about food?" A smirk crossed her face.

He smiled, and winked. "For the moment. Have a seat."

Sitting down at the table, she kidded, "I haven't seen anything here I didn't like."

He growled. "I've got more for you."

"We'll see."

"I saw all I needed to see last night."

"What do you mean?"

"The way you clung to me like your life depended on it. I've never had legs wrapped around me so tight."

Embarrassed by his comment, she lowered her eyes. "I'm sure you've had plenty of females cling to you."

"Plenty of females? Yes. But one who held me like she was about to fall off the face of the earth? Never."

"Why do I find that hard to believe?"

"Because you don't wanna believe it."

Monica smiled. "Did you get an invitation for the party that Rhythmhouse Records is throwing?"

He set their plates down on the table. "You mean the one for that singer, Asia?"

The aroma of French toast and eggs filled the air. "Yeah," she looked at her plate. "This looks really good."

"Thanks." He grabbed the orange juice from the counter and poured it into two small glasses. "The invitation's on my desk. It's this weekend, isn't it?"

"Friday night. Do you wanna go?"

"Together?" He sounded surprised.

She misunderstood his tone. "Well if you don't want to, I understand. I'll just . . ."

"Moni, baby."

"Forget it. I'll just go by myself."

"Monica, chill. We can go together. I didn't mean to sound like that. I want to go with you. I'm just not big on parties."

"I'm sorry."

"For what?"

"Rambling. I do that sometimes."

"You weren't rambling."

"Yes, I was."

"Whatever." Dray laughed. "You a trip, girl!"

They finished eating brunch. Dray had prepared scrambled eggs with green onions, hash browns, and his specialty, French toast. Monica added champagne to the orange juice for mimosas. Neither of them had gotten over the spell they were under. Monica couldn't remember when she'd enjoyed a man's company as much as she did Dray's. He was everything she ever wanted. She felt like it could be this way forever, and she wasn't alone.

CHAPTER 13

Monica waited outside the Swiss Hotel for Dray to arrive. He was supposed to be escorting her to the Rhythmhouse Records party. But he was twenty minutes late. He had a meeting after work. She hoped he wasn't standing her up. She paced the red carpet. Apprehensive, she checked her watch again. It was almost ten o'clock and still no sign of him. He hadn't called her cell phone because it still dangled silently from her wrist. After checking her watch one more time, she decided to go in.

She was dressed in a black leather dress with one side of the front cut out to expose her flat midriff. Her stiletto heels complemented her long, shapely legs. Her long hair was flat ironed bone-straight and fell past her shoulders. She wore a huge silver choker with turquoise stones and a small bracelet. She would definitely turn heads tonight, even if one of them wasn't Dray's.

The crowd was scattered around the room, each section blaring Asia's music from the speakers. The beats were catchy, but Monica still couldn't get past her sappy Jennifer Lopez-like vocals. If it weren't for the synthesizers, she'd sound like a squeaky mouse in heat. You could tell who the VIPs were, who the groupies were, and of course, the press. From the turnout it looked as if Asia had quite a few fans.

Monica made her way over to the bar and ordered a peach martini. The gladiator-looking bartender fixed her drink, casually staring at her. He was cute, with huge dimples and sappy brown eyes, probably no more than nineteen or twenty. Monica had a knack for attracting younger guys. He smiled sweetly and handed her the cocktail. She thanked him and slid a crisp ten-dollar bill across the bar. He looked prepared for conversation, but she rushed away.

"Monica Rose Holiday! Is that you?"

The eerie Southern drawl stopped Monica dead in her tracks. She'd know it anywhere. Please don't let it be. It was. Savannah Morgan, Hotlanta's very own media hoochie.

"Hey, Savannah," Monica said plainly.

"You just get smaller every time I see you, girl." Savannah gave her a quick hug.

She was a news anchor for Channel 4. A self-professed Georgia peach whose makeup spent too much time on her face. Her creamy complexion was matched with a pair of overgrown eyebrows and a faint mustache. Her Creole background was obvious, especially when she spoke French. She was also Bill Sanders' former mistress. It was pure cruelty for Monica to see her. Savannah had done nothing but torture her since she took the job at Handle Up. It was a job Savannah wanted. She held two degrees, one from Spelman, the other from Georgia Tech, and she was the first to inform anyone that she graduated magna cum laude from GT, the first black person ever to do so. She took a liking to Bill when he started the company while she was in college. She was determined to get her hooks in him and the company by luring him into her bed. Of course, when she didn't get the job after graduation, she was furious. And upon meeting Monica at the label launching ceremony, she found out why she didn't get the job. Monica was younger, prettier, smarter, and had more personality.

Savannah ended up being Bill's mistress for nearly two years. Once she landed the television gig, her ego inflated and Bill dumped her shortly after. When Monica's trouble with Rodney surfaced, Savannah jumped at the chance to make her feel worse all over again. During her news report, she casually mentioned how Monica's rapper beau had dumped her in a magazine article. She went on to quote the article, which otherwise may have gone unnoticed, to make a mockery of the situation. Monica's temper still burned when they were in the same room.

"Well, I see you're up and about. I know it's been hard for you, being dumped and all by a famous rap star like Rodney."

Monica gulped down her drink and walked back to the bar. Savannah followed. Monica looked her up and down and ordered another drink.

"If anybody knows about being dumped, Miss Morgan, it should be you," she said, turning back to Savannah. "It is still 'Miss,' isn't it?"

Savannah cocked her head to the side and put her hand on her hips. "If I was still at the AU, I'd probably say you were trying to start something, Miss Monica." Her drawl was just as annoying as she was. She flung her hair over her shoulder and stuck her chest out. "But since I'm not, I'll ignore you." She held her hand up in a halt position.

"Whatever you say, Savannah."

When Monica saw Dray coming her way, she was glad. He didn't stand her up after all. Coming towards her in a five-button black suit and a crimson silk shirt and matching tie was to Monica, the most handsome man in all of Atlanta. Dray looked like a Sean John runway model, with the smooth prowess of an athlete. And the way people parted as he made his approach made her heart flutter.

"Monica, baby. There you are." He kissed her cheek, rescuing her from Savannah in the nick of time. "I'm sorry I'm late, baby. He wrapped his arm around her gingerly. "Our meeting lasted longer than I expected."

Monica was relieved. "That's okay, I'm glad you're here." She shot Savannah a shifty look and slipped her arm around his.

"Did I miss anything?" he asked. "What are you drinking?" He looked tired.

She held his face. "A peach martini. If you want to leave, we can."

"What makes you say that?"

"You look tired, sweetie. I just don't want to keep you up if you need to rest."

He kissed her on the earlobe and held her close. "I'm fine. Bill just had me sit in on a couple of meetings. Then I had to make a trip downtown, but I'm cool. Besides, I'm not letting you slip away from me looking this good. "

She smiled. "Nothing interesting has happened so far." She peered at Savannah who was conspicuously checking him out.

"I think I'll order one of those drinks," he said. "Bartender." Savannah cleared her throat. "Monica, aren't you going to introduce me to your handsome friend?"

Monica sucked her teeth. "This is Drayton Lewis. He handles A&R for Handle Up. I thought you would have the inside scoop on that, Savannah."

"Well, I can't keep up with everything in this little old town, now can I?"

Dray extended his hand. "Nice to meet you Mrs. . . . ?"

"Miss Morgan. But call me Savannah, please."

"Savannah it is then." They shook hands.

"Pleasure to meet you, too, Mr. Lewis. Are you from the area?"

"No, I'm from Chicago."

"The South Side I presume? You can always tell men from the South Side of Chicago. They have such a presence."

Monica cut her eyes in Savannah's direction. She was pressing her luck.

"Is that right?" Dray looked over at Monica and raised his

brows. He could read through Savannah like glass. She was obviously trying to get under Monica's skin.

"So anyway, Savannah," Monica interrupted, "Why are you here?"

"I'm scouting real talent so I can feature them on my ATL People on the Move segment."

"Really now," Dray interjected. "So you're a reporter?"

"Yes, I am. Do you have something interesting I can report? Maybe I could feature you on my show."

"Nah. That's too much attention for a low-key guy like me."

"Oh, no, not with a handsome face like yours? You should be on TV, darlin'."

"We'll see you later Savannah," Monica pulled Dray by his sleeve. "Come on, baby. Let's go."

Just as Dray took a sip of his drink, Double R appeared with the singer Asia strapped to his side. They offered nonchalant glances as Savannah prepared to do what she did best, meddle. Monica quickly downed her cocktail. She was going to need a strong retaliation for this one.

"Looks like the gang's all here," Savannah chirped. "Monica, say hello to your former beau and the evening's star, the lovely Miss Asia."

Monica straightened up. "Maybe you should find a man, Savannah."

Dray took her hand and kissed it. "Chill," he whispered. "She ain't worth it."

Savannah wouldn't let up. "Isn't it nice to see your ex, Monica?"

Monica's eyes narrowed. She wanted to kill Savannah. Rodney was just as surprised at Savannah's comment. But he was really surprised to see Dray and Monica out together.

"Ain't this lovely," he blurted. "The new A&R man and the publicist on the town, that's alright." It was obvious he'd been drinking. Monica hoped he wouldn't make a scene. She eased closer to Dray, who offered her a shield of protection.

"This is some major shit," Rodney continued. "Where's the photographer? This is definitely a Kodak moment. Two Handle Up executives out on a date. This makes for very juicy conversation, don't you think? I think so."

"Rodney, why don't you chill? You've had too much to drink." Dray wanted things to simmer, and then he and Monica could make their escape.

"Aw, man, come on. It's a party. I'm supposed to be drunk." He lifted his arms in the air, swinging them carelessly.

"Rodney, you're embarrassing me!" Asia had sense enough to say. She poked him in the stomach and tried to pull away.

He kissed her cheek. "Sorry, boo. I'm tripping. Let's go say hello to some of these other bourgeois folks. Be cool, Mr. Lewis. See you later, Ms. Morgan. Bye Monica."

Savannah replied, "Nice seeing you again, Rodney." Relieved, Dray and Monica watched as Rodney and Asia disappeared into the crowd. Savannah straightened her dress and held up her drink. "It was a pleasure meeting you, Mr. Lewis." Her smoky eyes turned to meet Monica's. "See you later, Ms. Holiday."

When Savannah disappeared into the crowd, Monica, sighed, but it was more like a growl. "I can't believe the nerve of that witch."

"Damn, baby, I didn't know it was like that," Dray said. "What's up with you and her?"

"Savannah and I went to school together. She's a few years older than me. I've never liked her. She was always trying to compete with me for some reason. She's like an ant in your pants."

Dray looked puzzled.

"Maybe I should have used another metaphor. She's just a bitch, period."

"She's got a lot of nerve, that's for damn sure."

"Call it what you want, she's still a bitch. I've never come across a woman so full of it in my life. When I got my job at Handle

Up, she sent me and Bill threatening letters saying she was going to sue us and all kinds of stuff."

"Why would she send letters to Bill?"

"It's a long story. I'll tell you about it later."

An hour later, Asia gave the crowd her comical rendition of Patti LaBelle's *If Only You Knew*. Patti was a "singer." Not like some of the new singers who were getting away with whining over tracks produced by guys like Timbaland, the Neptunes, or Trackmasters. Some of the singers were better off dancing in videos rather than trying to carry a tune. Monica loved real vocalists. Girls like Missy who weren't what America would call the "ideal" vocalist, but could actually sing. She also loved Tamia for her breathy vocals, Brandy for her raspy spunk, and Teena Marie, the soulful white girl with honey-coated pipes. Unfortunately, Handle Up hadn't found a female singer it wanted to sign yet. But the Prima Donnas could sing. And Bill liked real talent, not some bodacious babe with a big booty who thought she could sing because some horny guy told her she could. Monica could hold a tune herself, but would never make an attempt to actually become a singer. She was more of a behind-the-scenes person.

Once the mini-concert was over, everyone hit the dance floor or went to the bar for drinks. Monica wasn't quite ready to go home so she decided to prolong the date. As they stood in the lobby, she wondered where the night would end. She pranced around him in a circle playfully.

"You wanna go dancing, Dray?" she asked grabbing his hands.

She pressed her breasts to his chest. "There's this little salsa spot I know in Buckhead." She gave him a quick peck. "We can get real close . . . and nasty."

He put her fingers to his lips and kissed them. "Ooh, you bad girl. You know how to salsa?"

"I know how to do a lot."

"Yeah, you do." He released her and they walked toward the

exit. "You tryin' to keep me up all night, woman?" He handed the valet their tickets.

Monica leaned to kiss him. "Yes," she blinked when she saw a flash. "What was that?"

Dray held her close. "What?"

"That light. Something just flashed."

"Probably nothing. Maybe a light from one of these buildings."

"You're probably right. And I'll keep you up if you promise to keep it up."

His lips brushed hers as he spoke. "I promise," he whispered. "Let's go."

The Salsa Club was dim and crowded. The music rhythm was upbeat and risqué. Everyone seemed to be having a good time. Monica led Dray to the middle of the dance floor where she wrapped her arms around his neck. He placed his hands on her hips as they moved from side to side, dipping every other beat.

"I see you know a little bit about Latin flavor," Monica said, playing with his hair.

"I know a little bit. How do you know about this place?"

"My girlfriends and I used to come here all the time when it first opened. I've always liked the music. It's so passionate and invigorating."

"You mean nasty?" Dray kidded.

"No, nasty is such a bad word. Can't I just like it? Is that alright with you?"

He could feel himself getting hotter by the minute. "Yeah, that's fine." He loosened his tie as Monica pressed her body closer to his. The softness of her breasts pushed up against his chest.

"Damn, your body is soft," he said, running his fingers through her hair. Carlos Santana's Maria Maria came on.

"Come on, baby, let's dance," Monica shrieked. "I love this song." She took Dray by the hand. "Okay, when you salsa, it's up on the left, back on the right. Come on." They danced for a few moments and then she took it to another level. She turned her back to Dray and pressed her butt up against his crotch, rounding her hips like a belly dancer. If she didn't stop, he would lift her and they would disappear into a secluded paradise of their own. He shook his head as he grinned back briefly. As she became consumed by the music, he joined her in the trance. Soon they were oblivious to everyone around them. The room was smothered with lovers, or people pretending to be in love. Latin music had a way of turning the dullest of characters into lust-driven specimens. Dray and Monica came together again, greeting each other with more kisses. She nestled her head into his chest and felt his lips brush her brow. Slowly his hands moved downward, skimming the sides of her body.

"Oooohh," she cooed while his lips played with her neck. "I'm ready to . . . "

"Go?" he asked, rubbing her cheek. "Where?"

"I don't know." Her soft curves molded to the contours of his body. "Anywhere with you."

His smile was intoxicatingly bright under the fluorescent lights. "We don't have to leave. I'm starting to like this, it feels nice." He unbuttoned his shirt and pulled his jacket off.

"I'm gonna go check my coat. You go get us some drinks. I'll be right back."

Monica went over to the bar and plopped down on a stool.

"What can I get you?" the bartender asked.

"Uh, I'm not sure. I need something sweet and exotic."

"How about a Mai tai?"

"Sounds exotic enough to me."

"And for your friend?"

Dray crept up behind Monica and wrapped his arms around her. "I'll have a margarita on the rocks. And let me get a shot of tequila too."

"Tequila? Are you trying to get drunk?" She spun around on the stool to face him.

"No, it takes a lot to get me drunk." He ran his finger across her collarbone. "I feel good right now." He wrapped his arms around her waist and kissed her neck. "Thanks for inviting me. I owe you."

She wriggled at his touch. "No, you don't. Call us even. I'll consider tonight your payback for my decorating your place." He flipped the long curls of her hair back over her shoulder and kissed her neck.

"Ooh, Dray," she moaned.

He laughed and drew a circle on her lips. "I thought the other night was payback for that."

She slapped his chest. "So does that mean I won't get anymore?"

"Hell no, you can get this anytime you want it."

Monica giggled like a schoolgirl as he kissed her neck. When the bartender set the drinks on the bar, Dray took a sip of his drink and pulled out an ice cube. He ran it down her back.

"Drayton Lewis, you're trying to get yourself in a heap of trouble, aren't you?"

He laughed. "I like trouble, baby."

♫

Monica and Dray found themselves at her doorstep playing with each other just before 2:00 a.m. He was trying to suppress his desire for her but it was hard, literally and figuratively. The tight-fitting leather dress with peekaboo holes didn't help either. She looked more seductive than a bowl of fresh peaches. She felt the same way about him. Her imagination had long overruled her senses. She pictured his chiseled body on top of her as she stood on the toes of her $200 Charles Jourdan stilettos. Warm in his arms, head spinning from his kisses, his arms encircled her at the small of her back.

"Damn, Monica. What are you doing to me?"

She had no desire to leave his embrace. "I don't want you to go," she said, smoothing his shirt.

"I won't. All you have to do is ask me to stay." His gaze was deep, piercing. "I just want you to ask me." He had to hear her say it, knowing he'd die if she didn't.

Somewhere she found the nerve. "Will you stay with me?" she asked as sweetly as possible.

He nodded and took the keys from her hand to open the door. Wrapping his arm around her waist he whispered, "Yes."

CHAPTER 14

A few days before the Prima Donnas' promotional tour was scheduled to begin, Bill called Monica into his office. He wanted to go over the itinerary and the complaints Rodney had about his representation. Monica sat nervously in the chair in front of his desk. Bill was finishing up a phone conversation. When he was done, he leaned forward.

"Monica, what's going on with you? Rodney says you haven't contacted him about his new releases. The Prima Donnas said they're seeing more of their stylist than they are of you."

She clutched her shaking hands. "Nothing's wrong. I've been trying to get some things together for them. I contacted some stores about selling their posters."

"Is your working relationship with Mr. Lewis becoming a problem?"

She was surprised by the seriousness in his tone. "No. Of course not."

"Good. You've never let me down. Don't start now." Monica nodded in agreement. Bill continued, "The first thing we have to do is get the Prima Donnas on the road. I know you made contacts with the most popular radio stations in the cities they're touring to offer a number of prizes to listeners. And that's good. We have to make sure this album is platinum."

"Okay."

"Now, let's join the rest of the staff in the boardroom."

Everyone had been waiting for Bill and Monica to come in. Rodney was the first to say something.

"About time," he said, looking at Monica.

She slipped into the seat next to Patrice. Bill gave Rodney the "don't start" look. "When are the Prima Donnas going to be able to record the vocals for the remix to my song?" Rodney yelled.

Bill looked down at the podium and then over at Rodney. "It will have to wait until we get the girls tour up and running. The Prima Donnas are our number one priority right now. Why don't you just do the whole track, and we'll add their vocals later?"

"That's a bunch of bull," he mumbled. "I've been waiting on this too long. They were supposed to do it a long time ago." He looked directly at Monica.

Bill would be damned if he listened to Rodney's bullshit any longer. "If you have a problem with that, Mr. Robinson, see me in my office."

Everyone waited for Rodney's reply. He took a deep breath, but decided not to say anything. He sucked his teeth and slumped lower in the chair. Monica looked at him and then captured Dray's eyes. She shook her head and snickered a little.

"What's so funny?" Rodney's grit caught everyone off guard. He was apparently aiming his comment at Monica, who sat poised as everyone stared.

"Excuse me?" she said calmly, setting her pen on the table.

"You're laughing, obviously you think something is funny." Rodney sat up and turned to face her. "It wasn't funny when I replaced you with another chick, was it?"

Everyone gasped.

"You could never replace me," Monica smirked. "And until your new album goes platinum, I wouldn't count my chickens. Oh, my bad, chicken-heads."

"My album has made more money than you'll ever make!"

"Enough!" Bill roared. His voice matched his size and everyone froze. "This is a business, and I will not have you two arguing back and forth like kids."

"It's not an argument. Monica just needs to know her place."

"Who the hell do you think you're talking to?"

"You, you bourgeois-ass broad." He jumped from his chair.

Dray stood and went to Monica's side.

"Fuck you, Rodney!" she yelled, jumping out of her seat. "I hope you never sell another record, punk!" Monica rushed from the room.

"Fuck you too!"

Bill darted from the podium into Rodney's face. "What the hell is wrong with you?"

"Ain't nuthin' wrong with me. That bitch just needs to know her place."

"Who the fuck you callin' a bitch?" Dray started toward Rodney, but Bill stepped between them. Everyone stared in disbelief.

"Calm down, Dray," Bill said. "Rodney, this is unacceptable. Sit down."

Rodney threw his arms up. "Unacceptable? Isn't Mr. Lewis fucking Monica unacceptable too?"

"Ooh, no, he didn't," Beverly said, covering her mouth.

Dray wanted to kill Rodney, but he kept his cool.

Rodney continued to rant. "Maybe that's why Monica can't do her work. She's too busy ridin' this niggas dick."

"Rodney that's enough," Bill said. "We will continue this conversation after this meeting."

Monica was in her office, her eyes filled with tears. She paced the floor for a moment and threw her notepad on the desk. Rodney had gotten under her skin, even though she vowed that he wouldn't ever again. *Stupid motherfucker*, she said to herself. She reached for a tissue. Then there was a knock.

"Monica?" Dray eased his way in and shut the door. "Are you alright?"

"I will be," she said.

"I'll whip his ass if you want me to."

She managed to laugh. "Yeah, I'm fine. I'll be back in a minute."

"The meeting's over. Bill is chewing Rodney's ass out."

"He's so stupid." She paced the floor behind her desk. "I could just slap him sometimes."

"Don't let that fool get to you, baby." He placed his hands on her shoulders and started to rub them. "Relax. He's just jealous. You're everything he wants to be and more. Don't let that shit bother you."

She blew her nose softly. "I don't know why I'm tripping. It's been so long ago. I feel stupid."

Dray wiped her eyes with his thumbs. "You're not stupid, you're human. And there's nothing wrong with being angry. You know he's a big bitch, so dry those pretty eyes so we can get his show on the road. A few days away will take your mind off work. And I promise I'll do my part to help you unwind."

She broke into a relaxed smile. "You're right, Dray. I do need some time off. Thank you."

"I'll talk to you in a little bit. I've got to take care of something right quick." He had a few things he needed to say to Rodney.

Monica wiped her face. "Okay. I'll see you later."

Once the meeting was over, Dray met with Rodney in Bill's office. He detested the way Rodney treated Monica and had to let him know about it. It didn't matter that Rodney was the label's top act, nor did his insignificant twenty-percent ownership of the company. He had no right to insult people. Bill sat calmly in his chair, his hands placed together in a praying stance. Dray stood near Bill's desk, eager to penalize the thug in front of him. He looked Rodney dead in the eyes. Even though they were around the same age, Dray felt like he was dealing with a child.

"I don't like the way you handled Miss Holiday. You were rude, and you made yourself look stupid in the process."

"Man, whatever." Rodney waved Dray off. "I ain't even trying to hear you."

"I agree with Dray, Rodney. You shouldn't have done that," Bill stated. "Monica's helped your ass out of all kinds of shit. Even after you lampooned her in that magazine article, she still saved your ass. She's kept a bunch of critics off your back and helped you stay out of jail. This is how you repay her?"

"It was totally unnecessary," Dray said firmly, making it a point to defend Monica. "I don't want to have to talk to you about this again, Rodney."

"Whatever, man," Rodney said, waving his hand again. "You're just taking up for her because you're fucking her!"

Dray wanted to punch Rodney in the mouth and end his rap career. "Dude, off this clock I'll whip your ass. Don't fuck with me."

Rodney blew Dray a kiss. "Come on pretty boy."

Dray shoved Rodney into the wall and raised his arm to punch him.

Bill jumped from his chair. "Not in here. Both of you get your asses out of my office with that shit!"

"Come on, B. You trippin'," Rodney said.

Dray released Rodney and fixed his clothes.

Rodney continued his ranting. "He is fucking her. You see he ain't denying it."

Dray stood angrily in front of him. "I ain't one of these punk ass dick riders you hand wit'. I'll fuck yo' ass up." He reached to open the door. "I'm going to lunch, Bill."

"No, wait. Rodney, take a walk."

Rodney sighed and turned to meet Dray's dark eyes. He mumbled something and left. Bill sat behind his desk.

"He's still the number one artist on this label, and I know he's crazy. I just don't want anymore shit from him, or you," Bill said. "Hopefully, this mess doesn't happen again."

"It won't," Dray said calmly.

"In the meantime," Bill began, "I need to ask you a question."

Dray knew what was coming next. "Yeah, what's that?"

"I told Monica, and I'm gonna tell you. Don't let your relationship affect your work."

"It won't," Dray said.

"It just did, son."

Bill had a point.

"I know you're both grown, and you're responsible. She's like a daughter to me. Please don't hurt her. She's been through a lot. And I don't want to see her hurt again."

"Bill, I care about Monica. And I'm not out to hurt anyone."

Bill relaxed a little. "Good," he said. "Because I don't want to have this conversation again." He eyed Dray sharply. "Now go get your lunch. I've got some calls to make."

When Dray left the office, Rodney was standing in the hallway. They looked at each other challengingly, but Dray decided to be the bigger man and apologize. Not that he was scared of Rodney, he just didn't want their bad blood to cause chaos among the other employees. He made his way over to where Rodney was standing and put a pound up.

"No hard feelings, dawg. I didn't mean to go off on you like that." Rodney nodded and reluctantly gave Dray a pound. "It's cool." Dray didn't care whether he was Handle Up's top-selling artist or not, Rodney was going to respect him.

Dray returned to his office, still boggled by his own behavior. He didn't leave Chicago to work for a company who let an artist get away with murder, so to speak, or to let his own checkered past resurface. The size of his hefty paycheck didn't matter. He left everything behind with the hopes of becoming a record company president someday. No two-bit hoodlum Detroit rapper was going to ruin it for him. Dray decided to get some lunch and trekked down to Monica's office to ask her to join him.

"Knock, knock." She was sitting at the computer. "Hey, you wanna grab some lunch?"

She spun around in her chair. "Yes, I'm starving. Just let me save this."

"I need to get out of here." Dray stepped in and shut the door.

"What's wrong?"

"I'll tell you about it at lunch."

"Okay, let me freshen up."

"I'll be downstairs," he said, loosening his tie.

The valet pulled Dray's Escalade to the front of the building. The platinum metallic paint and chrome wheels glistened beneath the hot sun. As he held the door open, Monica came from the building and jumped inside.

"Thank you," she said, sinking into the plush leather seats. She looked at Dray. "Penny for your thoughts?" she offered, as he pulled into the Midtown traffic.

He sighed and looked over at her. "I hope I don't have to deal with that bullshit your boy Double R keeps dishing out."

"What happened?" She sat up in the seat.

"Well, when I left your office I went to meet with him and Bill, and we got into it. He started talking all this shit about you and me messing around, and I just snapped."

"What did you say?"

"I didn't say shit. I pushed his ass into a wall. He pissed me off, and he told Bill about you and me. What do you want to eat?"

"Johnny Rockets is fine." She stirred uneasily in her seat. "Does what Bill said bother you?"

"No," he said to Bill. "Hell no." I just didn't want it to get out like that, you know? We don't have anything to hide. It's just that our business is our business."

They went inside and ordered their food and sat in a booth near the window.

"So what did Bill say?" Monica bit into her hot dog.

Dray shrugged. "Nothing, really. He just said for us to be careful."

She didn't believe that was it. "What else did he say?"

"Nothing. I don't think he likes the idea too much, but he didn't seem too upset."

"Bill doesn't really get mad. He's always been like a father to me. I guess he doesn't want to see me hurt."

"Yeah, he said that."

"Really?"

"Yep, but you don't have to worry about me hurting you." He stroked her cheek reassuringly. "That's the furthest thing from my mind."

Monica put her hand on his knee. "I know."

"Work, work, work. Is that what we're put here for?" Dray groaned. "To break our backs every day and get nothing in return? I thought I left the bullshit back in Chicago."

"Stop worrying about Rodney," Monica pleaded. "He'll dig his own grave. He does make it hard though, especially for me to do what I need to do. All he does is complain."

"Monica, you can handle him."

"Yeah. But do you think he told people about seeing us at the party?" she asked, worried.

"I don't give a damn what he tells people. And you shouldn't either. Who would believe Rodney anyway? If we're questioned, we'll do what you PR folks do best."

"And what would that be?" she asked.

"Deny it!" They laughed.

"I guess that makes sense."

He took another bite of his burger. "You ready for this tour?"

"Yeah. I'm ready for all the screaming fans, loud music, delayed flights, and lost baggage. I'm ready for all of that."

"I'm sure it won't be that bad. Frankly, I get a thrill out of shit like that."

"Yeah, you would."

CHAPTER 15

Houston was hot as hell. In addition to the weather being unbearable, the Prima Donnas were mobbed when they made their appearance at Sharpstown Mall on the southwest side of town. They were fierce competition for the local homegirls, Destiny's Child. The Houston police did what they could to control the crowd, but they could only do so much. Rochelle and Kim were enjoying the attention, but Amber was suffering from menstrual cramps and snapped at anyone she could. Monica's nerves were on edge, and the Advil wasn't doing a thing for her headache. Dray had to cancel his plans to come at the last minute. Bill needed him to sit in on some meetings with the label's distributor and finalize some plans with Rodney. Dray wasn't happy about it, but Bill gave it the go-ahead. Monica hoped Dray would come soon.

"Y'all ain't all that!" a girl yelled at the Prima Donnas from behind the ropes. She was wearing a Destiny's Child T-shirt.

"Shit, they look good," a guy yelled back.

"Why you bring yo' fat ass up here?" another guy yelled.

They were all that, and they had a gold album to prove it. The tour was just beginning. And the girls and Monica were already exhausted. After the mall appearance and a stop by the 97.9 radio station, they took a break for some much-needed rest. Monica busied herself in her suite by catching up on e-mail and music news. On the desk in the room were current issues of *Billboard, The Source*, and *Vibe* magazines. She also had a copy of *Entertainment Weekly* for an update of the top ten albums. After sending Bill an expense report and showering, she settled onto the couch for a nap. She was halfway asleep when she heard a knock at the door.

"Room service!"

She jumped up, startled from the loud banging. "I didn't order any room service," she mumbled.

She marched over to the door and flung it open. The irritability subsided when she recognized the smiling servant leaning against the doorway.

"Surprise, surprise, baby," he said in a husky voice.

Monica wrapped her arms around his neck. "Dray! What are you doing here?"

"Is that a good 'What are you doing here?' or a bad 'What are you doing here?'"

He lifted her off her feet and swung her around. "I missed you, baby," he said, putting her down. "And I told Bill I came to check on the girls."

"Ah, so you lied to him?"

"No," he said, pulling her body roughly to his. He kissed her neck. "I did come to check on one . . . special girl." He kissed her lips. "Umm . . . I missed this."

Monica smiled.

"And I came to check on the Prima Donnas too," Dray added facetiously.

She wound her arms under his shirt and rubbed his back. "When are you leaving?"

He looked over at her seductively. "When you kick me out. Nobody knows I'm here yet," he said, placing kisses on her neck again. "I may decide to keep it that way."

He sat on the couch and pulled her to straddle him.

Monica rubbed his head gently. "Where's your stuff?"

"In my room down the hall," he said, rubbing her legs.

"Oh," she said meeting his eyes. "You must have missed me a lot to come this far."

Dray slid his hand beneath her gown and stroked her butt. "Um-hmm. We did," he said, looking down at his crotch.

Monica punched him in the chest. "Very funny, bighead. What's going on in Atlanta?" she asked.

He threw his head back. "Same old, same old. You know Double R recorded the remix single without the girls?"

"Really?"

"Yeah. I'm tired and so pissed right now. That was their big chance to really blow up. Rodney did that shit on purpose."

"Don't sweat it. There'll be other opportunities for them. So who did the vocals anyway?"

"That broad from Rhythmhouse, Asia."

"Asia? Oh god, that chickenhead? Great," Monica said sarcastically. "And why would she want to do a song for her label's rival?"

"Exposure, and I think Rodney is putting the dick to her."

"Yeah, he's got a way with words."

Monica rubbed Dray's face lovingly. "Just do your thing. And don't worry about it. Bill said it was okay for them to do the song."

"I guess I shouldn't worry about it, huh?"

"Nope. You shouldn't."

His mouth met hers greedily. He slipped his hands beneath her shirt and rubbed her back. She arched in response and ran her manicured fingertips across the bulge in his pants.

"I see things are big in Texas," she teased.

"Let me show you just how big," he groaned as he unzipped his pants. He lifted her from the couch like she weighed an ounce, and placed her on the floor. Slowly he slid her floral-printed sundress to the floor, revealing her hardening nipples. He stood and licked each one, carefully outlining them with his fingers. She tilted her head to give him access to her neck. He kissed her there, and they glided toward the bed. She fell back and pulled him on top of her.

"What happened to my room service, Mr. Lewis?" Monica asked putting her tongue in Dray's ear.

He groaned with pleasure and pressed against her. "This is room service."

Monica clamped her legs around his waist. "I think I'd like to place my order now," she whispered hotly.

"Go ahead." He sucked her bare breasts and pulled her panties down and off. He rubbed her bare legs, kneading their soft flesh. His hands explored the silken lines of her back, waist, and hips.

She put her hands in his boxers. "I want, a large . . . " Her words were smothered by his demanding kiss. She drank in the sweetness of his mouth. She'd missed this terribly.

He groaned as she put her hands on his erection. "That feels good," he breathed.

Monica smiled as he climbed on top of her. He pulled her long legs around his waist, wading in their comfort. His mouth greeted hers again. He ran his tongue along the lines of her lips as she clasped her hands around his neck. She massaged it gently, dissolving the stress he held deep within. He held her waist, pressing it against his. Her body responded to his touch effortlessly.

Monica met the eyes of her Adonis. They excited every inch of her body. She had no desire to be anywhere else. She held him close, her limbs clinging. She felt a burst of excitement as he plunged inside of her. She enveloped him with her warmth as he thrust deeply inside her. She buried her face against his throat to stifle a cry. The explosions in her body clouded her thoughts of anything but him. His hot mouth tantalized her and teased her while the rest of him brought her to passion's shores. She felt his lips along her neck, shoulders, and breasts. He held her waist and grinded until climax claimed her. She buried her head in his chest and closed her eyes. Dray flipped her over gently and entered her from behind. She purred as he rode her, clutching the damp sheets until he delivered her another orgasm. She wound her hips to meet his stride. Seconds later he growled in release, collapsing on top of her.

Dray rolled over on his back and pulled Monica on top of him. She flicked her tongue in his ear and licked it until he rose again. She put her hand around him and stroked him until he was ready. She climbed on top of him and created her own storm. She rode him until he exploded inside of her. She smiled sweetly and snuggled at his side. Dray clutched her close and they slept.

♫

"The girls put on a good show," Dray said, helping Monica into the limo the next day.

"And so did you," she winked.

He laughed. "I'll have to see about what we can do for another performance."

She rested her head on his shoulder as they rode to the airport. The girls and their entourage were in a separate limousine. They were headed to San Antonio and then on to Las Vegas. He was flying back to Atlanta and would meet up with them again once they hit Los Angeles. When they got to the terminal, Dray didn't want to see Monica go. She held his eyes while the girls checked in at the counter. Once everyone else made their journey toward the gate, Dray and Monica shared a deep kiss.

"Damn, I'ma miss you," he said, pulling away.

"I'll miss you too," she said smiling. She pointed a finger, "Be good." She blew him a kiss as she stepped through the security check. He grabbed it and smiled.

"Always," he said.

Dray took a flight back to Atlanta. Once inside his apartment, Dray listened to his messages. There was one from Bill about the MTV award show coming up and another from his boy Adam. Once he finished unpacking he would return his phone calls. Dray was glad to have spent some time with Monica. He hadn't planned on missing the whole tour, but from the looks of things, that's exactly what he was going to do. Every moment away from Monica was pure agony.

He placed his dirty clothes in the washer and decided to take a shower. When he finished, he trimmed his hair and shaved. When he finished cleaning up, it was almost 11:30. He returned Adam's call. He figured Adam wouldn't mind, since he was a night owl and usually brought a lot of work home with him. Adam was an investment banker who made a ton of money, and he did some of his best work at night. Dray was sure he'd be up surfing the Web, and he was right.

"What's up, man?"

"Nothing much. Just checking on some stocks for a client. What's up with you?"

"I just got back from Texas. You know the Prima Donnas are doing that promo tour, and I kinda wanted to see Monica."

"Ah, I see you've been putting in some work with shorty. What's the deal, D?"

Dray rubbed his head. "Man, I told myself I wasn't gon' get involved. But now . . . "

"Now you realize you lied to yourself."

"I did, dude. I mean I enjoy being with her, for real. I've never met anyone like her in my life, and that's scary. She's my road, dawg. I can talk to her about anything."

"That's cool, man. Maybe things will get serious between you two after all. You know I saw your girl Lisa the other night."

Dray didn't seem surprised. "Ex-girl."

"Well, anyway, she was with that dude and like six of his homeboys. I think he's playing her."

"Oh, well, that's how the game goes."

"You think you'd ever get back with her?"

"Hell no."

"I think she wants you back."

"She can want me all she wants." Dray looked at the ceiling for a moment. "You know she had the nerve to call me asking for money."

"No shit?"

"Yeah. I couldn't believe her ass."

"Damn, that's wild, dude. I'll probably be down there next weekend. My job is sending us to a conference at some hotel down there."

"Which one?"

"I think the Hyatt, I'm not for sure yet."

Dray made a note on his calendar. "Well, let me know. I'll find something for us to get into."

"You know I was watching the countdown on BET. Those little girls are fine."

"Yeah, they're cool."

"Man, if I were ten years younger, one of them would be on my to-do list."

"You foul man," Dray joked. "They're way out of your league."

Adam chuckled. "Whatever man, just make sure you have some nice little honey dip you can hook me up with."

"I'll see what I can do, man, but I'm not making any promises."

"Do what you can. But listen, I'll rap to you later, man. I've got to run across town."

"Can't stay away from those loudmouth hoochies, huh?" he smirked.

"Naw, this is business. I'll check you later."

"Peace."

♫

Monica burst into the suite with food from McDonald's. "I know y'all are sick of this stuff but it will have to do. Y'all can fuss at Bill later."

Rochelle helped her with the bags by setting them on the table. "We don't mind, Moni. It's cool."

Amber disagreed. "Since we're in LA, can we get some Roscoe's chicken and waffles?"

"Come on, Miss Thing. One more night." Monica pulled off her denim jacket. She clipped her long tresses to the top of her head and took a seat next to Bruno, the bodyguard at the table. "Here's your filet-o-fish. They were out of tartar sauce."

Bruno slapped his cards on the table. "Damn! Is there a tartar sauce shortage in California or something? That's the second time!"

The melodic ring on Monica's cell phone interrupted them. "This is Monica," she answered.

"Hey, beautiful, it's Dray. I'm on my way over to the hotel. What room are y'all in?"

"Three-sixty."

"I'll be there in a little bit."

"Alright."

When Dray got to the hotel room everyone was glad to see him. He had good news too. Big Chief, a rap artist on the Atlanta-based Big Hits label's western division wanted the girls to appear on his upcoming album. People were calling him the next Tupac. His husky voice and political lyrics were making him a force to be reckoned with on the West Coast. His guest appearances on other albums had fans wanting more. He even hooked up with Dr. Dre, the force behind artists like Snoop Dogg, NWA, and Double R's Detroit homeboy, Eminem.

"We've got to get the girls to this recording session after the signing tomorrow. This could blow them up." Dray sat down at the table with Bruce, looking back and forth at him and Monica to see their reaction.

"Sounds good to me," Bruce uttered, even though his opinion didn't count.

Monica wasn't so sure. She knew the girls were exhausted, despite their bubbly impressions. Spending the day at a signing and the night in a recording studio wasn't exactly a good idea.

"I'm not sure if we should overwork them like that. They've been on the road nonstop. They need to rest, and at least have a day to themselves."

Dray's brows drew together in a frown. "Moni, this is the music business. These girls have to work hard if they want a quadruple platinum album. It's not going to come with just a pretty face and a big ass."

Bruce almost choked on his food. "Dang, Dray."

"Do you have to talk like that?" Monica asked, annoyed.

"Well, it's the truth, whether you like it or not. Until we have at least three million albums sold, we'll do whatever we have to."

"They have more than a million. And by the time they finish this tour, sales will be close to three million." She shook her head and put a few fries in her mouth. Dray glared into her eyes.

"You're missing my point, Monica. They have to do this. This guy is on a major come up in the rap game. He's gonna be a star. If they're the first females to sing on his album, think of what it could do for them." He sat down next to her on the couch.

Monica leaned back and closed her eyes for a moment. "They don't need him to be successful. They already are successful. He's the one who's up and coming." She settled back, disappointed.

"They're doing it." He hadn't heard a word she said.

"They're tired, Dray, and it's not a good idea."

He chuckled nastily. "Not a good idea for who? You?"

Monica felt her temper rise. "I told you, the girls are tired.

Hell, I'm tired. So yes, it's not a good idea for any of us. Couldn't you just wait until they finish the tour?"

He glared at her, frowning. "This is a once in a lifetime kind of thing. You can't put it on hold." He looked at Bruce. "Women. This is what you get when you work with women."

"Oh, please," Monica snapped. "Now you're going to say some sexist bullshit like that? Niggas, I swear y'all get on my nerves."

Dray stared with dark eyes. "Well, I've already agreed. So they're doing it anyway. End of story." He leaned back on the couch.

Monica's eyes blazed with anger. "I don't believe this." She rose from the seat next to him and put her hands on her hips. "You made plans for them without consulting me first?"

"I didn't have to consult you, Monica. I'm the VP in this camp. It's done, period."

"Fine." Monica snatched her bag and threw it over her shoulder. "I'm going to bed."

"Monica!"

"What?" She shot him a nasty glare.

"Why are you tripping? It's just one small detour from the tour. We have a couple more days here."

She snatched her drink from the table. "Why the hell did you ask me if you had already made up your mind?"

Dray blinked. She had a point there. "S-So you could prepare for it."

"Prepare for what? Damn it, Dray! You are such an asshole," she yelled. "I don't know who you think got these girls together. I've been working with them from day one. I don't appreciate your way of handling their schedule, shit!"

"Monica!"

She left and slammed the door behind her. Bruce laughed at Dray's frustration.

"What's so funny?" Dray asked angrily.

"Nothing." Bruce looked apologetic. "My bad, man. But I hope you know. She is pissed at you."

If the girls were listening, they pretended they weren't. Their eyes were glued to an episode of MTV Cribs on the other side of the suite.

Once Monica made it to her room, she showered and slipped into her nightgown. If Dray was going to be inconsiderate, two could play that game. After the record signing, she would leave the girls in his care. She'd let him be responsible for feeding them, listening to girl talk, and dealing with menstrual cramps. If he spent a day with them under excruciating circumstances, he'd see why the schedule was so important. After she brushed her teeth and wrapped her hair, she retired for some much-needed beauty sleep.

CHAPTER 16

After six hours in the studio, the girls were ready to go. They'd done vocals for two different songs, and the producer, Frankie, still wasn't satisfied. He sat at the boards with one of the engineers smoking cigarette after cigarette. Dray could see the distress on the girls' faces, and wondered what he'd gotten them and himself into. He watched Kim as she sat back in a chair pulling strands of her loose hair and dropping them on the floor. Rochelle, who had the most attitude, stood behind Big Chief with her arms folded. He was nodding his head at the playback, absorbed in his yet-to-be finished song.

"How much longer is this going to take?" she whined.

"As long as it needs to," Frankie snapped. "You in a hurry or something?"

"The girls have a flight to catch to New York in three hours." Dray's voice was harsh. "What's the problem?"

He was just as tired as the girls. The vocals sounded fine to him. He didn't see what the big deal was. He'd learned in college music theory classes, if something sounds good in a tune, don't mess with it. You only waste time when you could be moving on to the next song.

"Give us another thirty minutes," Big Chief pleaded. "I promise we'll be done." It was obvious he was the only one who seemed to be genuinely concerned for the girls. He was worn out too.

The girls went back in the recording booth for the last time to sing the hook for Chief's song *How Low Can You Go?* The catchy upbeat tune was mellow enough to peak the interest of urban adults, and cool enough for kids. The edited version would be released first, thus ensuring a crossover hit for all audiences. When the vocals were done, Dray ushered the girls back to the limousine and took them to Roscoe's Chicken & Waffles for a bite to eat.

When they got back to the hotel, the girls were exhausted and went straight to their room. Dray went into the hotel's bar and ordered a bourbon and coke. He gathered his thoughts for his conversation with Monica. He had to apologize to her. She was right about overworking the girls. He hadn't taken their feelings into consideration when he made the arrangements with Big Chief. They were teenagers, so he figured they could deal with the overexertion. He looked up at the television that was blaring the local ten o'clock news. He hadn't realized it was so late.

♫

Since she hadn't heard from Dray and the girls, Monica decided to make her way downstairs to the lobby to keep an eye out for them. After finishing the pastrami sandwich she'd gotten from the deli across the street, she headed for the lobby. They should be back by now, she thought. She put on some lipstick, grabbed her keys, and went to the elevator. When she got downstairs to the bar, Dray was sitting by himself. She hesitated at first, but then figured, *What the hell? They would have to talk to each other sooner or later.* Dray was finishing his drink as she made her way over. He set the glass down and ordered another one and stared at the pack of cigarettes the man next to him had. He was tempted to ask for one, but decided against it. He hadn't smoked in years and knew if he started again, it would be hard to stop. The bartender handed Dray his drink.

"Thanks, man."

Monica approached him from behind. "So, Mr. Lewis, how'd it go?" she asked, sitting in the seat next to him.

He was surprised to hear her voice and turned to meet her eyes. As she looked quizzically, he nervously picked up his glass again. "It was alright. The girls are tired." He took a quick sip.

"Did you think they wouldn't be?" she questioned, clearly unmoved by the remorse in his tone.

"Monica, if you're trying to insinuate that I made a mistake, don't bother. I should have listened to you."

Satisfaction showed in her eyes. "Hate to say I told you so, but I did. Bartender, let me have a peach martini, please." She turned to face Dray. "When I asked you not to do it, I knew how it would turn out. You'll have these girls exhausted and mad at you for nothing, and it's not a nice feeling. They're still kids."

"Yeah, yeah. And I know you enjoy being right. I knew that the first time I met you."

Monica shook her head and placed a ten-dollar bill across the bar. "I don't enjoy being right. It's just that I've been at Handle Up a little longer than you, so I know what I'm talking about. If you don't play by the rules, you'll fall flat on your face." She ran her manicured finger across the rim of her glass. "And floor polish tastes nasty."

"I hate it when you're right," Dray chuckled, taking a sip of his drink. "You ready for New York tomorrow?" He gave Monica her money back and handed the bartender a fifty.

"No one's ever ready for New York. Not even the natives."

She shook her head. "I just hope it's not as chaotic as it was in Vegas. That was crazy."

"Well, Vegas is the desert. It doesn't have much going on but slot machines, buffets, and lounge singers. The people there needed some soulful excitement."

They finished their drinks quietly. Dray was trying to think of a way to apologize. It was something he wasn't good at because usually he was never wrong. But if he was to win back Monica's affections, he had to. The pressures of the job were getting to him, and he was under a lot of stress. How could he not tell her about it? She'd been his closest confidante over the past several months. He desperately wanted her by his side. He ordered another drink and turned to look into her beautiful face.

"Monica, I want to apologize for the way I acted last night. I was tired, I was . . . exhausted. You know how stressful this job can be."

"Dray, you don't have to . . . "

"Apologize? Yes, I do. You were only trying to help, and I acted like an asshole. I'm sorry. If you don't forgive me, I won't be able to sleep."

"Why wouldn't you be able to sleep?" she asked, grinning.

Because I'm in love with you, he wanted to say. "I just wouldn't."

She smiled candidly and put her hand on his arm. "It's okay, really." She lifted her glass to toast. "Here's to new beginnings."

Dray smiled and tapped her glass with his. He wanted to take her in his arms and hold her like he'd done so many times before. He was longing for her body to be close to his, and to run his fingers through her hair. But for now they had to keep things professional. Once they finished the tour, he would do something special for her. For now, they would just have to take care of business.

♫

La Guardia Airport was worse than LAX. Monica hated the East Coast; she was a California girl. She could never understand how so many people could be crammed up into such a tiny place as New York City. *Guess you have to be a New Yorker to understand this crap,* she thought. She checked her watch again as they waited for the limos. She was growing more and more impatient. The loud honking horns and reckless taxi drivers in front of baggage claim scared her half to death.

When the limos finally arrived, Monica, Dray, the girls, and their entourage piled in. They were scheduled to appear on MTV after their CD signing at the Virgin Megastore on Broadway. Then they'd be free for the rest of the evening. Monica checked her cell phone messages as the limos sped through the New York traffic to get to the signing. When they arrived, tons of screaming fans were lined up outside. It was chaotic trying to get the girls into the store without the fans trying to get to them.

"Damn, they fine as hell!" some guy yelled.

"It's really them!" a young girl yelled. "They're so beautiful!"

"Oh, my goodness," Monica said as she walked alongside Dray. "This is crazy."

Once inside, the girls were seated at a large table in the middle of the store. Each was given a set of black-and-white photos to autograph as the fans piled in. Monica stood behind them with her earpiece. She flipped her sunglasses on top of her head and slung her bag over her shoulder. Dray talked with the store manager, who was excited about the girls' signing. Every few seconds, he and Monica would make eye contact and smile at each other. Dray blew her a kiss one time as she blushed and shooed him away.

Dray was pleased with what the manager had to say. "These people have been lined up since seven this morning. This is wild. We're completely sold out of the girls' album."

"Good, good," Dray rubbed his chin. "That's just how we want to keep it."

Dray then folded his arms and put his hand up to his chin, as if he were in deep thought. He looked over at Monica and then smiled to himself. He loved the power and grace she exuded.

Everywhere she went, people could feel her presence. She had an unforgettable essence. She must have felt him staring because she looked over and smiled. Her fantasies of him clung like static. All she wanted to do was get back to Atlanta and put her lips against his. She could see the ripples of his muscles bulging from beneath his shirt. His jeans hung loosely, disguising his well-proportioned body and other assets. She could have torn his clothes off right there in the middle of the store. Her daydream was disturbed by an eager fan who ran up to the table and nearly yanked Kim from her seat. Monica felt her heart skip a beat, but Bruce and the other security guys rushed to calm the young man.

"I'm sorry, Kim, I just want to touch you. Please . . . " he cried. He put his hand out to grab hers, and she shook it gently. "She touched me! Oh, my god!"

Kim's green eyes widened as she huddled next to Rochelle and Amber. "Was he gay?" she asked.

"Like, uh, totally," Amber said in her best valley girl impression.

Rochelle flipped her long hair back. "Oh-mi-god! Gag me with a spoon." They all laughed.

♫

Once the girls were inside the hotel, they went straight to bed. Their usual night of riff-raff and phone calls wouldn't take place tonight. They were exhausted, and they hadn't even been on stage. He hoped they would be alright because doing promo work often took more energy than performing. After making sure everyone was prepared for the trip back to Atlanta, he went to Monica's room to check on her.

"What's up?" she asked, opening the door.

"Hey, may I come in?" he asked.

She pulled the door open wide and waved him in, "What a

day, huh?"

"Yeah, it was a son-of-a-bitch."

"I know you're tired."

"Yeah." He sat down in a chair near the window. "I'm tired as hell. I think I need to take a couple of days off when we get back."

Monica continued to brush her hair as she sat on the bed. "This is only the beginning."

"I can imagine."

"Yeah, city to city and state to state. But don't worry," she said, smiling. "It's only entertainment."

They sat in silence, looking at each other. Neither of them had realized how much they needed each other until this moment. Monica was glad to have someone around to make her job easier. Dray had been a blessing from day one. It just took her a little time to realize it.

He got up from his seat and walked over to the bed. Monica met his eyes as he leaned in to kiss her. Slowly he lifted her chin and moved his mouth over hers. He devoured its softness, running his tongue around the corners of her mouth. As he stirred her passion, he was forced to ignore his own. He pulled away. It was getting late.

He checked his watch. "It's almost midnight. I'd better get some sleep. The flight leaves at seven, right?"

Still dizzy from his kiss, she whispered, "Yes, it is late."

As he moved away from the bed, she tried not to be caught staring at him. The strength of his body bulged slightly from beneath his clothes. He peered over at the television, which featured the evening's sports highlights.

"It's almost playoff time again. I think the Lakers may take it all the way."

"No, not this year, papi. You better recognize Iverson's game."

Dray smirked. "He's cool, he's cool. But if they don't make it, you owe me."

"Owe you what?" she asked followed him to the door. He

stopped abruptly and turned to face her. He put one hand on her arm and pulled the door open.

"Three days and three nights of lovemaking in every room of a summer house in Myrtle Beach. We can go there when the season's over."

"Sounds tempting." She tried to hide her smile as she looked up into his eyes. "And if I win?"

He whispered in her ear softly. "I don't lose, baby."

"There's a first time for everything," she cooed.

"Good night, Ms. Holiday." He stepped into the hallway and scanned it for strangers.

"I guess I'll see you in the morning. And if I haven't told you, thank you."

"For what?"

His eyes probed into her very soul. "For helping me with everything. I know we got off to a rough start, but I'm glad to have you around. You've helped me out a lot. Good night, Monica. Sweet dreams."

Though her body throbbed for his touch, she bid him good night. "See you in the morning, Dray."

"And in my dreams," he said.

CHAPTER 17

Monica couldn't wait to get back home. She'd seen enough of New York. She felt there were too many people, too few parking spaces, not enough land, and an excess of bad manners. She was elated to see the Atlanta skyline as she sat on the plane, reminiscing about the trip. There was one positive thing about New York City though, the shopping. In the few days she, Dray, and the girls and their entourage were there, she'd bought a Burberry rain hat, a pair of Gucci sandals, a coat from H&M on Fifth Avenue, and a silver bracelet from Tiffany's. If she had more time, she and the girls would have shopped in Soho too.

Once off the plane, Monica headed home. Dray stayed behind to make sure the girls got all their bags. Once they were gone, he got to ride home with Robert, his favorite chauffer.

"So how was your trip, young buck?" Robert asked, pulling away from the curb.

"It was alright. Exhausting, though. All I wanna do is take a shower and put my feet up."

♫

Monica opened the door to her condo and exhaled. The smell of potpourri greeted her. She felt through her purse for her wallet. Brian, her building's concierge set her luggage on the floor. When he finished, she handed him a twenty, thanked him, and sent him on his way before looking to see how many messages she had on her answering machine. It was a good thing she cleaned up before she left, she was too exhausted to lift a finger. All she wanted to do was settle into a nice bath. She placed her mail on the counter and peeked at her answering machine. There were six messages. The machine would have to wait. Right now, the tub was calling her name.

She went into the bathroom to run her water. As the tub filled, she added some Epsom salt for extra comfort, and a splash of bubble bath. She turned the water down and went to undress. She slid her white BCBG Capri pants and red DKNY top off. After she wrapped her hair and closed all the blinds, she hung her clothes on a hanger to air out.

The hot water felt delicious against Monica's skin. She propped her head up on her bath pillow and closed her eyes. If she had her way, Dray would be with her. She could just feel his strong body pressing up against hers, his stiffness protecting her. She pretended the bubbles were his arms, surrounding her with love. She could feel his lips as they glided down her skin. When he finished, he would make love to her, like he had before, filling her body with endless bliss. If only he were there, he could set her afire with a single stroke. The water made a bubbling sound as it escaped down the drain, awakening her from her daydream. Give me strength, Lord, please.

♫

Now that Dray was home he could take it easy. He wouldn't have to worry about getting three teenage girls to CD signings. The hoopla was over for the moment. After placing his bags on the couch, he took off his watch. The day had finally come to an end. It was almost 11:30. He pulled off his shirt and walked over to the window. The bright lights from downtown Atlanta lit up the sky. It was a clear night, and he could see all the stars.

Dray slid his Remy Shand CD into the stereo and *Take a Message* filled the air. He belted out the lyrics in his husky, baritone voice. It was the first time he'd sung in months. He surprised himself. He only sang when he was in tune with his emotions. He guessed it had a lot to do with the lovely Monica Holiday.

When he finished reading his mail, Dray went into the bathroom and stripped down to his birthday suit. He let the water warm up, and he stepped inside. The hot water felt refreshing up against his bronze skin. It was nice to take a shower where the water pressure was strong. Most of the hotels they'd stayed in had mediocre pressure and the water would barely heat up. He lathered his hair. He would have to get it trimmed some time this week. As he washed it, he could feel Monica's hand gliding over his wet skin. Her hands traveled down his chest and stomach, then finally to his firm need. She would press her breasts to his chest and then they would make love right there in the shower. Their bodies coming together in erotic harmony. Damn, he missed her.

♫

Rodney "Double R" Robinson's house sat atop a hill in the quiet area of Sandy Springs. The house was an elegant masterpiece that boasted five bedrooms, four baths, and an indoor basketball court and a pool. He'd bought it after his first album sold more than 3 million copies. Usually he was there alone, or surrounded by a number of friends. Tonight was a little different.

He was nestled into his Natuzzi leather couch watching music videos. There were two girls at his side, Shanty and Nicole. Shanty was a chocolate-brown honey from Cleveland. Despite her stripper-like appearance, she was pre-med at Spelman. Nicole was a pre-med major at Clark Atlanta. It was anyone's guess how they got hooked up with Rodney. He seemed to attract women from all walks of life, from the promiscuous dentist he boned in her office, to the nail technician in his favorite spa. He had more than his fair share of women. Shanty and Nicole were just a couple of more names to add to the list. They sat scantily clad in tank tops and short shorts. Nicole was asleep with her head resting on Rodney's shoulder. Shanty was leaning back with her eyes closed smoking a Black & Mild cigar.

The coffee table was covered with empty bottles of Moët, blunts, condom wrappers, and hip-hop magazines. Rodney's daily habits usually involved sex with his choice of women, alcohol binges, drugs, and video games. Even with his size, he was nothing more than a big child with a lot of money. He'd become careless over the years, despite his past run-ins with the law. He took a puff of his cigar and blew the smoke in Shanty's face.

"Stop it, Rodney!" She smacked his arm. "You play too much."

He inhaled again, and blew the smoke in her eyes. "Shut up, bitch."

"Stop, nigga. Damn. Why you always starting shit?"

"Because I can. This is my house. Don't question me."

Shanty put her cigar in the ashtray. "Forget you . . . stupid ass."

"Who you talking to?"

"You," she sneered. He yanked her by the arm.

"Don't touch me!" she screamed.

His expression clouded in anger. "This is my fuckin' house. You do what the hell I say."

"Fuck you, nigga!" she yelled. "I don't have to do nothing you say. You ain't my daddy."

The commotion caused Nicole to wake from her drug-induced sleep. She lay with her eyes open as Shanty and Rodney yelled back and forth. Calmly, Rodney set his cigar in the ashtray and backhanded Shanty. The force nearly knocked her off the couch.

She held her face. Her light skin had turned cherry red. "You motherfucker! I can't believe you hit me."

"Believe it, bitch!"

She jumped up and threw the remote at him. Nicole sat up quickly, yawning as she wiped the sleep from her eyes. Rodney jumped up and snatched the other girl as she stood holding her face in the middle of the floor.

"What the fuck did you say?" He grabbed her by the wrists and slammed her on the couch.

"Stop it, Rodney!" Nicole yelled. "Stop it!"

"Shut up, Nicole! This stupid bitch friend of yours just disrespected me."

"Rodney, leave her alone," Nicole pleaded. "Shanty!"

Shanty was crying hysterically, but it didn't matter. Rodney kept yelling at her.

"Get up, bitch!" He slapped her again. She put her hands up to keep him from hitting her in the face.

"Stop," she cried, as tears streamed down her cheeks.

He grabbed her wrists again and slapped her repeatedly. Nicole jumped on his back and started to punch him. He was tall and a bit stocky, so she was no match for him. Rodney threw her off his back, and she fell hitting the ceramic tile floor. As she struggled to get up, he kicked her in the ribs.

"Y'all hoes get the fuck outta my house!" He went ballistic and started to throw things. "I hate you fucking bitches. Get your black and high-yellow asses out of my house!"

While Shanty lay crying on the floor, Nicole was still trying to fight back. She picked up a champagne bottle and threw it at Rodney. He ducked, and it hit the wall behind him, shattering the framed picture of his last platinum-selling album. He went to where Nicole lay on the floor, grabbed her by the hair, and slammed her head into the wall, leaving a hole. He let go of her and she collapsed. He ignored the sobs coming from Shanty, who was lying on the floor holding her stomach.

"Shut that shit up!" he yelled. "I told you hoes not to fuck with me, didn't I?"

Nicole didn't reply. Shanty moaned and tried to sit up.

"Shut up!" he yelled again.

He picked up his blunt and lit it. He had resumed his position on the couch and started to watch television. When Shanty looked at her friend, she screamed. Rodney noticed the blood rushing from Nicole's head and rushed to see if she was still breathing.

"Oh, shit!" he yelled. "This bitch is dead?"

He dropped the blunt on the floor and ran.

♪♪

Monica's phone woke her up. She looked over at her alarm clock. It was 6:00 a.m. *Who the hell is calling me this early?* She struggled to pick up the cordless that was on the nightstand by her bed. *What is it now?* She picked up and put the phone to her ear.

"Hello?"

"Moni, its Dray. We got a problem."

"What kind of problem?"

"A problem with your boy, Rodney. Turn on the news and call me back."

She ran into the living room to turn on the television. The story was all over the early morning news. Rodney "Double R" Robinson was being charged with assault and attempted murder. He'd been arrested after calling an ambulance for Nicole Flowers, who at the moment was in critical condition. The news reporter indicated that the assault victim, Shanty Green was going to press charges. She'd suffered a broken wrist and broken ribs. As the police tried to shield her from the cameras, Monica could see she was hurt pretty bad. What the hell had Rodney gotten himself into now?

Bill Sanders was furious. He didn't know who to be more upset with, himself for letting Rodney get away with so much or Rodney for putting him in this situation. News reporters had been outside his house since one of Rodney's neighbors called the police. They heard the screaming coming from his house. Bill paced the grounds of his Alpharetta mansion, waiting for Monica. He wanted her to talk to the press. He was too upset and didn't want to say anything to damage the company's image. Bill had been in this kind of battle before, but only for minor incidents. His bread-and-butter was facing an attempted murder charge. How the hell was he going to get out of this one?

♫✺

After consulting with the Atlanta police and Bill, Monica addressed the press at Bill's house. She didn't give them much information. Rodney's lawyer, Warren Jackson, advised her not to.

"Mr. Robinson proclaims his innocence. And once the Fulton County police have finished talking to him, we'll be able to give you more information on his status. We'll be conducting our own investigation as well. Thank you."

Although the reporters weren't satisfied with her statement, there was nothing they could do about it.

Inside Bill's house, his wife, Karen, served hot tea and juice to Monica and the other employees. Everyone had gotten out of their beds to come to the house. Dray sat across the table from Bill, who was holding his head in his hands. What was he going to do? This was Rodney's third time getting into trouble with the law since he'd been at Handle Up. He was arrested at one of his concerts for assaulting a fan and another time for brawling with a rival rapper at a nightclub.

His bail hadn't been set. And Bill wasn't sure if it needed to be. Rodney might be better off in jail so he could have time to think about his actions. Bill scratched his head and pounded his fist on the table.

"Damn it!" Bill yelled. Everyone froze, hoping he wouldn't start yelling like he had when Rodney was arrested the first time. "This is too much."

Cameron came through the kitchen door. Everyone was surprised to see him.

"Hey, Cam," Monica said hugging him.

"What's up, Moni? You alright?"

"I'm fine. I guess you heard?"

Cameron nodded. "Yeah. So what are we gonna do?" he asked.

Bill shrugged. "How the hell do I know? I'm still trying to figure out why this shit happened."

Monica knew why. Rodney was a serious mental case. His mood swings were unpredictable. He was careless. This was the one time she wished she wasn't his publicist. It would be to everyone's advantage to let him sit in jail. He needed to learn a lesson. Dray watched her as she pulled her hair back and clipped it. She hadn't had a chance to comb it before making the thirty-minute drive to Alpharetta from Midtown. He could see she was still exhausted from the trip with the girls.

"Why don't we wait until they set his bail?" Terry Cole, the business manager, asked.

"I'm not gonna worry about this," George Jones, Rodney's road manager, said as he entered the room. He was dressed in a leisure suit and tennis shoes. His balding hair made him appear much older than his forty years.

Terry removed his wire-rimmed glasses and said, "We have to. This could damage our reputation."

Bill stood from his chair. "Everybody go home. I'm going back to bed. We'll meet up again at three o'clock. I don't feel like dealing with this shit right now. Rodney has a lawyer, let him deal with it."

"You can't mean that, Bill. Rodney is the best thing happening for you right now," Karen said.

"That may be true, baby. But he's also you and Warren's client," Bill replied.

Karen was a lawyer in private practice. She represented Rodney in some business matters.

"If you want to work it out, go ahead. I'm not doing anything until I talk to Warren. He's better at dealing with these situations."

Warren was also general counsel for Handle Up, and he ran his own firm. He represented athletes and entertainers. He had a reputation for getting them out of the stickiest of situations, and he was an expert on dealing with cases like Rodney.

"Well, I'm done with this mess," Terry mumbled.

Bill walked up his spiral staircase to the master suite and shut the door. Everyone sat around looking at one another until Karen came in.

"I guess you all can go," she said, wiping her hands on a dishtowel. "I'll have lunch ready for you at three this afternoon."

As everyone went outside, Dray pulled Monica by the hand. He led her into the kitchen and made sure no one was looking. The coast was clear, so he kissed her.

"Dray . . . please, not here."

"What?" he asked, wrapping his arms around her waist.

She pulled away from him. "There are too many people here."

He didn't believe that was what was bothering her. "Monica, what's really the matter?"

She folded her arms and walked out the back door. "Nothing."

They walked around the yard, past the pool to the gate. "Well, if nothing's wrong, why are you being so secretive."

"I'm not," she said. "I'm just not in the mood for all this drama."

Dray sighed. "Fine, let's just go get some breakfast."

They walked down the driveway to her car.

"Where?" she asked, unlocking the door.

Dray held it open for her. "I-HOP?"

"Sounds good." Monica slid into the seat and put her key in the ignition.

Monica slid on her Gucci shades and put the car in gear. "Just follow me."

He closed her door and slapped his hand on the hood. Monica pulled out of the circular driveway and waited for Dray to get in his ride. She pulled off as he approached her from behind, and headed towards the freeway.

CHAPTER 18

Dray sipped his orange juice and stared at the front page of the *Atlanta Journal-Constitution*. There was a huge picture of Rodney on the front with a headline that read, "How Will Handle Up Handle This?" Monica picked over her omelet and pancakes. She wasn't the least bit concerned with Rodney, but she did care about Bill. He was getting older, and she felt he shouldn't have to pay for his artists' mistakes. Rodney had put himself in the situation and she felt he should suffer for it. Dray was concerned with the company's image but knew that scandal sold records. Just like the controversy surrounding Tupac Shakur and the Notorious B.I.G and the infamous East Coast versus West Coast battle. Their label's CEOs, Puff Daddy and Suge Knight, had even exchanged verbal blows in the press. Although both rappers had been brutally slain in 1996 and 1997 respectively, the tension still haunts hip-hop.

"So what do you think?" Dray asked, pouring syrup on his pancakes.

Monica sucked her teeth. "You don't want to know what I think."

He wiped his hands on a napkin. "I asked you, didn't I?"

"You really wanna know?"

"Yeah, Monica, I do."

"He's a scandalous dog. I think Rodney should be prosecuted to the fullest extent of the law. He shouldn't be treated any differently because he's a celebrity. He's guilty. I know he did it."

"How can you be so sure, Monica?"

"Because I know."

"How do you —?"

"Just take my word for it!" she snapped.

Dray was shocked by her reaction. He'd never seen her get so upset, not even when he spilled his drink on her dress. "It's cool, baby. Forget I asked."

She simmered down. "I hope that girl is alright." Her thoughts drifted to the victim who was in critical condition at the Atlanta Medical Center. "What if she doesn't make it?"

Dray studied her closely for a moment. "She'll be fine. If it makes you feel better, we can send her some flowers."

"Flowers? You think flowers will make her pain go away?"

"No, Monica, I don't. I was just trying to make you feel better."

She pushed her plate away. "I'm not representing him this time." She took a deep breath and tried to relax.

"Come on, Moni. Think about what you're saying."

"I have thought about it, Dray, and I'm not doing it, period."

"Bill needs you ."

"I don't give a damn what Bill needs," she said, her voice raising, "I'm not doing it."

They were interrupted by a beep from Dray's two-way pager. He pulled it from his hip and read the screen. It was Patrice sending a message from Bill indicating that Rodney's bail had been set at five million dollars and that he needed to meet with them ASAP. His lawyer was on the way to pick him up from the Fulton County jail.

Since Monica had already made her mind up about Rodney, he decided not to tell her.

He got up from his seat. "I'll catch up with you later, baby." He tossed twenty-five dollars on the table and kissed her on the cheek.

"Where are you going?"

"I've got to take care of something. I'll call you later."

He dashed out of the door and hopped in his car.

"Great," Monica said, as she sat alone in the booth. "More drama."

She grabbed the newspaper and slid out of the booth.

♪♫

When Monica got home, she climbed back into bed. She set her alarm to wake her up for lunch at Bill's house. Her phone hadn't stopped ringing since she stepped in the door. She turned the ringer off. Dray called, too, but she didn't feel like talking to him or anyone else. She couldn't stop thinking about the girl in the hospital. She was only twenty years old. The newspaper didn't give very much information about Nicole Flowers, but it did say she was a college student. Monica wondered how she could ever have she put herself in a situation with someone like Rodney? What was she thinking? Maybe she'd been fooled by his charm and glitz. Rodney Robinson was a master with words. He could turn four-letter words into soul-wrenching art. It was one of things Monica loved about him when they were together. It wasn't until she found out about Rodney's dark side that she began to feel differently.

No one knew the real reason she hated him. It wasn't because he taunted her in a magazine article or made references to her on one of his songs. He nearly killed her while they were dating. They had gone out to dinner one night at a soul food restaurant in Decatur. Things were going fine until some guy who appeared to be more of a fan of Monica's than of Rodney's, disrespected him. Monica had only been friendly to the guy because he told her how beautiful she was.

Rodney was in the rest room when the guy started to push up on Monica.

"I don't care about your man," he told her. "He ain't my concern."

"Well, he's mine," Monica said.

"He must be good to you. You look like a million dollars. Is that how much I need to be with you?" The guy wouldn't take no for an answer.

"No. Why don't you go eat your food? I don't think it'll be good when it's cold."

Rodney emerged from the rest room to find the guy smiling in Monica's face. When he sat down, the guy mugged him.

"Oh, so this ya man?" he said. "This Double R ass nigga?"

"You got a problem wit me, nigga?" Rodney asked standing up. The guy stood up too, and so did his two friends.

"Yeah, I got a problem," the man said. "Rich niggas like you. That's my problem."

Once the first punch was thrown, Monica left. Rodney ended up breaking the guy's nose and firing a shot into the air to keep the guy's friends off of him. When he fled the restaurant, he came out yielding his gun and yelling. When she tried to calm him down, he snapped at her.

After arriving at his house back in Alpharetta, Monica told him how foolish he'd been.

"Why couldn't you just ignore them?" she asked. "Can't you ever just walk away?"

"Hell no!" he snapped. "I ain't no punk ass nigga. Fuck them!"

She reached for him to calm him down. "Rodney, please. You're gonna give yourself a heart attack."

"Shut up, Monica. I don't wanna hear this shit no more."

"Rodney!"

His nostrils flared with fury. "Didn't I say shut up?"

He grabbed Monica and started choking her on the couch. She tried to scream, but nothing came out. Rodney punched her so hard he broke two of her ribs. The only thing that stopped him from continuing was his cell phone ringing. After he answered it and talked for 20 minutes, he drove her to the hospital and made her lie to the doctors about what happened. She told them the guy and his friends attacked her, and Rodney came to break it up. Once she left the hospital, he gave her $10,000, and never mentioned it again. She was too petrified to disagree, but knew in her heart it wasn't a good thing to do. To this day, the money remained untouched in a money-market account.

Up until his display of abuse, he'd been a great boyfriend. He treated her well, bought her anything she wanted. She never considered him her type. But she was tired of dating white collar assholes with no stamina. She never expected him to become violent. Nor did she suspect he was using her. If he hadn't invested so much time and money in her, she might have believed it. It wasn't until he dumped her six months later that she realized what a mistake she'd made, aside from the beating.

After reading the article in its entirety, Monica folded the newspaper and tried to relax. If it were up to her, Rodney would never see the light of day. She wiped the tears from her eyes and pulled the covers over her head. She didn't want to think or hear about Rodney "Double R" Robinson anymore.

♫⌐

Rodney smoked his third cigarette down to the butt. He'd been sitting in his den, which was still in shambles from the accident. His lawyer, Warren, and Bill were trying to get him to calm down but realized it was easier said than done. Rodney had a history of drinking and drug use, but his domestic abuse was new to them. Dray had joined them, too, and Rodney was telling them everything about his past, excluding what he did to Monica.

Bill scratched his forehead. "How the hell could you beat up a woman like that? Broken ribs? You don't break a woman's fuckin' ribs!"

"Bill, this wasn't my fault. I didn't start that shit. Those stupid bitches did!"

Warren interrupted, "It doesn't matter who started what," he said calmly. "The fact is those girls were visitors in your home. And I know damn well they didn't attack you. I don't give a damn what you say. You have to be a big pussy to try to use that shit as an excuse."

Rodney jumped from his seat. "Man, those hoes brought that shit on themselves."

Bill threw up his hands. "I can't listen to this bullshit. Boy, you are crazy!"

"Come on Big B. It wasn't my fault!"

"Rodney!" Warren snapped, "sit down. Just sit down and shut up."

"Is anything ever your fault?" Dray asked.

"Man, fuck you," Rodney growled. "You and that bitch," he mumbled.

"What the fuck did you say?"

Rodney didn't say a word.

"Well, Rodney," Warren began, "you're gonna plead not guilty to an attempted murder charge."

Rodney closed his eyes and then looked up. "Is that gonna get me off the hook."

He clasped his hands together. "I guess so."

"Your court date is August 5th. You better pray nothing happens to that girl in the meantime. If I were you, I'd lay low, very low. And you are not to leave the state of Georgia. Do you understand me?"

Rodney put his cigarette out and reached for another. "Yeah, man, I hear you." He lit the cigarette and inhaled. As he exhaled the fumes through his nostrils, he looked over at Dray. "This is some bullshit, ain't it?"

Dray's eyes narrowed. "What's the real reason Monica hates you?"

Rodney lowered his eyes and rubbed his hand over his face. "It's a long story."

Bill slapped his knees. "Let's go. I can't stand to look at this boy another minute." He kicked one of the pillows on the floor out of his way. "And clean this shit up in here!"

"We'll see you later, Rodney," Warren said quietly.

Rodney threw up his hands as they walked to the front door. "Come on, y'all. Don't let this shit bother you."

Warren stepped out on to the steps and looked back. "It needs to bother somebody. Dray I'll give you a call tomorrow."

Dray nodded as he stood in the doorway.

Rodney stood in front of him and yelled. "Let Monica deal with it! She handles everything else." He shut the front door and turned to see Dray. "What the fuck do you want, man?"

Dray chuckled, "Monica declined to represent you on this one. Bill has to find someone else."

Rodney looked at him, his eyes filled with frustration. "Fuck, that bitch!"

Dray grabbed him and slammed him into the wall, not far from the hole Nicole's head made. "That's all the bitch's I'ma take from you. Call her out her name again and I'll whip ass all over this house."

A smirk crossed Rodney's face. "Pussy whipped ass nigga. It's good, too, ain't it? Does she still like to be on top?"

Dray threw Rodney across the room, straight into the mirror that hung on the wall. The glass shattered, and he slid to the floor. "I don't know what the fuck she ever saw in you," Dray said.

Rodney was bleeding. "Fuck you, man. I controlled her, that's what she liked." He grabbed a chair to help him stand. "All bitches like that wanna be controlled, and dominated. I gave her what she wanted." Rodney broke into a sinister laugh.

Dray turned to leave. "You're sick."

CHAPTER 19

The patio of the Sanders estate was packed with folks. Most of them were Handle Up employees, Bill's family, and industry heavy-weights. It seemed they were celebrating a Grammy nomination instead of the arrest of one of the music business' top entertainers. Rodney was loved, but most of it came from people who didn't know him or wanted something from him. Monica and Patrice sat on coordinating chaise lounges near the pool. They picked at the food Karen had prepared: fried chicken, potato salad, and macaroni and cheese. There wasn't much talk, only whispering. Patrice's upturned lip switched to a smile when she saw Dray coming to join them.

"Monica, you want some more tea? I'll be back." She didn't give Monica a chance to answer and quickly ushered Dray into her seat.

"Hey." He sat down holding a cup of iced tea.

Monica kept her eyes on her plate. "Hey."

"You been here long?"

"About thirty minutes."

He sipped his iced tea. "Heard anything else about the news?"

"No, didn't you meet with Bill? You know more than I do."

He shrugged dismissively. "Yeah, I did meet with Bill and Rodney."

"So what did Mr. Robinson have to say? More excuses, I presume?"

"Yep. I don't know how he's going to get out of this one. Have you told Bill you don't want to represent him?"

"No, but I will," Monica said. She peeled a piece of meat from her chicken and put it in her mouth.

Dray took a bite of the chicken he was holding and briefly took a swig of tea. "When are you going to tell him?"

She shrugged. "I don't know. Maybe before I leave."

"Don't wait too long, Monica."

"I won't."

He tried to read her dark eyes. Something was bothering her. "Are you okay?"

Patrice interrupted holding two cups of iced tea. "Here we go, Miss Holiday." She handed Monica a cup and returned to her chair. "So Moni, do you now what you're going to say about Rodney to the press."

She made eye contact with Dray and quickly looked away. "I'm not."

"Not what?" Patrice asked eating a pickle slice.

"I'm not representing him this time. He'll have to find someone else."

Patrice drew back. "Can you do that? I mean, I thought you had to do whatever Bill said."

"Not all the time," Dray said. His brows rose a little. "He'll get someone else."

Patrice put a chip in her mouth and frowned. "I sure hope so."

They sat and finished their food in silence, while everyone else headed into the pool house.

"Monica!" Bill called, waving her over. "Let me have a word with you."

She looked at Dray and set her plate down. "Here we go."

When she got to where Bill was standing, he was lighting a cigar. He took a puff of it and flicked the ashes into an empty cup he was holding.

"How's it going?" he asked. Despite everything he could still manage a fatherly smile.

"Fine," she answered plainly.

"You know I want to talk to you about Rodney." He took a deep breath. "I know he's been nothing but trouble. But I need you to really help him out this time, please."

"Bill, I . . . " He wasn't going to make it easy.

"We need to take care of this as soon as possible. The media is already all over his ass. The story even hit *USA Today*."

"Bill, I can't represent Rodney."

He looked at her mockingly as his mouth twitched with amusement. "For a moment I thought you were serious." He took a puff from his cigar.

"I am."

Bill struggled to breathe as he waved smoke from his face. "What?" he managed to say through smothered breaths. "You've got to be kidding."

Moments later, Dray and Patrice made their way toward the pool house. As they passed Monica and Bill, they could see they were in a heated discussion. Monica stood with her arms folded as Bill tore into her about her decision not to represent Rodney. Dray was tempted to interrupt, but Bill did not look too happy. As a matter of fact, he was livid. Dray and Patrice briskly walked past them and stood closer to the pool house.

"Monica, you can't back out on your responsibility just because you and Rodney have had some disagreements. How many times have I told you not to let your personal life interfere with your professional life?"

Monica turned her head away. "I'm not going to represent him."

"He needs you this time . . . I mean he really needs you."

"I'm tired of what he's doing to people. He thinks he's a damn king around here or something. And you treat him like he is."

With desperation in his voice, he said, "He's our number one act. What am I going to do? Rock the boat because of some little tantrum?"

"You'd rather see a girl cling to life in the ICU while Rodney just hangs out and parties all the time?"

"Monica, be reasonable. You know the boy has had some problems."

"I am being reasonable."

"You're not looking at it from a business point of view. He is the king, Monica. Do you know how many albums his last record sold? Eight million. Who's gonna argue with that? You think his fans will stop buying his records because of this? Hell no. Scandal sells records."

"I don't care what they do. Beating a woman like he did is attempted murder, and it's wrong. Have you even been to see the girl? Did you see how she looks? What about the scandal she has to deal with? What are you gonna do about that?"

"I'm prepared to compensate her."

Monica looked in disbelief. "I can't believe what I'm hearing. You of all people, Bill, should know! You're gonna try and buy this girl's pain away?"

He put his hands on her shoulders, "I know what he did to you, and it was wrong. But you can't ruin his career." He shook her lightly as if to emphasize his point.

Monica shook herself loose. "Bill, don't patronize me."

Bill pulled Monica's arm. "One last time," he said firmly, "please."

She snatched her arm away and stormed off. She went back to

her chair to grab her purse. Dray came toward Bill to see what was going on.

"What happened?" he asked.

Bill hung his head and flicked ashes from his cigar onto the ground. "She's not gonna represent Rodney. She is really pissed. I've never seen her like this."

"I agree. Something definitely happened between her and Rodney that she's not telling us."

Bill gave a quick nod. "Yeah," he said. "I just wish I knew what it was."

Dray patted Bill on the back. "I'll go talk to her," he said.

"Monica!" he called as she slid into her car. "Wait!" Dray put his hand on the door, forcing her to keep it open. "I need to talk to you."

"About what?"

"About you and Rodney. And about what Bill said."

"Why? Did he send you to be his errand boy because he knows we're sleeping together?" She yanked the door from his hand and shut it.

"Come on, baby, this is me, Dray. Don't do me like that. Tell me what's wrong."

Tears blinded her eyes and choked her voice. "Let it go, Dray." She backed the car up.

"Stop!" Dray yelled banging her window.
She rolled her window down. "Dray, I don't wanna talk about this anymore, especially not with you."

♫

Monica was sitting in her bedroom when the phone rang the first time. She sat on the edge of the bed staring out the window as she listened to her answering machine.

"Hi, you've reached Monica. Sorry, I'm unavailable at this

time. Please leave me a message or hit me on the two-way." Beep.

She didn't feel like talking to Dray, or anyone else for that matter. She needed to clear her head. She grabbed her keys and walked toward the living room. The phone rang again. She waited to hear the caller's message.

"Monica, it's Dray again. I was just calling to see if you were alright. I know you're angry, baby, but you can talk to me. Please don't shut me out." Beep.

I'm not shutting you out. I just don't feel like talking, she heard a voice say. She grabbed her purse and headed out the door.

♫

It was almost 8:30, and Dray was getting worried. He'd never seen her so upset, and wondered if there was more to her relationship with Rodney than she was letting on. The lights from his building shone down through his window as he sat in his truck. He closed his eyes and put his head back on the seat. What was Bill thinking trying to get Monica to do something she is totally against? She was too independent and headstrong to be coaxed into doing something she didn't want to do. Even in the short time he'd known her, he had figured that out.

"Mr. Lewis, are you alright?" said Chad, one of the building's concierges.

Dray opened his eyes. "I'm cool, just thinking about some things, you know?

"You want me to park your truck?"

"Not yet. I'ma chill for a minute. I need to get my thoughts together."

Chad pulled out a cigarette and lit it. "Just let me know. I'll be over there."

Dray's eyes widened. He knew he shouldn't, but he did anyway, "Let me get a square, man."

Chad looked surprised, but handed one to him anyway. "Here you go, dude."

"Thanks, man."

As Chad walked away, Dray lit the cigarette and took a drag. After a series of coughs, he realized why he'd given up cigarettes in the first place. He blew the smoke through his nose and tossed the cigarette out the window. He started the engine and pulled off into the night. He fiddled with the CD player for a minute and decided to go to the office.

He drove to Midtown, wondering what would happen at Handle Up. Would the company fall apart? Would Monica leave? All because of a hot-headed rapper named Double R. He let his lyrics go to his head and get him into double trouble. Not only did he assault one woman, he nearly killed another. Nicole Johnson was fighting for her life, and all anyone could think about was what Rodney's actions would do to his career. Dray wondered what the entertainment world had come to. It seemed as though money could solve any problem. He was caught up in the middle of his dream being in the music business and the realm of a woman he'd come to care about. Would he have to choose between the two?

CHAPTER 20

The smell of hospitals always made Monica sick. She clutched her purse tighter as she strolled down the hallway toward ICU. She was glad she'd worn her denim jacket. The building was extremely cold. As she approached the nurses' station, her two-way vibrated in the bottom of her purse. She figured it was probably Dray. No time for that now. She had to check on Rodney's victim.

"Excuse me."

She interrupted a nurse who was talking on the phone. The nurse held her pen up to let her know she would have to wait. Great, Monica thought as she looked around. She leaned on the counter, hoping someone else would come up soon. Another nurse, a stocky white woman wearing a blue scrub uniform, finally came to the counter.

"Yes, ma'am. Can I help you?"

Monica cleared her throat. "I'm looking for a young lady who was brought in the other night. She was beaten."

"Are you the press too? I swear, I wish y'all would stop coming up here. That poor girl needs her rest. They've been trying to get in her room at all hours of the night!"

"No, no. I'm not with the press. I-I'm a friend of hers." She had to lie. It was the only way she would be able to see Nicole.

The nurse eyed her suspiciously, and then took a deep breath. She looked harmless enough. "Alright. I'll give you a few minutes. Visiting hours are over at eight. You'd better hurry up. She's in Room 3C, just down the hall to your left." She pointed toward the yellow hallway.

"Thanks," Monica said.

The nurse smiled. And Monica headed toward the end of the hall. When she found the door marked 3C, she took a deep breath. She stuck her head in first to see if there was anyone else in the room. There was no sign of any other visitors. She stepped inside and shut the door behind her. Nicole's bed was in the middle of the floor. Surrounding her was a number of high-tech machines with wires and cords coming from them. She had tubes in her nose and arms, and the back of her head was wrapped with gauze. Her eyes were closed and her breathing was sporadic. Monica tiptoed toward the edge of the bed and took a deep breath.

She whispered, "I wish you could hear me. I hope you can hear me. I hope you get out of here alright."

She examined Nicole's injuries again, remembering her own a few years before. Tears filled her eyes. *How could this happen?*

When she left the hospital, she checked her messages. Her two-way indicated she had a call from Dray. She listened to his message and realized she was shutting him out. Just as she cleared it, he called again. Finally, Monica was ready to talk.

"Hello?"

Dray sighed heavily. "Where have you been? I was worried about you."

"I had to take care of something."

"How long are you gonna be mad at the world."

"I'm not mad at the world," she sighed. "I just don't understand the people in it."

"Nobody's perfect, Monica."

Monica's eyes filled with tears. "I went to see Nicole Johnson."

"Who?" Dray asked.

Monica sobbed loudly. "The girl Rodney beat up. I went to see her."

"Why did you do that?"

His words chilled her. "What do you mean, why did I do it? The girl is in ICU. Do you even care about that? Does anybody care about her?"

"Come on, Monica, of course, I care."

She shook her head and leaned against the window. "I know, and I'm sorry. This is a lot to deal with, and it's not easy." She wiped her eyes.

"I know that, but you can talk to me about it. Where are you?"

"In the parking lot of the hospital. But I'm leaving."

"Why don't you meet me at the Starbucks in Barnes & Noble in Buckhead."

"When?" She was glad he asked. She really needed to talk.

"Right now. I'm on my way there now."

"Okay."

"I'll see you in a minute."

Dray didn't see Monica's car when he got to Barnes & Noble. He hoped she hadn't changed her mind about talking. He wanted her to trust him. He parked in the lot and went inside to find a table. The bookstore was like a hot spot for intellectuals, and for folks who wanted to be trendy and drink coffee. For now, it would have to serve as the focal point for his and Monica's conversation. After picking up a copy of *ESPN* magazine, he found a cozy table near the window and waited. When Monica arrived, she looked as though she'd been crying. He hugged her, and her eyelashes fluttered against his cheek.

"Are you alright?" He helped her into her seat.

"No," she said, removing her jacket.

Dray leaned over the table. "Tell me what's wrong," he said, covering her hands with his. "I mean, what's really wrong."

She sighed heavily and closed her eyes. "It's a long story."

"We got all night. I'm listening. You want something to drink? A latte or something?"

"No," she said. "I'm fine."

He smoothed her hair. "So what happened at the hospital?"

"Nothing happened. I just went to see her."

"Did you talk to her?"

"No. She's in critical condition."

"Oh," Dray said, rubbing his forehead. "Moni, I want you to tell me the truth about you and Rodney. What did he do to you? I know something went down. I just want to hear it from you."

"Who told you something happened? Rodney?"

Dray sighed. "He talked around it. I almost kicked his ass tonight. But I want you to tell me."

"Why was he telling you? Did you ask him?" She slammed her fist on the table. "Damn it!"

Dray was surprised she was so angry. "Baby, I didn't ask him any-thing," he said calmly. "Why are you so upset?" He looked at her as if he just remembered something. "That night at the hospital. The doctor said you'd been there before. You didn't fall off a motorcycle did you?"

She spoke in a hushed whisper and wouldn't meet his eyes. "No, I don't want to talk about it. I want to leave."

They walked outside. Dray took Monica's hand and pulled her over toward the back of his truck. He kissed her gently.

"It's not going to go away until you let it out."

Monica started to cry. She buried her face in her hands and told him what happened. Dray took her in his arms as the tears dampened his shirt. He didn't like this vulnerable side of her. He was used to her fiery and combative nature. But seeing her cry made his desire for her stronger.

She stepped out of his encircling arms and sniffled, "I'm sorry about your shirt."

Dray assured her the shirt was fine. He wondered what she would do if the police found out Rodney attacked her. "Are you gonna give the police a statement?"

Monica backed away wiping her eyes. "I have to go, Dray." She looked at him once more and quickly ran to her car.

♫

At home, Monica undressed and put on her robe. She was listening to Aaliyah and sipping tea while pacing the floor. She froze when she heard her buzzer go off. She set the mug on the end table. She knew it was Dray. She wasn't going to be able to shake him, and it didn't seem like he wanted to be shaken. She went to the door and leaned against it.

"What do you want, Dray?"

"Monica, open the door, please. I need to see you."

She stepped back and closed her eyes. "Why are you making this so damn hard?"

"I'm not, baby, you are. You got me standing out here looking like a fool. Open the door please. You know Monica, I'm not used to this. Being open . . . I didn't think I'd want another woman in my life until I met you. Now you're pushing me away, and I don't like the way it feels."

She turned the lock and pulled the door open slowly. She let him in. She couldn't turn away the man she loved. She needed him too much. His eyes searched her face as he grabbed her hand.

"Don't walk away from me again, Monica," he said. "I need you, and I know you need me."

Her pulse pounded as he put his hands around her midriff. Her robe fell open, exposing her chemise, which came a few inches above her knees. His hands felt like fire at her sides.

"Are you okay?" he asked, lifting her chin.

"I don't know."

"I can take your mind off everything if you let me." He crushed her to him as his mouth persuaded her.

It didn't take long for her mind to forget everything else. She felt his hands on her hips. She never imagined them feeling so warm and gentle. But he was right. He could make her forget her troubles. Her body felt liquid as he glided his hands over her soft breasts. Her head fell back, and he lowered his mouth onto her neck. She moaned and pressed her body up against his.

She pulled his ear to her mouth. "I don't want to talk anymore."

"We don't have to." He took her in his arms.

His hands traveled up the small of her back as he pulled her toward the patio. He opened the door and they walked outside. The warm Georgia air was perfect. He set her up on the table and pulled off his shirt. She rubbed his bare chest as he bent to kiss her. He pulled the straps down on her gown and kissed her bare shoulders. Her skin was softer than silk. Dray eased her g-string off and went to his knees. She moaned with each seductive flick of his tongue, holding his head as he savored her. She turned to butter when he rubbed his hands up and down the insides of her thighs. Then, she exploded. It was so earth shattering she almost fell off the table. Dray decided they should go inside.

As he carried her to the bedroom, she could feel him pressing hard up against her. He put her on the bed and removed her clothes. He kissed every inch of her body. There wasn't a spot he missed. Monica was so heated she couldn't move. She lay still as his hands rubbed her breasts. He licked her nipples until they glistened. And she did the same. Consumed with passion, he couldn't remember what life had been like before her. She pushed him on his back and lowered her mouth on him. He growled as she pleased him, his body weak with desire. She licked his navel, his chest, and his neck. Her skillful play was a match for his own. When she straddled him, he was panting.

He lifted to take one of her breasts in his mouth. "I want you, Monica," he groaned against them. "I've missed you."

She arched back while he played with her, clutching his head to her breasts. She was so hot for him, she thought she'd die if he didn't take her. She kissed him hungrily.

"I've missed you too."

Slowly, he lifted her and placed her on her back. He plunged his hard love inside her, surrounding himself with her warmth. Her moans echoed throughout the apartment as he pulled her legs around his waist. She caressed the length of his back as he gripped her derriere. Sweat crept slowly from his face onto her shoulder as he thrust himself in deeper. Her damp locks fell into his face, absorbing his sweat. The warmth of his glide sent chills up and down her spine. He moved deliciously between her hips as he fought the waves of ecstasy. Monica rested her head on Dray's chest. She tried not to think about it, but the Rodney saga consumed her again. She sighed, and Dray knew something was up.

"What's wrong?" he asked, stroking her hair.

She took a deep breath. "Nothing really, I just keep thinking about Bill's reaction to what I said."

"Oh."

She lifted her head. "He didn't like it."

"Did you expect him to?" Dray cupped her chin. "You're one of his best employees. He can't have you set a bad example."

Dray gave Monica a lingering kiss. She was dazed for a moment.

"So, have you changed your mind?" he asked.

She came back to earth. "About what?"

"Representing Rodney. I think you should."

She sat up quickly and glared at him. "Is that what you were trying to do a little while ago? Persuade me to change my mind?"

"No, hell no. I was just asking. Please don't start tripping," he said, grabbing his boxers.

"So now I'm trippin'?"

"No, I'm just saying . . . damn, Monica. I just asked you a question. Stop being so goddamn defensive all the time."

Monica pulled herself up from the circle of his arms and clutched the sheet tight. "Dray, I'm not being defensive." She paused. "Why don't you just go, I need to get some sleep."

He knew where this conversation was headed. "Monica?"

"What?" She threw her head back. "Just get out. You got what you came for, so go home."

Her statement stunned him. He thought for sure after the fire they started, the last thing she'd want him to do is leave. He jumped out of bed and searched for his clothes. Monica pouted as she got out of bed.

Dray was angry now. "So you think I just came over here to screw you? Is that it?"

She didn't reply.

He continued, "Don't play me like I'm some nigga out to take advantage of you. You know me better than that."

She pulled on her robe and walked to the kitchen. "I didn't say all that, Dray. Stop putting words in my mouth."

He pulled on his pants and followed her. "You don't have to say it. You're talkin' to me like I just don't give a damn. I'm just worried about you, Monica. Is that so bad?"

"You don't need to worry about me," she said, pouring a glass of water. "I can take care of myself. Always have, always will."

"Can you?" He walked up behind her, pressing his chest to her back. He kissed her neck softly.

She turned to push him away. "Yes, I can. Why don't you just go? Please."

Dray was stunned. "Is that what you really want?" His handsome face was masked with anger.

"Yes. I need to be alone."

Monica wondered if Rodney was the real reason he'd come in the first place. He was wasting his time trying to convince her to represent him. Of course, she knew he'd say it was in the best interest of the company and that she'd be a team player if she did so. But what did he know? He hadn't been with the company long enough to assess anything or anyone. She knew he had ambitions of becoming a record company president one day, and that was fine. She just didn't think he had the knowledge or experience to deal with an artist in legal trouble.

"I think you're making a big mistake," Dray said, pulling his shirt on. "Not representing Rodney is going to hurt the company, not to mention your reputation as a publicist."

"So now we're back to talking about Rodney?" she said angrily.

Dray continued, "You think people will want to work with you after you turn your back on a client in his time of need?"

"I don't care what they think." She shook her head and hung it low. "You think you know it all, don't you? You don't know half of what I do. This game that's being played has no rules. And in case you didn't know, Drayton, this is the music business. It may seem like all fun and games, but it's business."

"I know that, Monica. What the hell do you think I am? Stupid? I hear every word you're saying, and no I don't know everything about this shit. But do you think for one minute Bill would have me move all the way down here from Chicago if I didn't know what I was doing?"

"I would hope that wouldn't be the case." She shook her head. "You don't understand how difficult this is."

"Yes, I do."

Her eyes clouded with visions of the past. "No, you don't! If I represent him now it will go against everything I stand for, Dray. You don't know what he did to me . . . the pain I had to endure. I can't just forget about it that easily."

"Monica, I know what he did was wrong. But you have to let it go." He entered the kitchen where she stood with her palms resting against the counter.

"I just don't see why I should do this. Is it just so the big rap star can keep from being attacked by the media when I know he's wrong? You know he's wrong."

He held her face. "I'm just trying to help you keep your job! What are you going to do if Bill fires you?"

"You sound just like him. And I don't need you to help me keep my job. I don't need you for anything."

Dray backed off. His expression was like stone. "Fuck it then, I'm gone."

"Bye."

He gave an approving nod. "Just remember who decided to break this off," he yelled.

CHAPTER 21

A few weeks after Rodney's arrest, things were starting to get back to normal. Handle Up's offices were extremely busy, mostly the press trying to get information on Rodney. Other than that, there wasn't much talk about what happened. The employees went back to their usual duties. Bill took a few days off, leaving Terry in charge. Dray was at the Georgia Dome negotiating the Prima Donnas' performance for the upcoming Atlanta Falcons football season. Cameron was out of town on business for another artist, and Monica used her time to catch up on some projects she'd been neglecting.

She wrote a press release announcing the film debut of their leading male vocalist. Tyrone Steele was a handsome Georgian with a syrupy tenor voice. He'd been generous enough a number of times to lend his background vocals on songs for the Prima Donnas and Double R. A few years earlier, Monica convinced Bill to sign him while he was a courier for a delivery service. She enjoyed having him as a client because he was hardworking and low-key. He lived a in a suburb outside of Atlanta, and the only time he was seen in public was if he was performing or attending a label function. There was an air of mystery around him, and Monica wanted to keep it that way.

Bill's assistant sent out a memo announcing his hiring of a freelance publicist to represent Rodney. Because of it, Monica's duties shriveled tremendously. It didn't matter, she was considering leaving the company anyway. She'd been getting dirty looks from a couple of the female staff members, mostly the ones who worked under Vera's wing. They envied Monica's position, and probably hoped she'd quit or get fired. She could care less. She had too many contacts and could easily start her own PR firm if she wanted. The only people who still seemed to be on her side were Patrice and Beverly. Dray might have been, but she didn't know for sure. They weren't speaking.

"Here's your mail," Patrice said, coming into the office. She set the stack on her desk. "So how've you been? I know things are weird right now. Those girls in accounting have been saying that Bill should have let you go. You know they love Rodney."

"I know, and I don't care. They just hate me cuz they ain't me," Monica sighed. "I'm just trying to finish reviewing these press releases for Tyrone's upcoming appearance in John Singleton's new movie."

"I heard about that. That should be cool."
Monica nodded and tore open the first envelope from her stack. Patrice nervously rubbed her hands. "Listen, Monica, I don't mean to be nosy, but is everything okay with you and Mr. Lewis?"

A shadow of alarm touched Monica's face. "W-what do you mean?"

"I was just wondering why I hadn't seen you two together in a while."

Monica gasped as if she were out of breath.

Patrice continued, "I just thought you guys were getting pretty serious."

Monica cleared her throat. "Mr. Lewis and I are coworkers, nothing more. I think it's in both of our interests to keep things professional. And I'm sure he feels the same way."

"If you don't mind my saying so, I think Mr. Lewis likes you a whole lot. I think he'd do anything for you."

The thought of that made Monica smile.

"Well, Patrice, that's sweet. But I don't think Mr. Lewis is concerned with me right now. He's busy too. Don't get yourself in knots trying to figure us out."

"Well, that shuts me up," Patrice replied, defeated. "I'll guess I'll go back to my desk now."

Good, Monica thought as she opened the rest of her mail. There was a party invitation from *Shazz*, a local African-American entertainment magazine having its awards banquet. Every month, the magazine has a new singer or actor on the cover. It had a circulation of probably a little over 500,000 readers. Handle Up had been nominated for a few awards, so Monica would definitely attend. Since she and Dray weren't on good terms, she would have to go to the party solo. She checked the box marked "RSVP" and slid it into the accompanying envelope. After proofing a press release, she printed it and saved it on disk. After lunch, she would get it out over the wire. It was easier to release press releases on the Internet, though she would still send them to all the magazines and newspapers via snail mail. She clipped the press release inside a file folder and went out into the hallway.

As she headed towards the copy room, she saw Savannah Morgan sitting in the waiting area. Monica wondered what she was doing there. Harassing people as usual? Savannah was dressed sharply in a gray suit, a blue blouse, and gray heels. Her blouse was open exposing an enormous amount of cleavage. Monica was embarrassed for her. She couldn't believe Savannah was going to such extremes to get Dray's attention.

Dray emerged from his office. He didn't even look at Monica. His eyes fell on Savannah.

"Ms. Morgan."

"Good afternoon, Mr. Lewis," Savannah purred. She didn't sound like someone who wanted just an interview. "It's so nice to see you again."

They shook hands.

"It's nice to see you too," he said smiling. Monica felt her face turn red. "Right this way, Ms. Morgan," he said, leading her to his office.

Monica's brow creased with worry. *What was Savannah up to? Was she trying to push up on Dray?*

Dray offered Savannah a seat and then sat down behind his desk.

She set her handbag down in the chair beside her and pulled out her notepad and pen. She smiled seductively and crossed her legs.

"So, Ms. Morgan, what can I do for you today?" he asked.

"Well," she said, tapping her lips with the pen, "I wanted to know if I could spotlight you on one of my segments. I'm doing a feature on young professionals in the area and you immediately popped in my head."

"Is that right?" He knew she was lying.

"Yes. You've successfully made the transition from Chicago to Atlanta, and I'm quite sure people want to find out about the real you."

"The real me," he smiled. "Well, I'm flattered, Miss Morgan. But I'm not anyone special."

"Of course you are. You've been here less than a year and you're doing such wonderful work with those girls, and you're handling that Double R business quite well. Bill said you're his right hand."

Dray looked surprised. "Bill said that?"

"Yes, he did," she said leaning forward. He could see how low her blouse was.

"I'm surprised you didn't want to interview someone like Monica. She's done more than I have these days."

Savannah's smile faded. "I think you're far more interesting than you realize, Mr. Lewis. Monica is . . . Well, let's just say she's not someone I would spotlight."

It was apparent Savannah had more than an interview in mind for Drayton Lewis. Little did she know he only had eyes for a fiery publicist named Monica Rose Holiday. Whether they were on good terms or not, her essence still soared through his veins. Nonetheless, Savannah Morgan wasn't easily daunted.

Dray sat across from her wondering what she was really up to. She'd been smiling at him non-stop since they'd come into his office. Wide-eyed and eager, she wasn't hiding her desire for him well. As he took in her overly made-up face, he wished she was Monica. If Savannah weren't so consumed with lust, she would see that his heart belonged to Monica. But Dray decided to play along, and see how far she would go.

"So, Mr. Lewis. Tell me a little about yourself."

He leaned back in his chair. "What do you want to know?"

"Where'd you go to school? Do you have any children? What kind of women do you date et cetera."

His mouth twisted. "Ms. Morgan those are very personal questions."

"I know. I'm just trying to break the ice."

Smoothly, he replied, "Consider it broken. And let's cut the bull. What do you really want?"

She sighed and straightened her back a little. After fiddling with the buttons on her blazer, she placed her notepad neatly in her lap and leaned over the desk. The gesture exposed her cleavage. Dray swallowed hard as he tried not to stare.

"I'd really like for you to accompany me to this magazine award ceremony on the twenty-fifth of this month. I know you got an invitation. Everyone in your office did. I'd like you to let me show you all of what Atlanta has to offer."

He hesitated, measuring her for a moment. What did she mean, offer? "Are you asking me out on a date, Ms. Morgan?"

"Only if you're accepting, Mr. Lewis."

He flipped open his date book and checked the date. He was free. In the back of his mind, he knew better. But why should his spat with Monica keep him from having a little fun? Savannah wanted more than a date, but he'd give her a fair chance to deny it. A mischievous grin crossed his face. "Well, Ms. Morgan, I guess you've got yourself a date."

As he marked the calendar and briefed her on his life, he realized it was lunchtime. He'd much rather be having this conversation over a bowl of pasta than in front of paperwork.

"Have you eaten yet, Savannah?"

A huge smile came across her face. "No. No, I haven't."

"Well, why don't you join me for lunch? There's a great Italian place not far from here."

"Spasso's," Savannah said. "I love it."

"Yeah, Spasso's."

Savannah felt as though she had won the lottery. "Sounds great. Just let me call the office."

♫

Dray let Savannah out in front of Spasso's and parked his truck around the back. It was a perfect day for dining outside, which is what he wanted to do anyway. He emerged from the parking lot, looking rather handsome in his steel-gray suit, an indigo shirt, and matching tie. He made small talk while they waited to be seated.

"So how long have you known Monica?" he asked.

Savannah sighed. "Too long. Since we were in college." She flipped her hair. "She was always everyone's favorite co-ed." She slipped her arm in Dray's. "But I don't want to talk about Monica."

They followed the hostess who took them to a cozy table near the edge of the patio, away from the sun. He knew Savannah enjoyed being the center of attention. It gave her a chance to be seen by some of her news-watching fans. As soon as they sat down, an Italian looking guy placed two glasses of water on the table. The waitress came over soon after.

"Good afternoon. My name is Rachel. I'll be your server. She handed them menus and pulled out her pen and pad. "Can I get you something to drink?"

"Yeeess!" Savannah put her hand on Dray's, making him very uncomfortable. "I'll have a glass of Chardonnay. What would you like, Mr. Lewis?"

He pulled his hand away nervously and placed it under the table. "I'd like a Corona, please." He usually didn't drink while he was on the clock, but he figured it might help him relax. Savannah was too aggressive for his taste. He liked his women subtle. He contemplated telling her he had a meeting.

The waitress returned with their drinks and asked, "Are you ready to order?"

"No, not yet," Savannah said, "give us a moment or two."

"Okay," the waitress said. She smiled and slipped the pad in her apron. "I'll give you a little more time." She left.

Dray didn't like Savannah's bossiness. He found it a bit overbearing. Since he invited her to lunch, he figured he may as well go through with it.

"You know, Dray," she began. "I've had my eye on you since we met at that party a few months ago." She slipped her hand on his again.

Jaded, Dray eyed her sharply. "Oh, really," he said.

"Yes, really . . . So tell me, Mr. Lewis, have you gotten your feet wet in our lovely town?"

He chuckled nervously, and carefully moved her hand. "I've done alright. I don't have any complaints."

Savannah wouldn't let up. She moved her chair close to Dray and put her hand on his thigh. "Well, if you need me for anything, I'm always available. I'm a good shoulder to lean on."

221

Nervous, Dray took a sip of his water and looked around. When his eyes found hers she was gawking. The type of leaning she wanted him to do definitely didn't involve a shoulder.

♫

"Patrice, I'll be back shortly," Monica said. "I have to run over to Kinko's and a couple of other places." She checked her watch. "When the girls get here, have them wait in the boardroom for me. I need to talk to them about their contract."

"Did they get the gig?"

"Yes, but I don't like it. I need to have Terry go over the contract with me in depth. Some of that legal mumbo jumbo is over my head. I'll be back in a few."

"Okay."

Monica headed downstairs and had the valet bring her car around. She slid onto the cool leather seat and flipped her mirror up. As she pulled out into the street, she reapplied her lipstick. She almost hit a black Range Rover that was double-parked in the street.

"Great," she said, tossing the tube in her purse. "Why can't people pull over out of the way?"

Just as she was about to try and go around the car, Rodney appeared. He'd been standing on the side of the truck, and she hadn't seen him. She waited for him to pass, but instead he approached the car. Fear knotted inside her as he stuck his head inside the window. She gasped as he grabbed her face.

"What's up, Moni?" His eyes darkened.

Monica felt her heart pounding in her chest. Rodney tightened his grip on her face. "I'm a little pissed at you, baby. Why you didn't wanna represent a nigga? You know I can't go to jail. And I know you want me to."

She gasped, panting in fear.

"I know you gon' tell Bill you changed your mind, aren't you?" He didn't give her a chance to reply. "You better."

She was too terrified to respond.

"Okay?" he growled.

Monica nodded. When he released her, she tried to catch her breath. When she calmed down, she managed to pull out of the parking lot. She could feel her hands shaking on the steering wheel. She drove two blocks before she realized tears were streaming down her cheeks. She was dazed as she headed north, scanning her surroundings like a paranoid schizophrenic. When she got to Buckhead, she got another surprise. Dray sitting outside Spasso's having lunch with Savannah, and he seemed to be enjoying himself. She glared at both of them as the light turned green. *What the hell were they doing together?* she wondered. *And why did he look so happy?* She flipped up her visor, and burned rubber.

When Dray and Savannah got back from lunch, Dray couldn't wait to ditch her. He was tired of hearing about country clubs and cotillions. He made an excuse as to why their lunch date couldn't continue and showed her to her car. He almost regretted agreeing to lunch, and he knew he'd be in trouble when he escorted her to the magazine award dinner. She talked too much, and it was always about her. As he waited for the elevator, Monica returned from her errands. She held her lunch in one hand and her keys in the other. They made eye contact, but neither of them said a word. Dray wanted to but feared her reaction. As they waited, he smiled to himself, admiring her cute little suit and heels. She was still a classy lady, whether she was speaking to him or not. When the elevator arrived he allowed her to enter first. She thanked him silently, and kept her eyes on the buttons as they rode to the seventh floor. His cologne brought back memories. She'd loved the way it smelled when it lingered between her sheets. It reminded her of him. When the elevator stopped, Monica rushed to the door. She stormed out and went straight down the hall to her office, shutting the door behind her. Dray walked to his office and did the same.

In her meeting with Terry, Monica voiced her opinion about the Prima Donnas' cosmetic endorsement contract with Star Cosmetics.

"I'm not feeling this contract. It's not enough." She paced the floor of the boardroom with her hand to her chin. "This deal is nowhere near the one they gave those white girls a couple of years ago. They had a platinum album. But they weren't close to having a triple platinum album."

Terry flipped the papers back and forth and shrugged. "Really, Monica, it's not that bad. This is a standard deal. I mean, consider that this is the girls' first album. It's platinum, which is a good thing, and they're doing really well. If this is what the company is giving them, why rock the boat?"

"Whatever. I just don't like it. I mean, I know I don't have the final say, but they should get more money."

"Monica, $300,000 per person is not a bad deal. It's almost a million dollars."

"So why couldn't they make it a million. What? They aren't worth the extra $100,000?" She took the papers from him. "They're going to get a million, believe that."

"Monica, you can't tell these people what to do with their money. This isn't even really your area. Bill just asked you to look at the contract to see if it was fair. And it is. The girls get an equal amount of money." Terry rubbed his eyes and sighed. "This is a prestigious cosmetics company. They're not going to appreciate you marching in there like the Queen of Sheba and telling them what to do."

"Watch me. Bill knew I wouldn't like it."

"Well, I'm not gonna tell the girls you lost their contract, if you screw it up."

"You won't have to."

Dray's eyes fell hard on Monica as she emerged from the conference room. He was standing in the lobby talking to Double R. Seeing them together, she hurried past them carrying papers to her office. Her heart was beating nervously in her chest. She sat down and took a sip of water, wondering why Rodney was there. As she took a deep breath, she stepped out of the office. He wasn't about to ruin what she'd worked so hard for.

"I'm not representing you," she said as she marched up to where Rodney and Dray were standing. They looked at each, other and then Dray handed her some paperwork.

"You will represent him, if you don't want to be replaced," Dray said.

Rodney snickered behind his hand, but Dray hushed him.

Monica's neck rolled. "What do you mean replaced? You don't have the authority to hire or fire anyone."

Vera and Beverly were coming down the hall when they heard the commotion.

"Actually, I do. You fall under my realm on the tier of personnel. Since I'm the director of A&R, I tell you what to do. Now, if you'll excuse me, I have some work to do." He walked toward his office as Rodney stood with Monica. "Keep the copy of the contract. It's yours."

She glared at him with burning eyes and went back to her office. "Not again," she said to herself. "He is not going to win again."

CHAPTER 22

Monica pulled up in front of the Grand Hyatt in Buckhead. The valet, a handsome young black man, helped her out of the car. He gawked at her as she slipped a twenty-dollar bill into his hand. She went inside as he got behind the wheel and pulled off toward the parking lot.

As she made her way to the Grand Ballroom, she stopped to sign her name in the guest book and looked up to see a huge fish bowl.

"It's for the contest," the white woman behind the table whispered. "We're giving away three thousand-dollar gift checks for Lenox Square and Phipps Plaza."

"That's a lot of money for a gift check," she said, dropping her card into the bowl. I guess the magazine is doing well."

"Very," the woman said, winking. "Enjoy yourself."

Maybe I should drop in two, Monica thought. It would give her a better chance at winning. When the woman turned her head, she slipped another card in and shuffled the bowl. Nothing beats a fail but a try. She clutched her purse and went inside the ballroom.

Every entertainer in the city wanted to be featured in *Shazz*.

Despite its lack of quality editorial content, their features on business people and celebrity homes were always nice. Most of the crowd were business professionals, news media, and of course, the honorees themselves. As she searched the room trying to see who's who, she found Bill at the bar with his wife, Karen. She didn't expect to see them. Bill had been out of sight since Rodney's arrest. He was tired of being harassed by the press. She adjusted her dress and decided to go and say hello. A band was playing soft music as she made her way to the bar. Karen was dressed in a long white Armani sheath, and Bill in a black Armani tuxedo. They looked like the ultimate power couple, the beautiful young wife and the wealthy husband. Monica strutted toward them as they sipped martinis.

"Monica!" Karen squealed. "How are you, darling?" Karen offered her a hug and the bourgeois folks' kiss of a fake smooch on each side of the face. She took Monica by the hand and examined her fitted tube dress. "You are working it tonight, girl," she joked.

Bill nodded in agreement and said coolly, "She's always a class act, baby, you know that." He set his drink on the bar and turned serious for a moment. "Did Dray talk to you about Rodney?"

Monica's smile disappeared. "If you call telling me what I have to do to keep my job talking, then I guess so."

"Don't take things the wrong way, Monica," Karen said. "We don't want to lose you."

Bill continued, "We need you to stay with us. Now if you're not happy, we'll have to see what we can do about that."

Monica watched them, silently.

"Honey," Karen said, tugging Bill's arm. "There's the mayor and his wife. Let's go say hello." She waved goodbye to Monica and pulled Bill away.

Monica checked her watched and ordered a Cosmo. She needed one to loosen up. While she waited for her drink, she fumbled to find her seating assignment. The crowd began to disperse toward their seats because it was almost time for the program to begin. She slid the bartender a ten and took her drink. Table fourteen was in the middle of the room, close to the stage. She made her way to her seat and nearly spilled her drink when she saw Dray and Savannah seated at the table. She looked around the room to see where Bill and Karen were, wondering if the extra chairs were for them.

"Hello!" an older man said, as he stood up to help her into her seat. "Let me get that for you, dear."

"Hi," she said softly. "Thank you."

"You're welcome, dear. I'm Dr. Marvin Mitchell." He extended his hand. "This is my wife, Ruby." They were a nice-looking older couple. Ruby smiled and nodded. Monica had heard Dr. Mitchell was one of Atlanta's most prominent black physicians. His family had been in the city for more than fifty decades.

She shook their hands and set her purse on the table. "Nice to meet you. I'm Monica Holiday. I'm the publicist for Handle Up Records."

Their eyes widened. And Mrs. Mitchell spoke. "Oh, honey, she works for Bill." She leaned toward Monica. "What a mess that rapper has gotten you all into."

Monica nodded and looked around the table. Everyone had started eating their salads. Dray kept his eyes on her as she sat down. She placed her napkin in her lap and bowed her head to say grace. When she finished, she poured dressing on her salad. Monica couldn't believe Dray was bold enough to show up with Savannah, who was busy talking to a woman seated behind her. She hadn't even seen Monica come to the table. Monica started to eat her salad. By the time she finished, Savannah was done chatting. She turned around, and her eyes grew wide with surprise.

"Monica!"

Damn, Monica thought. "Savannah," she said as she sipped the iced water in front of her. She set the glass down.

"Oh my God, we — I didn't expect to see you here."

"Really now, Savannah? Everyone at the office got an invitation. I didn't expect to see you here."

Savannah rattled on and on as Monica ate her salad. "Hey, baby," she heard Savannah say to Dray.

Monica froze and looked up from her plate. Dray. She cast her eyes in his direction, but he didn't look at her. Now he was Savannah's baby? She couldn't believe he stooped so low. Savannah turned around to greet some other guests. Dray watched Monica, but didn't say anything. She couldn't get over him showing up with Savannah. Of all the things he could have done, this was the lowest. He figured it would be best to keep his mouth shut with all the tension in the air. He knew Monica was upset, but what could he do? He was a gentleman and would never leave a lady stranded on a date. But that same gentleman longed to be in the arms of the woman who sat so dignified across from him. What was he thinking escorting Savannah to an awards dinner when he could barely stand her?

"Hey, Monica," he managed to say.

She pushed her hair behind her ear. "Drayton."

He knew she was angry. She never called him by his whole name. He parted his lips to speak but was interrupted.

As the mistress of ceremonies approached the podium, everyone stopped eating. She gave a short welcome and told everyone dinner was on the way to the tables. Once everyone was served, the awards ceremony began. The waiter brought out dinners that consisted of either chicken or fish with a fancy array of rice and vegetables. Monica chose the fish and examined it closely as it was placed in front of her. Visually, it was appealing, taste could be another story.

"Not bad," she said as she took a bite. It was grilled filet-of-sole. Monica hadn't eaten any since her last visit to California. She tasted the vegetables, which were a bit dry and buttered her rolls. Since the dinner was free, she was going to make the best of it. Savannah and

Dray ate quietly. He felt uneasy and couldn't look Monica in the eye. Monica ignored him. It didn't matter that he had the softest touch she'd ever felt or that his lips gave her the kiss of life. They'll be kissing Savannah tonight, she thought. She prayed for the night to end.

After Handle Up received its two awards, Monica decided to leave early. She wanted to make it home before the press could question her about anything going on at Handle Up. She wasn't in the mood to answer questions about anything. While everyone went to congratulate one another she slipped out the door. The still-eager valet happily brought her car around. He held the door open for her, and she graciously handed him another twenty-dollar bill.

Shortly after the announcing of the raffle winners, everyone began to clear the ballroom. Dray tucked Monica's gift certificate into his coat pocket. She'd won the thousand-dollar certificate for Lenox Square. He couldn't wait to give it to her. He escorted Savannah to the lobby as they prepared to leave. She'd been hinting that she wanted him to stay over, but he wasn't interested. It was bad enough she didn't tell him she used to date Bill. When Savannah made her exit to the rest room, Bill excused himself from Karen and approached Dray.

"I see you escorted Ms. Morgan tonight. Is she driving you crazy yet?" he asked.

Dray managed a smile. "Yeah. Is it that obvious?"

"It is." Bill pulled a cigar from his coat pocket. "Well, Savannah is an easy lay but hard to get rid of. Better watch your wallet too." He gave Dray a swift pat on the back. "Good night."

"Good night, Mr. Sanders."

Dray pulled up in front of Savannah's apartment in Lithonia. He was more than happy to let her out. He was sick of seeing her and listening to her. He'd never heard a woman talk about herself as much as Savannah did. She talked about herself all night. About everyone she knew, who was seeing who, about the city's local politicians. Dray had heard enough. All he wanted was to get rid of her and get back to the city. He pulled the envelope that he'd gotten from his coat pocket and made his way back to Buckhead.

♫◡

At home, Monica slipped into her pink Victoria's Secret chemise and prepared to lie down. She brushed her hair and clipped it on top of her head. Since she didn't have to get up early, she'd spend time reading the newspaper articles about Rodney so she could draft a press release. She knew in her heart what he did was wrong, but she had to keep her job just a little while longer. She was prepared to meet with his new publicist and pick up where she left off. She pulled her robe on, went into the living room, and settled on the couch.

"No Change in Victim's Condition," one headline read. "Atlanta Woman Wounded by Rapper Still Clinging to Life," another read. Monica closed her eyes for a moment. The news made her sick to her stomach. With all the talk about and concern for Rodney, people forgot about the victims. Monica threw the papers aside and went to fix some tea. As she filled the pot with water, someone rang the buzzer.

CHAPTER 23

When Monica opened the door, Dray was standing there holding an envelope. She closed her robe and tied it.

"What are you doing here?" she asked.

He smiled as he handed her the envelope. "You won one of the thousand-dollar gift certificates," he said, loosening his tie. "They called your name after you left, so I accepted it for you."

"And what did Savannah think about that? Isn't she waiting for you?"

"No," he said, "I took her ass straight home."

"Really," she said sarcastically. Monica didn't want to let his handsome ass in. He'd already turned her world upside down. But the way he looked in that damn tuxedo made her forget how mad she was.

He looked deep into her eyes. "I didn't come here to talk about Savannah."

Monica's eyes were filled with skepticism.

"Do I have to stand out here all night? Or are you going to invite me in?"

She showed him in.

Monica looked down at the floor, and then up at Dray. "You didn't have to come all the way over here to bring me this."

"I know, but I wanted to see you. I would have called, but I didn't think you would answer."

She shrugged. "You're probably right," she said softly. She put the gift certificate on the end table.

Dray's eyes filled with tenderness as he came toward her. "I figured it would be harder to turn me away if we were face-to-face."

He was right about that. She shot him a withering glance. "Dray, this really isn't a good time. It's been a long night."

He pulled her hand gently. "I know, but we need to talk. I don't like this distance between us, Monica."

"Well, I'm sure Savannah can fill whatever space you need to have filled." She rolled her eyes.

Dray couldn't argue. "I guess I deserved that one. But it's not what you think. I'm not interested in Savannah, Monica. I was just being polite because she asked me to go with her to the dinner. She's not even my type. She talks too damn much."

"And what about your lunch date the other day? I guess that was courtesy, too, huh? You seemed to be enjoying her conversation then."

He stared blankly. He didn't know she knew about that. "It was a business luncheon, Monica, nothing more. Please believe that."

"I don't know what to believe." Her voice trembled. "It doesn't matter anyway, because I don't care."

"If you don't care, why are you shaking?" Dray asked. He ran a finger across the base of her neck, feeling her skin.

A soft gasp escaped Monica as she closed her eyes. "I'm not shaking," she told him, pulling away.

He stepped in front of her. "Yes, you are," he said, lifting her chin.

Monica avoided his eyes. If she looked at him she would crumble, and then he would know how she really felt. She wanted to wrap her arms around him and feel the warmth of his body one more time. He could sense her aching as he put his hand to her face.

"Why are you here?" she asked, pulling away from him again.

"I wanted to see you, Monica. You looked beautiful tonight. When I saw you in that dress, sitting across from me, I wanted to make Savannah disappear."

"I guess I should be flattered."

Dray rested his hands in the pockets of his tuxedo and followed her to the couch. "It's the truth."

Monica sat down on the couch and cut him off. "Yeah, I know."

"Could you just hear me out?"

Monica folded her arms. "If this is the part where you get really sentimental and mushy, save it. I've had enough shock for the evening."

"Monica, I'm just trying to be honest with you. You know I care about you."

"I wonder sometimes."

"You don't have to wonder. I do care about you." He decided to change the subject. Monica was still upset. "You know Savannah is jealous of you."

Monica rolled her eyes.

He continued, "Seriously, she talked about how well you've done for yourself. And how everybody loved you on campus. I think that's why she has tried to compete with you all this time."

Monica remained blasé. She could care less about Savannah.

"Listen, Monica," he continued, "I know we've screwed things up over the last couple of months. I just want us to be friends again. It's driving me crazy that we're not as close as we once were."

She shook her head and closed her eyes. "Dray, we would never work. You and I are on two different pages, and neither of us is turning."

"I'm trying to," he said, "but you keep fighting me on everything."

Monica searched the heavens for guidance. "Here I was trying to focus on my career, and then you came along and made me fall in love with you. I realize now that I can't have both."

Her revelation broke his heart. Even after he promised himself he'd never let a woman hurt him again, he let his guard down for her. What more could he say at this point? He would return to work and talk to her about nothing more than business. If he had to know about anything else that was going on in her life, it might tear him apart. He wanted to touch the strands of her hair one last time as they dangled down her back, to feel their softness. Then, at least he'd be able to go home somewhat happy. She got up from her seat and quickly rushed to the door.

"You'd better go. It's getting late," Monica said. She dropped her eyes to hide the hurt.

Dray checked his watch. "I guess so."

Just then a highlight from the evening news flashed. "Breaking news tonight," the announcer began. "Nicole Johnson, the young woman who was assaulted by rapper Rodney "Double R" Robinson two months ago, has died from a massive brain hemorrhage. Ms. Johnson was a twenty-year-old college student from Miami . . . "

Monica felt her chest heave. Sorrow knotted in her. "Oh, my God!" she yelled, burying her face in her hands. "He killed her!"

She sobbed and felt Dray's hands on her shoulders. He pulled her close and turned her around. Slowly he moved her hands away from her eyes.

"Come here," he whispered. "Let me hold you."

Monica clutched him tightly, sobbing. The tears she shed were for her and Nicole. Dray held her until she let all of her pain out. She needed him now, and he wouldn't walk away. He was still holding her hand when she pulled away suddenly.

"I'm sorry," she said.

He lifted her chin with his finger. "For what?"

She avoided his eyes. "You see. This is exactly what I was trying to tell you. Rodney is dangerous. I can't believe you want me to represent him. What am I supposed to say now?"

Dray shook his head. "I know, I should have listened to you."

"But you didn't!" Monica snapped.

He shook his head regretfully. "I know, and I'm sorry."

"Most men are," she mumbled.

"What?" Dray couldn't believe what she just said.

When she didn't respond, he decided it was best if he left. If he stayed they would do nothing but argue, and he didn't want that. He wondered if Bill had heard the news yet. If he had, he'd be calling him at any moment. He wondered if the police had gone to pick up Rodney. He'd been lying low ever since his release from jail. Things were about to get really bad for him.

Dray realized Monica wasn't going to say anything else. "I guess I'll talk to you later," he said, scanning her face. He left without another word, and Monica let the tears flow.

The police station was swamped with reporters and fans. Since Rodney's early-morning arrest at his Sandy Spring's home, the city was in an uproar. After Nicole Flowers' family arrived from Miami, they were rushed to safety after they left the police station. Rodney, Bill, Dray, and Rodney's lawyer, Warren, sat in an interrogation room where Rodney was held, handcuffed with his ankles shackled. Warren reviewed Shanty Green's statement about the incident that took place in Rodney's home. He held his hand to his mouth as he read the graphic details.

"I can't believe you slammed the girl's head into the wall," he yelled. "What the hell were you thinking?"

Rodney ignored the question. "I feel like a slave," he said with his head hung low.

"You should feel like a damn fool!" Bill snapped. "I can't believe you let yourself get in this mess. I knew you were crazy, but this unfuckin' believable."

"Damn, Bill, I didn't kill her on purpose. She attacked me. What the hell was I supposed to do?"

Bill slammed his hands on the table. "You think a jury gives a fuck about you attacking her? You're a grown man, nigga! You slammed a woman's head into the wall, someone more than a hundred pounds smaller than you. You think her parents want to hear about her attacking you?"

"No," Rodney said, holding his head down.

"Well, you better hope they don't find out about what you did to Monica," Dray said, folding his arms.

Rodney looked up wide-eyed. "What?"

Bill's eyes widened too. "What did he do to Monica?" he asked angrily.

"I'm sorry man," Rodney said, looking at Dray. "I know how you feel about her. I messed it up for you, didn't I?"

Bill hadn't gotten his answer. "What did you do to Monica?" he repeated to Rodney. His tone was demanding.

"Tell him, Rodney," Dray said. "Go ahead."

"Tell me what?" Bill asked, looking up at Dray.

Rodney settled back in his chair. "Monica's not like any woman I know," he said, lighting his cigarette. "She doesn't fuckin' listen."

Dray's expression clouded with anger. "Why'd you do it?" Dray asked.

Bill interrupted. "Rodney, did you hit Monica?" he asked calmly.

Rodney put his head down and then held it up. "Yeah." A bitter jealousy stirred in him as he looked at Dray.

"I'm listening," Bill said, cracking his knuckles.

Rodney continued, "This dude tried to holler at her while we were out one night." He took a drag off the cigarette. "She was being friendly to him. I thought she wanted to get with him, but she was trying to tell him we were together. I ended up fighting the dude and she told me I overreacted. I just snapped. I lost it."

Bill stared in disbelief. Now he knew the real reason Monica didn't like Rodney.

"Well," Warren began, "you haven't exactly made up for it either. This isn't going to look good. When's the last time you've been to a doctor?"

"For what?" Rodney asked angrily.

"To see if you have some type of mental disorder."

"Man, hell naw! I ain't got no damn mental disorder."

"Well if you get bail, you're going to see one tomorrow. Something in your head is causing you to go off, and I want to find out what it is."

As they got up to leave, the guard opened the door. "Times up," he said sternly. He helped Rodney up from the chair to escort him back to his cell.

"We'll see you later, Rodney," Warren said. He closed his portfolio and followed Bill and Dray out the door. When they stepped outside the precinct, Bill pulled out a cigarette. He lit it and took a puff.

"This boy's gonna do some time. I can feel it," he said. "But he's our bread and butter. What am I supposed to do? Cut him off?" Dray put his hands in his pockets and looked around. "So you think he'll do some time, huh?"

"I know so." Bill flicked the ashes from his cigarette and pulled his car keys from his pocket and sighed. "I'll see y'all later."

They watched as he got in his car, then Warren left. Dray waved goodbye and stood on the steps for a minute. He wondered if he had made a mistake leaving Chicago. He thought he'd left all the drama behind.

CHAPTER 24

Monica couldn't believe it was almost July. It was so hot outside, the sun needed shade. She and Robin were enjoying drinks at Robin's townhouse overlooking Piedmont Park.

"You think he's gonna do time?" Robin asked Monica as they sat in Robin's backyard.

Monica stretched her legs out on the chaise lounge and flipped up her sunglasses. "Yes. The other girl will probably testify."

"You think they'll dig that stuff up about you?"

Monica looked out at the lush greenery. "Not unless they find out about what happened." She groaned and buried her head in her hands. "I just wanna get away from all of this. I'm tired of Handle Up. The Prima Donnas are selling, but nobody's paying attention because of Rodney. Bill has his head somewhere else."

"Is Terry still doing operations?"

"Yep. He's been lying low since Rodney's arrest. You know he avoids the limelight."

Robin got up from her chair. "You want some more lemonade?"

"Yeah, thanks." Monica shifted in her seat. She closed her eyes, but opened them when she heard her cell phone ringing. She reached in her bag to grab it. "Hello?"

"Monica, its Dray."

"What's up?" she asked solemnly.

He sighed. "I was at the police station with Bill, Warren, and Rodney early this morning."

"And?"

"And nothing. We were just trying to see what we could do to help him out. Warren thinks a doctor should examine him. He says he might have a mental disorder or something."

"He does. He's bipolar."

"Bipolar? How do you know?"

"Rodney's always been bipolar. He used to take medication for it. After his second album he felt like he didn't need to take it anymore."

"Monica, how could you keep something like that from everyone?" His voice hardened. "What the hell were you thinking?"

"What?" She jumped up from her chair, nearly knocking it over. "I'm not no damn doctor. I can't believe you have the nerve to ask me that? He's a grown man. You're his A&R rep, why don't you deal with it?"

"I am dealing with it, Monica. You're his publicist. And I'm trying to deal with you too. You're the most difficult woman that I've ever met in my life. You make things harder than they have to be."

"How am I making things harder? You act like this is all my fault. A girl is dead. And for some reason everyone at Handle Up wants to make Rodney out to be a saint. He has a problem that he needs to deal with. No one told him to slam that girl's head into the wall. You're making it seem like she did something wrong. What about him taking responsibility for his own actions?"

"Forget it," Dray said. "If he's crazy, he can't be responsible for all of his actions."

"So who gave you a Ph.D. in psychology? And what are you going to do about your actions?" Monica fired back.

"Bye, Monica." He didn't want to argue.

She searched the phone for an answer as she heard the dial tone. There was no way she and Dray were going to make things right again. Now, she didn't even see the use of trying.

"Here we go," Robin said, as she emerged from the house. Monica took the glass and fell into her seat. "What happened?" There was concern on Robin's face.

Monica set the glass down on the small end table near Robin's chair. "That was Dray."

"I take it, it didn't go well."

"No, it didn't. He had the nerve to go off on me because Rodney screwed up. I can't believe the girl died." Monica wiped away the tears that had formed in her eyes. "I give up, I can't do it anymore. I'm going to forget all about him."

"No, you won't," Robin said. "You love him." She sat down. "Don't worry, you'll work it out. Just wait and see."

"No, we won't. We should have never been together in the first place."

"I hear what you're saying, but I know you don't mean that, Monica. Maybe he's not the one being the jerk."

"What? Are you trying to say that I'm wrong?"

"I'm not saying either of you is wrong because I don't know all the details. All I know is that you can be a bitch at times."

"I was born on a cusp. You know how we Aries-Taurus people are."

"Whatever. But seriously, you know how you are. You get into that bitch mode." Robin shook her head. "What's Dray's zodiac sign?"

Monica leaned back and closed her eyes. "Come on, Robin, that sounds like a line from a *Superfly* movie. And I don't know what his sign is. But I think his birthday is in August. Leo, Virgo. Who knows? Who cares?"

"Call it what you want. If you weren't so in love with that nigga, you wouldn't be so upset."

"I am not upset, Robin!"

"Well, then why are you yelling?"

"I'm not!" Monica's two-way went off. She fumbled through her purse and pulled it out. There was a message from Bill requesting that she come to his house immediately for a meeting. Rodney was out of jail. She slammed the thing shut and jumped out of her seat. "I am so sick of this shit!"

Robin stopped in her tracks. "What shit?"

"This Rodney shit!" Monica scrambled for her keys. "Why is everyone trying to save this son-of-a-bitch's ass? I've had it with this mess. And Dray, you would think he would be on my side." She almost spilled her drink.

Robin's eyes grew wide. "Here," she said, handing her a coaster, "and calm down please before you have a seizure."

♫

The cars parked at Bill's house stretched all the way down the street, as if there weren't a soul in all of Atlanta who wasn't visiting him. Monica parked her car directly behind Dray's Navigator. Her tail end hung out of the driveway a little, but she didn't plan to stay long. She clutched her Gucci bag under her arm and slid past the other cars in her snug-fitting denim dress. She had her hair neatly pulled back into a ponytail and a sweater thrown across her shoulders. When she came to the door, Patrice greeted her.

"They're in the back praying," she whispered. Monica nearly fell to the ground. *Praying for what? Rodney to not kill again?* She shook her head. *Why did some black folks only run to God when they needed to get out of trouble?* she wondered. She stepped inside and didn't utter a word. She just followed Patrice to the sunken den in the back of Bill's mansion. Everyone was bowing their heads, including Rodney, who was in the center of the room near the preacher.

"And see us through this dark time, Lord . . . and help this young man to straighten out his life. In Jesus' name we pray. Amen."

"Hello, Monica. I'm glad you came," Bill said, coming to greet her. She returned his hug half-heartedly.

"Nice to see you, too, Mr. Sanders."

He stepped back and looked at her strangely. "The last time you called me Mr. Sanders, you were mad at me. Are you?"

She didn't reply.

"Don't be," Bill uttered. "Come on and get something to eat."

"Hey, Monica," Dray said as he approached them.

"Hey," she replied dryly. She avoided looking at him, but could feel his gaze.

"So Monica, are you staying for dinner?" Bill asked. "It's being catered."

"Yeah, I guess so," she said, looking at Dray.

"Good, good. I'll see you in a minute. I've got to speak with Rodney alone for a moment."

They both nodded. "Dray, excuse me for a moment."

His mouth fell open, but no words came out. He couldn't figure out how she could be so distant. They'd shared so much over the past few months, including each other. He finished the rest of his beer and watched as she left and made her way over to the kitchen where there was an assortment of snacks. He stood alone as she fixed a plate of appetizers. Their tension was thick and obvious.

"Hey, Monica," Cameron said, appearing from the patio. "Come here for a minute." He'd seen the way she was acting toward Dray.

Monica walked toward him slowly. He looked a little heavier since she'd seen him last.

"What's up, Cam?" she asked.

"What's up, baby girl," he said, giving her a quick hug. He bent to whisper, "What's the deal with you and Dray?"

"What do you mean?" she asked smiling.

Cameron picked up a beer from the cooler. "Y'all beefin' or somethin'? You were a little hard on him a minute ago. What's the deal?"

"Nothing for you to worry about," she said, nibbling on cheese and crackers. She watched people make their way up to greet Rodney and Bill. "What a joke," she mumbled.

Cam saw what she was looking at. "So, what do you really think of all this mess?" he asked. "You look like you wanna kill somebody."

"You know what I think. What about you?"

Cam took a swig of beer and shrugged. "I'm sorry that young lady had to die behind this . . . But I try not to associate myself with a lot of this shit. I guess that's the reason I'm gone so much. I hate my job when drama arises." He shook his head. "But you know he's an adult. He knew what he was doing."

Monica nodded in agreement. "Yeah, that's exactly what I've been saying." She looked down for a minute and then met his eyes. "I guess you've heard about me not wanting to be his PR rep, huh?"

"I heard a little something about that. And I guess you wanna know my opinion on it?"

She nodded.

Cameron placed his hands on her shoulders. "You didn't do anything wrong. You should never have to do anything you don't want to. I'm behind you 100 percent, no matter what Bill or Dray or anyone else has to say. Do what you feel is right."

"I'm trying, but people are making it very hard."

"What people?"

"Everybody. Bill, Dray, Rodney. I'm sick of being looked at like I caused all this mess."

"Come on, Moni, you know better. Bill is just stressed out. And speaking of Dray, what's up with you two. I heard y'all had been hanging kinda tight these past few months. Don't let work get in the way of your feeling for him. It's just a job."

She bit her lip and looked away, "It's over, so just leave it alone."

"I know you, Monica. That's bullshit. There's more to you and this dude than you're telling me. I will say this, I haven't known you to lie. But if you do, don't let it be to yourself. You only get one chance in this life. There's no going back when it's all over." With that he kissed her cheek and dashed off. *When did Cameron become such a prophet?* she wondered. He'd taken one look at her under a microscope and told her what she needed to hear. Monica felt strange. Cameron hadn't seen her and Dray together since the Prima Donnas release party. Was her attraction to him that obvious?

She was prepared to take a seat out on the patio with the rest of the guests, but Karen Sanders had something else in mind. Clad in a yellow knit halter and floral-printed Capri pants, Karen graciously glided toward her.

"Monica, darling, come with," she said. She looped her arm in Monica's and led her to the kitchen nook that overlooked the pool. With a drink in hand, she sat down at the table and guided Monica to sit across from her. Reluctantly, she obliged her.

"So," Karen began, clasping her hands together and giving Monica her first up-close-and-personal glimpse at her eight-karat diamond solitaire. "What's going on? Have you gotten over this hump about representing Rodney?"

Monica stared at Karen's brilliant ring. The sun reflecting off it blinded her. "Huh?" she said, shielding her eyes.

"Are you going to continue working at the company or have you made some other plans?"

What concern is it of yours? Monica wanted to ask. "No, Karen. I don't have any other plans, at the moment."

"Well," Karen began, "You don't want to step on any toes. Bill and I care about you a whole lot and would hate to see you leave." Her long eyelashes batted swiftly and then she changed her tune. "However, if you don't get it together soon, Bill and I will have to replace you."

Monica's nostrils flared with fury.

"Karen?" a woman's voice called. "The caterer is here."

It was her younger sister, Sheila, who resembled her so much people thought they were twins.

"I'll be right there." She stood up and looked at her Ellen Tracy clad frame in the window. She gave Monica a hostile stare. "Get it together, Miss Holiday."

Leaving Monica stunned, Karen glided off toward the front door. Monica looked around the room at all the people with whom she once had something in common. She realized how much she'd outgrown her coworkers over the past few months. Everyone seemed to be turning against her; there was no one she could trust. She felt more alone than she ever had before. It was then she decided to slip out the back door and leave. She had made it almost all the way around the house until she ran into Rodney. He appeared out of nowhere and stood firmly in front of her with a desperate look in his eyes.

"Where you going?"

She swallowed, but the lump in her throat rendered her speechless.

"You can't leave, baby. We haven't had any fun yet." He grabbed her arm firmly. "I may be going away for a long time. This is my freedom party."

"I'm not your baby."

Rodney bent to kiss her. "Come on, girl, give me one for old time's sake."

She yanked away from him and nearly fell on the walkway. "You're crazy, Rodney. Get your hands off me."

"I recall a time when you liked these hands on you."

She pulled away from him. "That was a very, very long time ago — before I came to my senses."

"Sorry," he said apologetically. "I'm tripping," he said. He moved away.

"You probably hurt that girl on purpose," Monica said.

"Hey," Rodney yelled, coming toward her. "That's bullshit. She attacked me." He paced the ground. "You know I meet a million hoes a day, and all they want to do is be seen with Double R. They don't care about me. I'm just a thirty-million-dollar dick to them. They want me to buy them shit. They wanna sleep at my house. Why is that, Monica?"

She shrugged smugly, "You tell me, Rodney. You got what you always wanted. You've never cared about anyone but yourself."

"That's not true!" he snapped.

Bill appeared from around the corner. "Is everything alright out here?"

"Everything's fine," Monica said sharply. "Excuse me."

"Are you leaving?" Bill asked.

"Yes."

"Well, you'll miss dinner. It's soul food."

"I know, but a friend of mine is waiting for me." It was a lie, but Monica definitely couldn't stand another moment at the Sanders home. She was furious about Karen's "threats" earlier and the casualness of everyone inside. It was as if the Handle Up family was celebrating Rodney's crime rather than contesting it.

That night Monica decided to quit working for Handle Up. She felt she had to in order to maintain her sanity. The more she thought about it, the more logical it seemed. She would go to work the next day and turn in her resignation. As she tossed and turned beneath her comforter, she couldn't help but wonder what would happen to her relationship with Dray. She always loved her job, but seeing his smiling face always made her day.

CHAPTER 25

Bill sent Monica a note saying he wanted to meet with her. She knew he probably was going to try to work things out with her. But Monica didn't want to work things out. She wracked her brain trying to see the logic in what everyone was asking of her but she couldn't. She still came to the same conclusion. She was leaving. She had to move on. Things would never be the same there. And why should she pretend?

Monica went back to work as usual. She hadn't made her announcement yet. She wanted to be sure she had another position first. She had a job interview with a public relations firm downtown, Johnson and Brown Communications. It was known throughout the nation for its savvy public relations. She'd caught the ad in a copy of the Atlanta Journal-Constitution. She e-mailed them her resume and got a call a few days later. The company's sassy vice president, Irene Johnson-Brown, wanted to meet with her.

Monica put on her fitted black suit and stretch gray top. It was cute enough to say stylish and practical enough to say classy. She slipped on her black pumps and left.

She hoped her departure wouldn't cause too many problems,

but she expected the worse. She hadn't seen Dray all day. And she knew he would be upset.

After a twenty-minute drive from Handle Up's offices, she was ready for her interview. When she arrived, a bubbly receptionist seated her in the waiting area. The office was decorated with bright colors and eclectic art that jumped off the walls. Nervously Monica, shook her foot. She hadn't been on a job interview in years. A glamorous-looking young woman appeared from behind the corridor.

"Mrs. Johnson-Brown will see you now, Ms. Holiday."

"Here we go," Monica said to herself. She was led to a huge corner office that overlooked the hills of Atlanta. Irene Johnson-Brown was busy chatting away on her headphone but waved Monica in. Monica liked her already. She was dressed to kill, spoke with authority, and ran a successful business. Her client list read like a who's who in the entertainment world. She even represented a few corporations.

"Well, Ms. Holiday," she began, once Monica sat down. "It's obvious you have excellent references. I don't know if you'll enjoy the boring world of corporate PR, but we desperately need someone in our events department. We're looking for someone to coordinate fundraisers, membership drives, et cetera. We have full medical, dental, and vision benefits that are paid for by the company, of course. And a vacation package. You know, ten years ago I would have killed for a job like this. It will be a lot of fun, what do you think?"

Irene spoke so fast, it took Monica a moment to process what she'd just heard. But it did sound good. "The position sounds really interesting. I think I'd enjoy it."

Irene smiled. "I know you will love it here. With your contacts, good looks, and personality, you could really set this town on fire. We want to really leave everyone else in the dust, especially for the holidays. We did the *Shazz* magazine awards dinner a month ago. Were you there?"

"Yes, I was. It was very nice."

"That was one of our better events." Irene's eyes narrowed. "If you don't mind my asking, why do you want to leave Handle Up? It seems like such a great company. I was just wondering."

"It's a long story, but I feel that I've done all I can do over there. I'm looking to be a bit more creative."

Irene nodded. "I see. Well, don't worry. You won't get any gripes from me. We'd love to have you work for us."

"I would love to accept, but I'd like a few days to consider all my options."

Irene lifted her hand to her chin. "Have you had any more offers?"

"Yes," Monica lied. There were none, but she needed to tie up some loose ends first. "I'll let you know by Friday. Is that okay?"

"Sure, take all the time you need." Irene stood. "I look forward to hearing from you."

Monica joined her stance and shook her hand. "Thank you."

♫

Dray was sitting on pins and needles. He was contemplating whether or not the Prima Donnas should start their tour. It was a tough decision, and no one else seemed to be interested at the moment. Part of him wanted to ask Monica what to do, but he didn't know if he could see her without thinking about the two of them. Bill was busy dealing with the press, Terry was out of town again, and Cameron was in meetings all day. Everyday, Cameron would come to work, go in his office, and usually not come out until it was time to go home. Dray wondered if he was contemplating a move to another label. As impractical as the idea sounded, Dray couldn't help but wonder if he should do the same thing.

"Mr. Lewis," Patrice said through the speakerphone.

"Yes?"

"Savannah Morgan is here to see you."

Damn, he wanted to say out loud. *What the hell does she want?* "Give me a minute."

"Okay," she said.

She hung up the phone and turned to Savannah. "He'll be with you in a minute, Miss Morgan," Patrice said. "Can I get you anything?"

"No, not really," she replied snobbishly. "Where's Ms. Holiday?" she asked, shifting her position in the chair.

"I'm not sure . . . probably at lunch."

"Speak of the devil," Savannah said as Monica entered the office.

Monica smiled at Patrice and stopped at the desk. She set her lunch down and turned to face Savannah.

"Miss Morgan, you making rounds again?" she asked.

Savannah gave a faux smile. "No, I'm not. I'm here on business to see Mr. Lewis. You know your good friend, Mr. Lewis."

Monica wanted to snatch her from the chair. *Still running behind men who have no interest in you, aren't you?* "Any mail for me?" Monica asked Patrice.

"No, it hasn't come yet."

"Well, I'll be in my . . . "

Dray appeared from his office. He looked at Monica with burning eyes. They both smiled.

"How are you?" he asked, not taking his eyes off her.

She smiled, his presence gave her intense joy. "I'm fine," she said. "How . . . "

Savannah cleared her throat and got up from her seat. "Mr. Lewis, shall we go in your office?" She gave Monica a smug glance.

"No." He put his hand up to halt her. "What are you doing here, Miss Morgan?"

Monica couldn't hide the grin on her face as she watched Miss Savannah being put on the spot.

"Well, uh . . . Mr. Lewis, I was coming to see about that interview."

"Did you make an appointment, because I don't seem to recall one? Patrice, does she have an appointment?"

Savannah flushed to a shade of crimson as heat rode into her face. She lowered her head and then looked at Monica furiously. Without another word, she straightened herself and stormed out of the office. They all had a good laugh, including Monica, who hadn't smiled in weeks.

"Well," Monica began, "I better get back to work."

As she turned to leave, Dray called her name, "Monica."

She turned around, "Yes?"

"Can I see you for a moment please?"

"Dray, I really have a lot of work to do."

"It will only take a minute," he said, waiting for her.

Monica set her things back on the counter. "Watch these for me, Patrice."

"Sure," Patrice said, smiling. "Go get him, girl."

Dray graciously held the door open for her, and she stepped inside. Her intoxicating perfume filled his nostrils as he shut the door behind him. Instead of offering her a seat, he stood in front of her. She wouldn't meet his eyes, fearing they'd give away her secret longing for him. He placed his hand on her cheek, upsetting her balance. He stroked the side of her face as she reached to pull his hand away. She couldn't meet his eyes.

"Dray, what do you want?" she asked nervously.

"You," he said softly.

He placed his mouth over hers. He missed the taste of her lips, and he missed her fire and spunk. Most of all, he missed the spark she gave him when they were together. Monica couldn't turn away. He made her so weak in the knees that she couldn't move an inch. As his hands slipped up the front of her blouse, she shivered. He found his way to her breasts and teased her nipples until they stood at attention.

"I've missed you, Monica," he whispered

She went limp hearing his words and took a minute to catch her breath. Her world came to a halt. What was he saying? What did he mean where had she been all his life? Her thoughts drifted back to days they'd made love. How could she tell him there would be no more lovemaking, no more kisses? Even though this man had rocked her to the core, she still had to say goodbye. But his lips tasted so sweet, so soft, so inviting, she didn't want to pull away. As if struck by lightning, she threw herself in his arms. His thumping heartbeat pounded against her breasts. He kissed her neck, ears, nose, and everywhere he could reach without struggling. She eagerly returned his kisses, trapped in love as the hairs on his goatee teased her ever so slightly. He moved his body downwards, stopping to kiss her board-flat stomach along the way. He wanted to take her right there, but it wouldn't have been appropriate. It wouldn't have mattered; she wanted him to take her. As he made his way back up to her face, she stopped him.

"Dray, I have to tell you something," she said, pulling away.

"Can't it wait?"

Her body still craved his warm hands as he stared with anticipation. She parted her lips and felt them tremor. He looked so intent on listening. Part of her wanted to say never mind and continue kissing his full, supple lips. If she was going to tell him, now would have to be the time. She didn't know when she'd have him alone again.

"What is it?" he asked, seeing the seriousness in her eyes.

"I wanted you to hear it from me. I-I'm leaving the company."

He stood still for a minute and then turned his back. "What?"

"I can't work here any longer . . . And I have another offer."

He breathed in deeply and shook his head. "So you're leaving just like that?"

She straightened her blouse and flipped her hair back. "Yes. I can't stay here. You know the pressure I've been under."

"Yeah, and I thought you could have at least come to me to talk about it."

"For what? You were so mad at me for not representing Rodney. I didn't know if I could trust you."

"Trust me?" His eyes were dark and stony. "Monica, I know your deepest secret. We've been open with each other. You think I would do something like mess over you for a paycheck?"

She looked away.

"I'm wondering how you would even think I would do something like that."

His handsome face was masked by disappointment. He was hurt. But what could she do? She'd much rather hurt him now than hurt him later on. He stood by the window staring out into the midday traffic.

"You don't know how hard it is to have people looking down at you and wanting you to fail so they can say 'I told you so.' I didn't want to represent Rodney, and I can't pretend that it doesn't bother me because it does."

He looked at her. "Monica, I'm sorry about all of that. But it's no reason for you to leave. Let me talk to Bill again."

She shook her head. "It's too late for that, Dray."

"What do you mean it's too late?"

"I told you. I have a new job offer."

"Where?"

"It doesn't matter where, Dray. I'm seriously considering it. Why can't you just support me?"

He didn't answer, he couldn't. He didn't want her to leave. He turned his attention to the street again. As much as it hurt, he tried to make light of the situation.

A broad smile crossed his face. "Who am I going to go to lunch with now?"

They both snickered.

"I don't know. Maybe Miss Savannah will come and take care of you when I'm gone."

"Not likely. I can't stomach that woman. She's like a diaper, always on your ass and always full of shit."

Monica giggled. "I'm definitely going to miss your sarcasm."

"You act like you're leaving town or something."

"I'm not, but it will definitely feel like it. If I take the position, I'll be working downtown."

"Oh, so you're moving downtown, huh?" His left eyebrow arched indicating his huge surprise. "That's a big move. Just don't forget about the little people."

She settled her eyes on his as she parted her lips. "Some people aren't easy to forget."

His gaze was as soft as a caress. "I'd better get back to work," he said, backing away. *If I keep looking at you, we'll both need to make a move and it definitely won't be to an office.* "I have to catch up with Bill to see if he's going to postpone the girls' tour. All this Rodney mess has screwed up everything."

"Why would he postpone their tour? It was already planned. They've been working hard for it."

"Don't worry. I'll take care of it," Dray said.

"Uh-oh. Okay. I guess I'll see you later then."

"Wait," he said, coming toward her. "Can I at least have a hug?"

She wanted to give him more than that, but held back. "Sure," she said, as he opened his arms.

They embraced, and he held her body to his like a blanket. He had to feel her one more time. Without looking away, she backed out of the embrace.

"I better go. I have to finish some things before I leave in a couple of weeks."

"Sure, sure," he said nervously. "I'll see you later."

CHAPTER 26

After going home a little early to change clothes, Dray drove to the airport to pick up Adam. He was visiting the city on business again and decided against renting a car since Dray didn't mind picking him up. They rode back to town listening to Tupac and smoking cigars. Adam had gotten them from a guy off the street who bought them from a Cuban importer.

"These are pretty good, man," Dray said, exhaling. He relaxed in the seat a bit and took in the cool night air as they rode up I-85.

"I know, dawg. These go for like sixty dollars a pop. My man gave them to me for twenty."

"That's a steal. How many did you get?"

"About nine or ten. This is my first time lighting one up since I got 'em. You now I wanted to put you up on 'em and shit."

"Yeah, I hear that."

"We need to get some beer, dawg, before we get to your crib."

"That's cool," Dray said, choking on the smoke. "Damn!" he rolled his window down to let the smoke out. "These thangs are potent."

"Too much for you?" Adam asked. "You've been off the squares a long time."

"Nah, I just should've kept my mouth shut. They're a nice ass gift, though. I've been stressed out lately."

Adam cocked his head to the side with a sly grin. "What's up with shorty? You still kicking it or what?"

Dray shook his head, "No, we're over."

Adam was surprised. "Damn, just like that? What happened?"

"What didn't happen?" Dray said, sighing. "I guess I blew it. We blew it."

"So you just gon' let it go like that?"

"It what?"

"The relationship, nigga!"

"I have to, man, or look like a fool. And it wasn't no relationship."

Adam knew better than that. "So you telling me you don't care about this girl?"

"I'm not telling you nuthin'."

Adam chuckled, "Why you scared to look like a fool, dawg? That's what love does to you."

There was a long silence.

"Once bitten, twice shy. I've been down that rode before. I'm not trying to do it again."

Adam flicked his ashes out of the window. "Well, at least you had fun, right?"

"I guess so, man. I guess so."

♫

Monica sat patiently as Bill read her resignation for the third time. He couldn't believe it. She was leaving, and her reasons why were clearly stated in her letter. He pondered a way to make her stay, but to no avail. She wasn't going to stay. He hadn't been as understanding as he should have, and now it was too late. She checked her watch. It was almost seven. She wished he would hurry up.

"Monica, I really wish you would reconsider your decision. We need you here." Bill paced the floor of his office and stopped behind her as she sat in front of his desk.

"I'm sorry, Mr. Sanders. I've already accepted another position with another company."

"Another record company?"

"No, a small, but prestigious PR firm. You've heard of Johnson and Brown, haven't you?"

"Come on, Monica, don't tease me, of course, I have. They're the best PR firm in town. It's bad enough you're leaving. I don't want to hear about how great the other company is."

"I'm sorry."

Bill sat in his chair. "Well, I guess your mind's made up."

She nodded and placed her hands in her lap.

"You know, my wife told me you were thinking about leaving. She said you seemed dead set on doing so at my house the other week."

Monica looked puzzled. Karen had ticked her off, but she never mentioned resigning to her. As she recalled, Karen did all the talking.

"I didn't tell her I was leaving then."

Bill rubbed his head as he leaned on the desk. "Maybe she misunderstood."

Yeah, she misunderstood alright. "Bill," Monica said sharply, "Karen sort of . . . well she threatened me. She said I needed to get my act together and . . . "

Bill raised his hand. "Monica, I know my wife. And she wouldn't say anything to threaten or offend you."

No, Monica figured, Bill didn't really know his wife.

"Well," he said, "I want you to know I've been blessed having you here. I want you to know how grateful I am for everything you've done. I hope that you'll remember us when you leave."

She smiled. "I'm not leaving the city. I'll just be downtown, Bill."

"Yeah, but you know people get downtown and forget where they came from."

"Not me," Monica reassured him.

"Well, Rodney's court date is right around the corner," Bill said.

She lowered her eyes. "Yeah, I know."

Bill threw his head back. "It'll be interesting to see what happens."

I won't be around to find out, Monica told herself.

Back in her office, Monica straightened up the mess on her desk and put her files in her tote bag. After shutting her computer down, she gathered the rest of her belongings and grabbed her purse. The other offices were extremely dark, and there was no sign of Patrice. Even Dray's office bore no light. She wondered where everyone had gone that fast, but didn't really pay it any mind. After a once-over of the office, she threw her bag over her shoulder and left.

Thirty minutes later, Monica pulled up in front of her building. She let the valet park her car and went on inside. She clutched the stack of letters she pulled from her mailbox. She balanced her purse, briefcase, and laptop as she waited for the elevator. "Come on. Come on, come on," she said impatiently. She rode the elevator up to her floor, humming to the corny elevator music. Inside her apartment, Monica put her things on the couch and went through her mail. One letter caught her immediate attention. She opened it and read it. Fulton County was subpoenaing her to testify in Rodney's case.

"Damn," she said, reaching for the phone. She called her homegirl, Raven Wallace, a sports lawyer in Dallas.

"Moni? Oh, my goodness. Girl, this is a surprise," Raven said.

"I know, girl. I've been busy, busy, busy. What's up in D-town? How's your love life?"

Raven chuckled. "Don't ask. It doesn't exist, but I do have this football player on my tail."

Monica's brow rose. "Who, girl?"

"Jefferson Davis."

"The football player? Girl, he is fine," Monica said, forgetting all about the subpoena.

"I know. But I can't stand athletes." There was long silence. "But enough about me. What's wrong?"

Monica sighed. "Girl, I got a subpoena."

"For what?"

"You remember Rodney, don't you?"

"Crazy Rodney?"

"Yeah." Silence. "He killed somebody. It was an accident . . . well he says it was. And now he's facing jail time."

"I know you're not still seeing him, Monica," Raven said with concern.

"No, I'm not. I was seeing our new A&R director, but that's another story." She held her breath. "I think they want me to testify against Rodney for what he did to me while we were dating."

"So?"

Monica was uncertain. "Should I do it? I mean what if he goes to jail for life?"

"Don't tell me you care?"

"No, Raven, but . . . "

"But what? That dude broke your ribs. And he killed someone. Why should you care about what happens to him?"

"I know, but I just don't want to do it."

Raven cleared her throat. "You have to do it, legally anyway. Were there any other witnesses?"

"One. He attacked her too," Monica said in a low voice.

"If you're lucky, they won't need your testimony. But since you know first-hand about his violent temper, the district attorney is going to get whatever they can out of you. Just be ready. Because his lawyers will try to get in your head too . . . especially if you show one sign of weakness."

"I know, Raven. Believe me. I know."

"Well, just don't ignore the subpoena. If you need me to fly out one weekend, I will."

"Thanks, Rave, but I don't think that'll be necessary."

Raven's voice was suddenly vibrant. "So, tell me about this A&R director you've been making nice with."

Monica couldn't help but blush. "His name is Dray, he's from Chicago. He's tall, about six-two, toffee brown, nice body . . . and a big stick."

"Ooh, okay. Cut the bullshit. Is he good in bed?"

Monica laughed. "I can't believe you asked me that!" she said, walking into the bathroom. She sat up on the countertop.

"Well?" Raven pressed.

Monica closed her eyes and purred. "Oooh, yes! He's great in bed."

"Well, I see somebody's been taking care of business. So, what's the real deal?"

"What do you mean?"

"What do you do besides screw him? Does he take you out? And how on earth did you end up fucking somebody you work with, girl?"

Monica shrugged as she looked at herself in the mirror. "It just happened. You know? It was just one of those things. He was good to me, we clicked, and that was that. But somehow work got in the way."

Raven heard the sadness in her friend's tone, and was serious when she asked, "Do you love him?"

At first, Monica couldn't answer. Sure she cared for him, but did she love him? Even with all they'd been through, Dray was always there. She couldn't deny it any longer.

"Yes, Raven, I do."

CHAPTER 27

The August heat hit Georgia like a left hook from Roy Jones, Jr. For the eleventh day in a row, the temperature was more than ninety degrees. Monica was nestled into her new office working on the details for an upcoming music convention's cocktail party. She thought back to all her days of party planning at Handle Up and smiled. She'd thrown some of the best the city had ever seen. This event would be held at the Georgia World Congress Center, and Monica wanted it to be her best event ever. As she jotted down some more notes, the theme came to her: Listener's Paradise. Perfect, she thought, "An Oasis of Music." *I love it!* She had two more weeks to finalize the details. And if she was going to do it right, she had to get on the ball.

She showed the plans to Irene who approved them. Irene assured her that the promoters had a huge budget and money was no object. The convention would bring the city at least ten million dollars, probably more. Since the center was already reserved all Monica had to do was get the ball rolling. On Monday, she would start by calling the promoter to get the event schedule for the evening of the party.

Monica climbed out of bed and made her way to the bathroom. It had been almost three weeks since she left Handle Up. When she finished, she went to the living room and turned on the television. It was rare for her to be up early on a Saturday unless she had some promotions to do. She fixed herself a bowl of cereal and sat down on the couch. With the sun shining through her blinds, she wondered if the heat would ever stop. The sun's rays warmed her mocha brown skin. She thought about Dray as she finished her cereal. She missed him. She would give anything to look in his eyes and inhale his scent one more time. Waking up in his arms would have been more exciting than waking alone. She stared at the phone, wanting to dial his number, but couldn't bring herself to do it. The last look in his eyes let her know she'd made a mistake letting him slip away. When she closed her eyes at the memory, tears fell. She shook her head as if they would magically disappear and collected herself. "Get it together girl," she told herself. "Get it together."

Later that day, Monica went shopping at Perimeter Mall. Shopping was her favorite pastime when she wanted to clear her head. As she wondered through the mall, she decided it would be a good time to find a dress for the party. She found a green, floral-printed, silk wrap dress in BCBG that would match a pair of Jimmy Choo stilettos she already had. She made a mental note that it might play into the "paradise" theme for the party. After leaving there, she headed for Illuminations, where she spent more than seventy-five dollars on scented candles. With no steady man in her life, she would be forced to drown herself in bubbles in a hot bath and surround herself with candlelight.

She headed back to the mall parking lot and hopped inside her car. Before she started the engine, she slid in her Maxwell CD. She turned the volume up and remembered it playing when she and Dray were alone fixing up his apartment. It reminded her of the fun they had. She started the engine and pulled out of the parking lot. After making a couple of stops at the grocery store and Wal-Mart, she headed home.

♫♪

That evening, Dray met Cameron at his house to watch the Lakers and Knicks game. He invited him to sort of break the ice between them. They hadn't had much time to get to know each other since Cam spent a lot of time out of town. Dray welcomed the invitation. He thought Cam was pretty cool. And he cared about Monica too.

"Make yourself at home, man," he told Dray as he showed him to the back of the house. "I know we haven't seen much of each other, but I wanted to make my point clear."

He stopped walking. Dray met his eyes and Cam continued, "I love Monica like a sister. I don't like what Rodney did. And I know, you and Monica have been together. In short, I'll always support her. And if you're a good nigga and can treat her right, whatever level you take your relationship to, I approve."

Dray was speechless. And he appreciated Cam's honesty. "Thank's, man," he said, slapping five. "I appreciate that."

"Good," Cam said. "Now, let's see if I you can whip my ass at pool."

"This is a nice house," Dray said, holding his Corona. He looked outside past the den's French doors. "Damn, a pool too? You're doin' it, man."

"Not really," Cam said, toasting him with his beer bottle. "This is just a little something. I'ma have a house built the way I want it in another year or so," he said, sharpening his cue stick.

"It's still cool, man." Dray made his way over to a shelf that held a bunch of pictures, all framed and neatly placed. He looked them over once and then again.

"That's my hall of fame," Cam informed him. "Everyone who's ever been to my house usually ends up having their picture taken. Most of those are from parties I had here: pool parties, Superbowl parties. You see your girl?" he asked, nodding toward a picture of Monica on the top shelf.

Dray looked at it. Cam was standing next to her with his arm around her waist and Rodney was on the other side of her. They were all holding drinks and smiling. Monica looked extremely beautiful dressed in a hot pink halter and denim shorts.

"That was the Fourth of July last year. We had a ball. Double R performed and shit. It was cool."

"So Monica was still seeing him when this was taken?"

Cam shrugged. "I guess. It was a lot of shit going on between them, you know? Double R put her in the hospital one time. She had broken ribs, I think."

Dray remembered his conversation with Rodney the night he assaulted the two girls in his home. The same bad taste filled his mouth again. Monica was such a beautiful person. He couldn't see anyone wanting to hurt her. He looked at some of the other photos and took a seat on the couch.

"You think Monica loved Rodney?" he asked Cameron.

Cam shrugged. "Maybe, but I think she liked the notoriety more. You get mad props being an entertainer's woman."

Dray nodded. "I hope these Lakers get wit' these New York tricks," Dray joked.

"Nah, I have to disagree," Cam said, taking a seat in his armchair. "I need my boys to come through."

"You wanna put some money on it?" Dray asked slyly, pulling money from his pocket.

"A gambling man. My kind of nigga exactly. One C-note says the Knicks get in that LA ass."

"Bet that!" Dray said, slamming his 100 dollar bill on the

table. They both smiled and relaxed as the sports anchors gave a run-down of the match ahead.

"Say, man," Cam began, as if he just remembered something. "Have you talked to Monica since she left?"

"No."

Cam took a sip of his beer and looked at Dray. "Why not?"

"I don't know. I just didn't feel I had a reason to."

"Love is always a reason, man."

"I never said I loved her."

"You never said you didn't either." Cam had a point. "So, do you?"

Dray didn't answer.

Cam looked out into the yard for a moment. "I lost my girl Angie like that. I couldn't tell her I loved her because I thought it would make me look weak."

"So what happened?"

"She left me and married some nigga who plays football."

Dray frowned. "My ex left me for some football player, too. Dig that."

Cam turned his nose up. "Does Monica know about your ex?"

"No. I don't even bring her up. She's not even important."

Cam shrugged. "Well, anyway, like I was saying. I looked like a fool when I lost my girl. By the time I was able to get up the nerve to tell her how I felt, it was too late. I couldn't even look at her without wanting to roll up in a ball and die. She's close to my family, and that was really hard. My mother was so mad at me for not trying to get her back. At the time, I couldn't compete with that nigga. I mean he was a baller, and I was just coming into my own. I was alright financially, but I got so scared of losing my freedom, I just let her go."

"You think she's happy?"

Cam shrugged. "I don't know. I think about that shit all the time, and it always gets me. Every once in a while, she'll visit relatives here, and I always end up seeing her out somewhere. You want some chips man?" He stood up and walked toward the kitchen, and the conversation ended.

♫✍

Monica wasn't a coffee drinker, but right about now she needed some. The upcoming Third Annual Hip-Hop and R&B Convention was receiving a lot of media attention. Rodney had a few more days before he was to appear in court, and Monica hoped she wouldn't be called to testify. With less than a week to go, she was busy with the party plans. She'd been up since five making trips to the hotel, the caterer's, and the liquor distributor. Since the music convention party was being sponsored by a private entity, the hotel was willing to let her bring in liquor from an outside vendor. Hip-hoppers liked to drink, and since the big money-makers would be on hand, she had to make sure there was plenty of Cristal, Moët, and Belvedere. The rap industry, in particular, was making those drinks so popular. They were flying off the shelves. Luckily, she was able to find the Moët at Sam's Club. She nearly fainted when she saw the total for all the 300 bottles they had in stock. After composing herself, she remembered she didn't have to pay for it.

The set-up for the party was coming along nicely. The palm trees would arrive on Thursday morning from California. They were sure to cause a ruckus among partygoers, many of whom hadn't left their home state except to attend the function of the year. By the time she finished supervising the table-and-chair setup, she went back to the office to finish reviewing all of the vendor contracts. Later, she took a lunch break and went to Spasso's to get a to-go plate. When she got there, she was surprised to see Drayton eating alone on the patio. She ordered a plate of lasagna, a Caesar salad, and lemonade. When her order was ready, she carried her bag outside to the patio.

"Excuse me, sir. Is this seat taken?" she asked Dray.

He looked up from his food, surprised to see her. "Monica," he grinned, standing. "What are you doing here?"

She shrugged. "Just passing through."

He planted a gentle kiss on her cheek. "Have a seat."

They exchanged a subtle look of amusement as Monica opened her bag of food.

"Surprised?" she asked.

"Very," he said in a sultry voice.

"I saw you, and I thought it would be nice if we talked," she said. He nodded. "So how are you?" she asked with a serious look on her face.

"I'm alright, I could be doing better, though."

Monica put a forkful of lasagna in her mouth. "How so?"

He remembered what Cam said as he glanced down the street. If he was going to say the words, now would be the perfect time.

"I miss you, Monica. I can't stand being away from you, not talking to you, touching you."

His words ripped through her, making her warm all over. She felt lightheaded and she couldn't move.

"Dray . . . "

"Wait," he said. "I'm not done. I'll understand if you don't feel the same way and it's cool. I know it sounds crazy coming from me, but since the first time I saw you, I wanted you in every way a man can want a woman, and I still do."

"Dray," she said, closing her eyes and shaking her head, "I'm afraid of us failing. What if it doesn't work out?"

He put his finger up to silence her. "Don't be afraid. Just think about what I'm saying."

♫♪

Monica met Dray at his house for dinner that evening. When he opened the door, a smile crossed his face. She was wearing his favorite color, blue, and looked absolutely beautiful. Her dress was short-sleeved and revealed the slenderness of her arms. Her mocha skin glowed beneath the dim track lighting in his dining room. He'd prepared fried catfish, cabbage, mashed potatoes, and strawberries with whipped cream for dessert. They talked briefly over dinner and sipped homemade Sangria. After dessert, they stepped out onto the balcony to talk.

Dray couldn't keep his eyes off her as the night breeze whipped through her hair. Monica stared out into the night. The sky was filled with stars and the view of downtown Atlanta was crisp and clear. There was a twinkle in Dray's eyes as she looked at him. She traced his profile with her eyes and took in the fullness of his lips. He sensed her staring and turned to meet her gaze.

"What's wrong?" he asked, as he leaned over the railing.

"Nothing," she said softly. "I've just never known anyone like you before."

"Is that a good thing?"

"It's a great thing," she said, wrapping her arms around his neck. She pressed her breasts to his chest and put his hands on her butt. He squeezed it gently while she rubbed the back of his neck.

"Kiss me," she whispered.

He put his mouth to hers and took in all its sweetness. Monica was so hot she could barely stand. She felt her body throbbing against his. She wanted him more than she had ever wanted a man. Dray pulled away and pushed her back into the cement portion that supported the balcony. She grabbed it as he knelt to pull up her dress. His soft hair brushed her thighs as her knees melted. After teasing her a bit with his tongue, he came up and kissed her neck, sucking it like candy. She pulled his shirt from his pants and felt the length of his back. Then, her fingers traveled to his nipples to stroke them.

"Ooh, that tickles," he moaned.

Monica turned him around and pressed him against the railing, gently running her hand over his manhood. With the moon as her light, she slid down beneath him and took him in her mouth. He almost lost it when he felt the warm softness surround him like a summer breeze. Not able to contain himself any longer, he picked her up and carried her to the bedroom.

"You smell so good," he said, pulling her on top of him.

He squirmed beneath her as she kissed his neck, chest, and stomach.

"Let me take off my dress," she said, getting up. Dray removed his clothes only after watching her. She pushed him on his back and climbed back on top of him. She leaned over and put her breasts to his mouth. He took turns sucking and stroking them. Monica was so wet she could barely stand it. She lifted and slid Dray inside of her. He closed his eyes and surged into her warmth, meeting her sensuous rhythm. His fluid strokes made her explode right on top of him. But she wasn't done. She rode him until a loud growl escaped from his throat and his eyes went back in his head.

Monica leaned to kiss his chest. He smiled. "You keep doing that, and you'll be on your back next time."

Monica laughed. "Good. That way I can feel every inch." She purred at the thought.

"I'll be right back," he said, climbing off the bed.

He left the room and returned with a bottle of honey and a cup of ice.

"What are you going to do with that?"

Without a word, he turned the spout and let the honey pour. It dripped onto her stomach, and its coolness made her twitch. He used his fingers to put some on each of her nipples as she squirmed in delight.

"Dray, you are so bad."

He let out a sly grin. "I know." With a gleam in his eye, he began his descent down toward her. He started from her neck and worked his way down to her breasts. The sticky substance became warm as his tongue flicked her nipples. She was so excited she thought she'd come right then. Her eyes fluttered like butterflies as he blew cool air on each spot he'd licked. Monica ached. She parted her lips to speak, but there was only a gasp. She was so hot. Dray stiffened even more watching her climax. She reached for him, gently placing her small hands in his large ones. He held them as she squirmed against the bed.

Sticky and hot with pleasure, Monica wanted him to take her now. He couldn't, not until he'd made her scream loud enough for people to hear it in the Carolinas. He moved his mouth to the warmth between her thighs, and taunted her until her grip on his hands became tighter. As she began to tremble, he held her so she couldn't move. He wrapped her legs around him and took pleasure in watching her wiggle. The surrendering moan that escaped from her mouth excited him. As she came back from her orgasmic spell, he laughed.

"Are you alright?"

"I'm not sure," she moaned.

"Woozy?"

"Yes."

"Good. That means I'm doing my job right."

He kissed her again, and followed up with his slow entrance. Monica loved the way he filled her. He felt her shake a little.

"Aftershocks?" he joked.

"Yes."

He smiled, and she gasped as his strokes deepened. She met them with the full force of her hips causing him to moan deeply. He kissed her neck and ran his tongue over the hills of her breasts. His skin felt like a warm blanket next to hers.

"Oh, Monica," he moaned. "You're so warm, baby. You gon' make me come." He growled in her ear.

"Go ahead," she whispered.

He grabbed her long hair gently and held it tight. As she cooed beneath him, he felt her body begin to shake. The sensations met his own. He couldn't hold off any longer as she cried out and decided to come with her. Their combustion of ecstasy sent them into a sanctuary of passion. Dray collapsed on top of her, their bodies wet with love. He removed the slightly melted ice from a cup and slid it down her hot thighs.

"What are you doing?" she moaned.

"Trying to cool you off."

They laughed.

CHAPTER 28

The next morning, Monica awoke to feel Dray's hands sliding down her thighs. She moaned out loud as he placed his lips against her neck. He rolled her over onto her back and kissed her neck. She hoped he didn't want to kiss her yet because she hadn't brushed her teeth. She couldn't help but giggle as he slid beneath the covers to suck her breasts and stomach.

"What are you doing?" she asked.

"Waking you up," he said, taking her left breast in his mouth and sucking it. He did the same thing with the right.

For a moment, she forgot the English language. She ran her fingers through his slightly curly hair as he eased his way inside of her. But as their journey of lovemaking began, the phone rang. It startled both of them.

"Damn, who the hell is calling me this early?" Dray asked.

Monica rubbed his shoulders. "Maybe it's important. Answer it."

He reached for the handset. "Hello?"

"Drayton Lewis?"

Dray didn't recognize the man's voice. "Speaking. Who is this?"

"My name is Oliver Gordon, district attorney with Fulton County."

"Yeah?"

"Is there a Miss Monica Holiday there with you?"

Dray looked at Monica and frowned. He wondered why on earth they were calling him. "No, she doesn't live here."

"Yes, sir, I know. But we can't seem to reach her at home. We were told you might know where she is? We need her to be in court today at two."

Dray sat up in bed. "Well, I don't. But if I see her, Mr. Gordon, I'll have her call you." He hung up the phone and threw the covers back.

Monica sat up. "Who was that?"

"The D.A. looking for you."

"For me? For what?"

"They want you to be in court at two. I guess they're going to put you on the witness stand." Dray went into the bathroom. "I don't know how the hell they got my number. And what made them think you would be here?"

Monica hadn't heard what he just said. "Witness stand?" she mumbled. "I thought I wouldn't have to testify." She clutched the covers to her breasts. "Damn."

Dray could hear the fear in her voice. "You want me to go with you?"

Monica stared at his magnificent nude body. She would rather stay in bed all morning with him. Her thoughts drifted back to the matter at hand. "Yes," she said with certainty.

Dray turned on the shower. "Let me get dressed and then we'll go to your place."

♫

Monica clutched Dray's hand tightly as they walked up the courthouse stairs. She didn't want to discuss what happened between she and Rodney. She wanted to put all of that behind her and didn't see the point of regurgitating old memories. After she met with the D.A., she was asked to sit with the rest of the people who had come to hear the trial. Some of them were Handle Up employees, including Bill, Cameron, and Vera. The rest were news media, the victim's families, and the family of Shanty Green. Shanty was seated behind the plaintiff's side, and Monica was one row behind her. Dray had a few phone calls to make so he opted to wait outside. When Rodney came in, he gazed at Monica for what seemed an eternity. She stared back at him, hoping the D.A. wouldn't need her on the stand.

After Shanty Green's testimony, the jury took a recess. She was so upset, she cried when she got off the stand. When they reconvened fifteen minutes later, what Monica feared most happened.

"The prosecution calls Miss Monica Holiday to the witness stand," the D.A. said.

She felt her knees weaken when she got up from her seat. She clutched her purse tightly and looked for Dray. He still hadn't come back. She sighed deeply. Now she had to face this alone. After being sworn in, Monica took a seat in the witness chair. She tried to relax as district attorney Gordon looked her in the eyes. Then, he began his questioning.

"Miss Holiday, what was your relationship to Rodney Robinson in 2000 and 2001?"

She took a deep breath. "We dated." *Don't give too much information.* Monica could feel Rodney's dark eyes on her. *And don't look at him,* she told herself.

"And during this time was Mr. Robinson ever abusive?"

Monica nodded.

"I'm sorry, Miss Holiday we didn't hear you."

"Yes. Yes, he was abusive."

"According to a report from the Atlanta Medical Center, you suffered from broken ribs last spring. However, at the time, an ER physician said he suspected foul play. What really happened, Miss Holiday?"

For the first time, Monica looked up and saw Dray. She held his eyes for a moment and then looked down. Everyone was waiting for her to explain. Monica began telling the details of what happened the night Rodney attacked her. When she was done, everyone stared in awe. Monica didn't hear the D.A. ask her to step down. With the bailiff's help, she was finally able to. She headed straight for the lobby, right past Dray. He ran out after her and took her in his arms. "It's okay, baby. It's over," he said, holding her face.

Monica was rambling about her testimony hysterically. She hadn't heard a word he said. She went on and on as he tried to calm her. He finally had to shake her a little to let her know it was over.

"It's over, baby," he repeated. He kissed her softly, and met her eyes.

She was still shaken as she looked in his eyes.

"Monica, I love you," Dray said.

"He was just looking . . . " She thought she heard the words I love you fall from Dray's lips. "What did you say?"

He lifted her chin. "I said, I love you."

He kissed her to confirm his confession. Monica thought she was dreaming. She felt tears forming in her eyes and quickly wiped them away. Dray wasn't saying he loved her. She had to be hearing things.

"Dray, I have to go," she said breaking free of his arms and dashing off. She headed toward the exit of the courthouse, and she didn't look back.

When Monica got outside there were a few reporters waiting outside. They shoved microphones toward her as she brushed past them.

"Miss Holiday, what is your opinion of your ex?

"Is Drayton Lewis your lover?"

"Why did you leave Handle Up? Did Rodney threaten you?"

Monica couldn't believe the questions they were throwing her way. She hurried to her car and got inside. She sped off into the midday traffic. She had too much to deal with right now.

♫

When Monica got to the Congress Center, she was amazed by what she saw. The huge room was taking on the appearance of a tropical oasis. Even the blue tarp that was neatly placed near the sand by the wall to look like water made the scenery somewhat authentic. The artificial birds that would be placed in the palm trees would really set things off. Since there were a few artificial trees thrown in here and there, the effect would definitely be unforgettable. She was having trouble forgetting something too. Dray's confession of love. *I love you, Monica,* he said. As she instructed the workers on where to place the palm trees, Irene appeared from the hallway.

"Monica, this is fabulous! Oh, my God. I thought I was back in the Caribbean. How did you do it?"

The forty-something woman glowed as she looked around the room. She was dressed casually in a black skirt and a striped black-and-tan silk sweater. On her head was a pair of Dior sunglasses, almost buried in her silky black curls.

"This is absolutely wonderful. When is the press conference? I want all of Atlanta to see this. We'll be famous!"

Monica smiled at Irene's hoopla. Irene was more excited than she expected her to be.

One of the tree installers approached Monica with a clipboard and pen. "Ma'am, I need you to sign here verifying receipt of the merchandise." He smiled as he handed her the pen and wiped sweat from his pink-toned face.

"Here you go. Thank you." She gave him his pen back and smiled.

"Thank you," he said.

"Monica, I'll see you later, darling, I'm meeting Savannah Morgan for lunch."

"How come?" Monica asked, trying not to sound sarcastic.

"She wants to feature the company on her show."

"Oh, that's great," Monica said.

"How did it go at the courthouse, Monica? Is everything alright?" Irene asked.

Dray said he loved me. "No. I mean yes . . . everything is fine." She sensed Irene didn't believe her, but now wasn't the time to care. "I'm just a little tired."

"Well, get some rest. I'll see you tomorrow if I don't see you back at the office."

"Okay."

♫

Dray sat in his office in the dark when he got back from the courthouse. He hadn't been able to think straight since he and Monica parted. He told her he loved her.

But why didn't she respond? Maybe she was afraid or upset with all that was going on.   Dray didn't know. But he wasn't going to let her get away that easily. The phone rang.

"This is Dray."

"What up, dude. It's Adam. I'll be at your place around eight."

Dray rubbed his eyes. "Yeah, alright, man."

Adam sensed the tension in his friend's voice. "What's wrong, man? You alright?"

Dray snapped out of his trance. "Yeah. I'm cool. I'll see you later."

♫

Monica sat in her desk chair the following day and picked up a copy of the newspaper. Her eyes widened when she saw the headline: "Will Rapper Double R's Ex Get Him Double Time?" The article talked about Rodney's trial and Monica's testimony. She finished the paper and her small snack of shrimp fried rice. She shut down her computer and picked up her bag. She took the elevator to the parking garage and hopped in her car. She rolled her windows down and let the warm night air seep inside. She had about a twenty-minute drive to get home. As she drove home, her thoughts drifted back to what Dray said at the courthouse. She hadn't meant to run off like that. He probably thought she was the cruelest woman on earth.

♫✍

Dray and Adam sat in Dray's living room watching television. Dray whipped up some spaghetti and fish for dinner while Adam sat at the bar. He watched his friend make a mess in the kitchen and chuckled at the sight of cornmeal scattered over the ceramic countertops and spaghetti sauce splattered on top of the stove.

"Man, this is hilarious. I never imagined your ass in the kitchen like this. That girl must have put some shit on you."

"Fuck you, man. And I'm cooking because I'm hungry," Dray said, stirring the sauce. He sprinkled in some basil and oregano and took a whiff. "Smells good, don't it?"

"Yeah," Adam said. "It does. So what's up with this party tomorrow night?"

"Oh, it's a part of the conference. I guess like a 'Welcome to Atlanta Party.' It's supposed to be off the hook. Monica's throwing it with her new company."

"Yeah, you told me. You seen her lately? Better yet, when's the last time she spent the night."

"Get out my of business, fool. We ran into each other at this little Italian spot in Buckhead. She joined me for lunch."

"And?"

"And nothing. We talked, we ate. " Dray didn't want to let his friend know that he bared his soul and Monica didn't respond the way he hoped. He didn't want to tell Adam anything until Monica was sure of her feelings for him. Adam was sure to make a mockery of him if he knew how love struck his friend was. "You'll get to meet her tomorrow."

"She have any friends?"

"Probably. She works a lot though. One lives here, the rest are all over. And no, I'm not going to ask her to hook you up. You might treat one of them like shit, and she'll be looking at me with green eyes."

"I wouldn't do that!"

"Yeah, right. Come on, man. Let's eat."

CHAPTER 29

When Friday rolled around, the city was packed. The malls were full of people, most of them trying to get suited for the party so they could mingle with all of the stars: Dr. Dre, Outkast, Angie Stone, and a slew of actors. Monica had time to chat with Vivica A. Fox in the lobby before she "went on duty" to man the party. Vivica was her favorite actress, so she had the firm's photographer take plenty of pictures. Once she was done, they said their "see you laters" and went their separate ways.

At nine o'clock the crowds began to pour in. Monica saw all the partygoers were dressed in summer gear: linen suits, Capris, tank tops, slip dresses, and short outfits. She was glad people were going along with the theme. It was a very casual event, and the promoters even allowed people with tennis shoes in. They didn't have much choice. Some of the male entertainers were dressed in T- shirts and shorts complemented by tennis shoes.

Security was heavy. Those who didn't have a hologram invitation or VIP passes were promptly turned away. The only other way you were getting into the party was with a fifty-dollar pre-sold ticket.

There were several parties in the area, but none of them would compare to the crowd at the Congress Center. As the elite enjoyed the paradise party, all the other guests were allowed in a ballroom downstairs where a lot of local artists performed. Some people just wanted to be seen around the center. And promptly filled the lobby with their entourages.

Monica moved around the party chatting with the employees she hired for the evening. With security in place, everything was going as planned. She smoothed the ruffled edges of her dress as she stood near the entrance watching the long lines outside. She wondered if Dray would show up since he'd gotten an invitation. The rest of the staff at Handle Up had been invited too. She had mixed feelings about seeing Bill. But she hoped Cameron and Patrice would show. When Monica surveyed the room again, she was surprised to see Cameron's ex girlfriend, Angela, coming towards her.

Angie was dressed in a black, fitted tank top, khaki Capris, and mule sandals. Her long auburn tresses hung at the sides of her face in a sleek wrap. On her finger was a dazzling diamond ring that rivaled the one Bill's wife, Karen, had.

"Monica!" she screamed over the loud music, excited. She gave Monica a quick hug and stepped back to look at her. "Girl, you haven't gained an ounce since I left! How are you?"

"Fine, chica, fine." They gave each other a cheek-to-cheek kiss. Chica was their pet names for each other from back in the day. "So, Angie, where's that football-playing husband of yours?" Monica could never remember his name.

"James is here in Atlanta, but not with me. We're separated."

"Separated?" Monica was stunned. "What happened?"

Angela shook her head and shrugged. "Can't keep his dick in his pants." She looked away for a moment. "You know, I never had to worry about shit like that when I was with Cam. But I guess that's life."

"Well, you know, I'm not at Handle Up. I had to leave. My new company threw this event along with the promoter folks who sponsored the convention."

"Damn, girl, you loved that job. What happened?"

"A whole lot." Which she didn't care to discuss right now.

"Have you seen Cameron tonight?"

"No, but I'll keep an eye out."

"I need to get your number too. I think I'm going to move back to the ATL. Life in the Big Apple is not for me."

Monica nodded.

"So, is there any special man in your life since you and Double R split?" Angie asked.

"Not really. There was this one guy, the new A&R director at Handle Up, Dray."

"So, what happened?" Angie snapped her fingers. "I need a drink, girl. You want one?"

"No, thanks. I'm working."

"Oh, girl. Come on. One little drink. And you can tell me about this A&R director."

They walked toward the bar. Monica folded her arms while Angie ordered two apple martinis.

"Now, tell me about this man," Angie said, handing Monica her drink.

"I don't know what happened. It started off with us bumping heads. Then we had to work with the Prima Donnas, and then the Rodney mess came up. It was just one big mess."

Angie sipped her drink. "So I guess you starting a new job didn't help either."

Monica continued, "We made up. He's a great guy, handsome, smart, everything I ever wanted . . . but . . . "

"But, what, girl?"

"He told me he loved me."

Angie looked confused. "And?"

"And I panicked." Monica threw her hands up. "I was just like, now what?"

Angie rolled her neck. "Girl, you heard the words every woman dreams of hearing. And you're scared? You better suck that shit in and get that man."

"I just don't want all the drama," Monica said, sipping her drink.

Angie waved her manicured hand in the air. "Well, honey, no two men are alike. If they were I'd be desolate in the woods somewhere."

"Yeah, probably so," Monica added with a smile.

While they walked and talked, the party filled up. In a few minutes, the first act would give a mini-concert on stage. As Nelly's *Hot in Herre* blasted through the speakers, Angie started her shimmy of a dance move.

"Girl, this place looks spectacular. I know you had to be the one to do it, huh?"

Monica answered humbly, "Yeah, it's okay."

"Please," Angie said. "For you to turn this drab place into an oasis like this, girl, you're the bomb."

As much as Monica wanted to stay and chat with Angie, she had a job to do. She decided to get her number and move along. She needed to get backstage to see if the artists were ready.

"Angie, do me a favor, call my house and leave your number on my answering machine. I have got to get backstage."

"Okay, I'll be around here seeing who I can see."

Monica cracked a smile. "Don't hurt nobody."

"As long as I don't see R. Kelly, everyone else is okay."

"Whatever, girl, I'll see you later," Monica said. "And I'll keep an eye out for Cam." She dashed off and headed backstage.

As the night slowly came to an end, Monica felt herself tire. It was almost two o'clock, and she was beat. The crowd began to slowly leave the room. It was covered with empty glasses, tattered decorations, tipped over chairs, and teetering groupies. The crew would start cleaning in another fifteen minutes or so. Their work was cut out for them. Once Monica got the word from the head of security, she would leave and come back in the morning and check out the damage, if there was any.

"Hey, girl," Cameron said, approaching her from the side. "What's the damn deal? These people getting' on your nerves yet?"

She gave him a hug. "Hey, Cam. And to answer your questions, yes."

"This was a nice ass party, kid. I've got to hand it to you."

"Thanks." She went into Diana Ross mode, "Thank you very, very much."

Cam laughed. "You silly girl. What's up for the night? You finished here?"

Monica sighed and leaned against the wall. "Well, I have to make sure everything gets put where it's supposed to."

Cam nodded as she looked around the room. "Did you see Angie?"

"Yeah." She watched his face light up. "I talked to her." Monica knew Cam was up to something. "And?"

"And what?" he smiled.

"I was just wanted to know if you talked to her." She paused. "Cam, you have that look in your eye. You still love Angie don't you?"

There was a glow in his eyes. "Do you love Dray?" he countered.

Monica looked away. "We're not talking about me and Dray. We're talking about you and Angie."

"I'm not going to put myself in a situation where I'm with her one minute and she's back with her nigga the next," he said coldly. "Fuck that."

Monica heard the pain in his voice. "They're separated, Cam."

For a moment he didn't say anything. Then he asked, "Do you love Dray, Monica?"

"Yes," she said, avoiding his eyes. Then they were interrupted. "Well, Miss Holiday, you definitely know how to throw a party," one of the guests said. Monica didn't recognize him immediately, but she knew he was a rapper from New York. His platinum jewelry glittered under the dim lights as he and his posse lingered, apparently waiting for someone else.

"Thank you very much, Mr . . . ?"

"Just call me D-Nut," he said, offering his hand.

She shook it and looked up at the brown-skinned baldheaded gentleman. "Well, then, you can call me Monica, D-Nut."

"I'd like to call you at home."

She was flattered, but had no interest in dating another rapper. "I'm sorry, I don't date musicians."

"Would you date a lonely A&R rep?" a strong male voice asked.

Monica didn't have to turn around to know who it was. Her heart fluttered as she took a deep breath. He moved to kiss her. She welcomed him, clutching his body tight. She was glad to be in his arms again. When they parted everyone was staring.
"I love you, too, Dray," Monica breathed.

He kissed her again.

"Nice talking to you, Monica," D-Nut said. "I see you've got somebody to take you off the market." He whistled for his crew and they moved on.

Dray laughed. "Me and my boy decided to stroll in finally, but I see we missed most of the activities. Looks like you had your hands full."

"Yeah. It's been a long night. I'm ready to go home an sit in a hot tub."

"I think I'll join you," Dray said.

Once Monica was free to leave, she and Dray made their way to the lobby. Dray dropped Adam off at his suite and told Monica he would meet her at her house. When she left, she saw Cameron and Angie outside near Cam's SUV. She walked over to tell them goodbye.

"Is everything okay over here?" she asked.

Angie smiled, though she looked as though she'd been crying.

"Everything's fine, Monica," Cam said. "Go deal with your man. We'll be alright."

Monica smiled and left them alone.

♪♥

Monica filled the tub with water, scented oils, and bubble bath. She lit candles all around the tub, took off all her clothes, and slid her robe on to wait for Dray to arrive. When he did, he came to the door with a bottle of Cristal and a small bag. Monica smiled as she let him in.

"What's in the bag?" she asked.

"Rose petals, massage oil, some freaky dice."

"Oh, Dray. You shouldn't have."

He pulled her close and ran his tongue over her lips. "Umm . . . well I did. So let's proceed with the evening."

"Is that like a vernacular for seduction?"

"Of course, it is, so come on."

Dray undressed and climbed into the tub first. Monica took her robe off and joined him. She scattered the rose petals all over the water and straddled Dray. Her fingers traced the firm lines of his jaw.

"Damn, you're a handsome man," she purred.

She felt his manhood stiffen against her.

"Well, thank you, baby. Thank you."

Monica snickered at his imitation of The Mack. "You are silly," she said tapping the top of his head.

"And you're a beautiful woman," Dray said, washing her back.

"But tell me one thing. Did that dress you had on tonight cost $600 too?"

She punched him in the arm, "Very funny, Mr. Lewis. Will you ever let that rest?"

He grabbed her wet thighs and rubbed them. "Maybe, if you make it up to me."

Monica wrapped her arms around his neck and started to rotate her hips. "How can I do that?"

"Let me show you," he said, easing inside of her.

Instinctively, Monica arched her body to him. He held her waist, guiding her in their rhythmic dance, splashing water outside of the tub. His hands explored the wet curves of her body. He brushed his lips against her nipples, tormenting her in ecstasy. Their eyes met, exposing their desires. Monica clutched the back of Dray's head. She rubbed the soft hairs on his neck while meeting his strokes. She lowered her eyes onto his part-ed lips, observing their soft lines. She put her fingers to them, as he grabbed her hand. He took each finger in his mouth and licked them sensuously. The softness of his tongue made her tremble. Her free hand squeezed his shoulder. He dipped in her until she came, the water splashing with each shudder. Dray's strokes deepened until he erupted, holding Monica so tight she couldn't move. When he opened his eyes, she was looking at him.

"Are you alright?" she asked holding his face.

He threw his head back. "Yes, I just need to catch my breath, baby."

They rested for a moment and then got out of the tub. They took turns drying and oiling each other. When they were done, Dray carried Monica to the bed. They slid beneath the covers and slept until morning.

♫

Monica awoke to find Dray propped up on one elbow staring at her. She reached for his handsome face and stroked it. She tried to assess his unreadable features.

"Good morning."

He kissed her nose. "Good morning."

"How long have you been looking at me?" she asked, yawning.

"Not nearly long enough," he said, smoothing her hair.

She laughed and rolled on her back. Dray's hands glided over her flat belly and up to her breasts. Monica liked the way his hands felt against her skin.

"Tryin' to seduce me?" she asked.

"No, baby," he said. "I'm tryin' to marry you."

Her eyes lit up and she propped herself up on one elbow. "What?"

"Are you ready to become Mrs. Drayton Lewis?" She didn't speak, so he asked her again. "I said, are you ready to become Mrs. Drayton Lewis?"

She was so happy, she had to make sure she wasn't dreaming. "Are you serious, Dray?"

"Hell, yeah. I ain't lying here with all this mornin' breath for nuthin'. They shared a laugh. "Of course, you might get a couple of babies out of the deal."

Monica was so excited she screamed. She rolled next to him and held him tight. "I hope I have sons as handsome as their father? I think I could flow with that," she said, snapping her fingers.

"So your answer is yes?"

"Yes, it is." Monica hopped out of bed. "Let me go brush my teeth so we can seal the deal. Dray climbed out of bed too. He went into the living room and turned on the television. He flipped through the channels to CNN and sat on the couch to watch the broadcast.

"Rap star Rodney 'Double R' Robinson was scheduled to appear in court Monday morning, but guards found the multi-platinum artist unconscious in his cell this morning. Robinson was rushed to the Atlanta Medical Center, and is listed in stable condition . . . "

EPILOGUE

Monica couldn't stop staring at the brilliant diamond ring on her finger. Dray smiled as he watched her examine the Tiffany's five-karat Lucida cut diamond framed by smaller pave diamonds. He knew he made a good choice because she couldn't stop grinning.

"This is so beautiful," she told him. She'd been staring at it since he put it on her finger at breakfast. "Thank you, Dray."

"You're welcome, baby." He kissed her forehead. "Now stop staring at it before you go blind.

It was Friday morning, and Handle Up was having their employee appreciation luncheon before the Labor Day weekend. Dray was getting ready to go. He pulled on one of his best suits and let Monica pick out the shirt and tie. She chose a lilac shirt and a tie that was a shade darker to complement the gray suit.

"I'll try not to miss you too much," Monica said, adjusting his tie.

"Okay, just miss me a little," he said, wrapping his hands around her waist. They shared a deep kiss and then Dray left.

Nothing pleased her more than having him in her life. She was looking forward to becoming his wife. They were planning a spring wedding next year. They wanted plenty of time to plan their special day. Monica was busy at work, and Dray was going to be doing a lot of traveling. They planned to hire a wedding planner so they wouldn't have to worry about the details. Monica hopped in the shower and dressed for work.

After a noon meeting, all of the Johnson and Brown staff went to lunch. Monica stayed behind to catch up on the work she had neglected over the past couple of weeks. She was so excited about being engaged, she could barely concentrate. She was busy writing press releases when she heard some knocking in the main office.

"Hello?" she said.

No answer. She figured it may have been the mail man and continued working. She heard the knocking again and decided to go see where it was coming from. She checked all the offices that were open, the break room, the copy room, nothing. There was no sign of anyone. Standing in the middle of the hall, she rested her hands on her hips. That's strange. When she turned to go back to her office, she met the darkest eyes she'd ever seen. She froze and felt her knees lock in place. Rodney.

ABOUT THE AUTHOR

layinka "Yink" Aikens was born and raised in Oakland, California. She holds a bachelor's degree in psychology from Southern University and A&M College. A member of Romance Writers of America, Yink is currently working on her second and third novels simultaneously. She is a licensed real estate consultant and a freelance writer. She divides her time between Dallas and Atlanta.